# THE LAST CENTURION

* * *

# THE
# LAST
# CENTURION

A NOVEL

BERNARD SCHOPEN

BAOBAB PRESS

Printed in the United States of America

ISBN-13: 978-1-936097-14-2
ISBN-10: 1-936097-14-1

Library of Congress Control Number:
2016954383

Baobab Press
121 California Avenue
Reno, Nevada 89509
www.baobabpress.com

*The book was typeset using Kepler Std.*
*Named after the German Renaissance astronomer,*
*Kepler is a contemporary type family created by*
*Adobe type designer Robert Slimbach in 2003*
*in the tradition of classic modern*
*18th-century typefaces.*

*Printed by Thomson Shore, Inc.*

*Cover design by Travis Bennett*

FIRST PRINTING

18   19   20   21   22        5   4   3   2   1

★ ★ ★

*To my sons*
*Kyle and Mac*

I N THE WARM AUGUST NOON, traffic hissed on the motorway edging the site of the old Roman fort. Seen from speeding vehicles, the ruins, now free of the apparatus of archeology, seemed only patches of scraped earth, smooth-sided holes, a scattering of stones, here and there a crumple of ancient wall. Not so to Tad Fellows. Standing sentry-like beside a collection of boxes and crates near what had once been the Praetorian Gate, he discerned in the angles and arcs pressed on the land the geometry of military purpose. Where stone was yet mortared to stone, he saw the will of empire, Rome enduring.

The fort was surrounded by England Bucolic—copse and rivulet, drystone wall and briar hedge, pasture and sheep, in three directions the swell of low hills, and to the north the miles of fields made from the great flat fen. Rather than admire the landscape, however, Tad traced on it the outlines of fortifications and buildings and grounds destroyed by nearly twenty centuries of unrelenting greening and dying into rot. So it must be, Marcus Aurelius told him, an endless cycle of growth and corruption.

. A decade of archeological effort had uncovered what once had been. Now the soft breeze, as if it passed through not space but time, carried that long-ago world to Tad's senses. In the stirred air he tasted the bile of desperate exertion, smelled the reek of gore and fear, heard the clatter of weapons and the cries of war and death.

He tasted and he smelled and he heard, or, after a night alone and a morning in the sun, he dreamed. Or he remembered. But Rome or America, England or Afghanistan, Picts or Taliban—to a young man such as Tad Fellows, no matter.

He watched and listened, on guard, as if still a soldier. He had enlisted right out of high school, a couple of months before 9/11, and he had been a soldier for nearly four years, until at a checkpoint near Kandahar the bomb of a burqa-clad zealot had bruised his brain, ruined his shoulder, and riddled his side and thigh with shrapnel. He recovered slowly. His concussed brain began to repair or adjust to the damage it had suffered. His flesh wounds healed. But the joint of his shoulder was irreparable: he would not soldier again.

Still, he could do some of what a soldier does. He could guard, if only ruins. He could protect, if only ancient stones from tattooed local louts and their litter and their spray paint. He could defend a decaying greatness from small spite. Thus he was almost content.

So he had been all summer, his fifth—two as an undergraduate and three as a graduate assistant—working the site. If not on watch, Tad was at ease in the world only when he had in his hand a tool or a piece of the past. Shaving or scraping or brushing away soil, hauling and sifting dirt, exposing a shard of pottery or a scrap of metal long buried in the layered and constantly transforming earth, he connected. He felt as he had as a fire-team rifleman, a small part of an entity large and powerful beyond reckoning. He thought himself a cog, anonymous and unremarkable and necessary, fated to a future he could neither anticipate nor avoid.

Now the dig was finished, for the summer and for good. Tad alone remained on the site, the others involved having departed over the previous weeks. He had packed the remaining site records and tools and equipment, arranging containers in a neat stack for the movers. Then he had policed the area, filling trash bags with the litter of end-of-dig revelers. He had spent the night in his small tent watching the boxes and the fort and the stars. He still watched, for the truck due that morning had not come.

He watched from under the brim of a faded US Army camouflage boonie hat, to which he had pinned a Combat Infantryman Badge.

Mid-sized, slight, he wore an old gold UCLA sweatshirt and tan cargo pants and hiking boots. Outfitted thus, he stood so still that passing motorists might momentarily have taken him for a commemorative stone. Had they been able to look on his rather delicate features, they would have thought him younger than his thirty years. Had they found themselves fixed by his grave blue gaze, they would have believed him older, and odd.

Those who knew Tad Fellows understood that he was different. He was bright enough, although his professors allowed that his academic achievements were won by diligence rather than brilliance: he worked hard, steadfastly, at the edge of his abilities. He was not unfriendly, if usually unsmiling and, indeed, rather solemn. But what he thought and felt were for the most part a mystery to others. He did not often say. He usually spoke only in reply to direct address, and not always then. He was not merely a quiet young man. He gave the impression of one who lived in a reality somewhat aslant.

War and wounding were responsible for his silences, most assumed, and for his remoteness, his memory lapses, and his impulses to order and his reliance on routine, for his headaches, and for incidents like that three years earlier when he had disappeared from the site and come to himself fifty-six hours later, forty miles away, sitting on the rail of a bridge over a stream, flipping a shilling. He didn't know how he got there, and he didn't know how he came by the shilling, a coin not in currency for decades.

Army doctors, assessing the results of the pre-discharge tests they had given him, and noting his detachment and small compulsions, as well as his need to read the world in military terms, had told him that he suffered from PTSD. Tad understood the diagnosis but not how it applied to himself. He believed that he was as he had always been, only more so. He had been prescribed medications, but the drugs made him feel other than himself, so he didn't take them.

No one thought him dangerous. He did not think himself so either.

He believed that his life was a fateful unfolding. He believed himself one destined.

NOW HE STOOD in the sun and dust of the English countryside, Tad Fellows, and he watched and he waited as the shifted breeze brought him the scent of the sea and the sounds of passing traffic. After a while he heard the whine of a decelerating engine. A thin plume of dust puffed up as a silver BMW pulled into the entrance to the site. Soon the purring machine came to a stop in the graveled circle before the stacked boxes.

Behind the tinted windshield, the driver, her face a pale smudge, spoke into a cell phone. Tad felt something in his chest shift and settle into place.

Her passenger climbed out, offering a wave of greeting in the same motion with which he smoothed back his undulant silver hair.

"The English Heritage people failed to procure the necessary authorization from the lorry drivers' union, Tad. The truck will be a while yet."

The rich warm baritone fell into practiced rhythms, to which the man's rawboned frame and pleasantly homely features offered a folksy counterpoint. Robert B. Garner—"Professor Bob" to a generation of students and archeologists and middlebrow viewers of his PBS shows on Roman Britain—had made stones speak to the masses. He had made the Americans understand that they were heirs to a tradition both civilized and brutal, and the English understand that they were conduits through which the beauty and blood of the past passed into the present.

Professor Garner was the most important person in Tad's life. He had shown the wounded young ex-soldier how to live after war, helped him find a vocation in his long interest in ancient Rome, become Tad's advisor and mentor.

"The museum will be closed when you get to town. I tried to arrange for you to be allowed to unload then, but Sylvia Stuckey couldn't find the time to return my calls." The professor's smile deepened the squint marks around his eyes. "You'll have to do it in the morning. But maybe that's better—you can settle in at the B&B and get a decent night's rest before you start work."

After a glance at the young woman still in the car, Garner touched Tad's elbow to urge him down what had been a main wagon road into the fort.

"There's another problem in Cambridge, possibly," he said. "A few students are protesting the Horatio move. I hear a politician named Quarles has taken up the issue, but most of the energy and encouragement seem to be coming from Sylvia Stuckey."

Tad knew that Professor Stuckey, the director of the museum, was fighting to keep Professor Garner's remarkable find in England. Elected into the office the year before, she had immediately announced her opposition to removing from the country any part of the national patrimony.

"Be careful with her, Tad. She'll try to goad you into rashness. She'll want you to give her an excuse to withdraw all museum assistance from our project."

Tad looked out over the land, the dips and humps in the earth that might conceal sappers, the breaks through which an enemy might funnel in force.

Garner brushed at his hair. "She's like so many of these intellectual Brit females—*Guardian* readers, middle-class Marxists and committed anti-Americans, and perpetual do-gooders. If there's a committee to save or defend or protect something, Sylvia Stuckey is on it, usually as chair. She's made an impressive, if unorthodox, academic career, but for her the professional is always the personal. She'll take your presence as an insult, if not a threat."

That might be the case, or it might not. Robert Garner's view of the museum director was not objective. He and Sylvia Stuckey had, Tad knew, a history.

"You'll need to watch over Horatio, too. Museum security doesn't inspire confidence. The way they've got him displayed, he's vulnerable, he could be damaged, ruined. Somebody could even waltz right out with him."

Tad tugged the brim of his boonie hat down against the angling sunlight.

The professor smiled again. "I'll be back at Christmas, commitments in hand. Then as soon as you finish—by the beginning of the new term, we agreed?—we can take Horatio back to California and start on the book."

For a moment, standing before an emptiness that had been the fort's headquarters, both men were silent. Then Bob Garner turned, taking in the site that had occupied his professional interest for ten years. "I did some good work here, Tad. I made some people rethink their theories."

That was true, if to Tad of no great consequence. He had little interest in theories, per se. And while he loved humanity, as instructed by Marcus, he had little interest in what people thought.

"Ten years." The professor's voice thickened. "You know this was the last actual digging I'll do. I'm not the type to dodder about in the sun till I drop. Another couple of television shows, the book, and I'm done. Still . . ."

Tad knew what was coming.

"I want to be recognized, Tad, and remembered, if only for a while. Fame is ephemeral, your friend Marcus Aurelius tells us, but I want my moment."

Tad had heard, more than once, of the professor's aspirations, as he had of his family affairs and academic intrigues and erotic adventures. Bob Garner often made Tad privy to his considerations. The younger man's presence was so unimposing that, for Professor Garner, talking to Tad was like talking to himself.

"'Look on my works, ye mighty, and despair.'" Garner smiled ironically. "The Ozymandias complex. Or maybe the proper reference is Ecclesiastes."

His voice had taken on a bitter edge. Robert Garner had in the last decade been denied, twice, an honor for which many in the archeological community, including himself, believed him to be the most worthy candidate—an endowed chair in the UCLA Classics Department. The selection committee, word was, deemed him to possess insufficient gravitas. He was to their collegial mind perhaps less scientist and scholar than panderer to popular tastes, a performer amusing the multitude.

The horn of the BMW honked expensively. The professor smiled. "I've got a plane to catch. Ginny's running me down to Heathrow."

As they turned and started back, Garner adjusted his expression and his tone. "Are you doing all right? Headaches under control? You've got your meds?"

He took Tad's silence as an affirmative response.

"Everything else is as it should be?"

"The coin is still missing," Tad said.

"From the votive hoard?"

Two months earlier, almost by accident, they had found the coins in an urn buried in a small grove before what appeared to have been a shrine to local gods. Somewhere in transit between the grove and the museum lab, one of the fourteen denarii—a Marcus Aurelius, A.D. 194, showing surprisingly little wear—had disappeared.

The door of the BMW opened and the young woman got out. Her silky summer dress, splashed with bright colors, shimmered in the sunlight.

"It could have been the Picts," the professor said.

Local yobs, wildly tattooed and weirdly coifed, ill mannered and looking to steal or vandalize, had lurked about the site for several summers. This year they had also, by way of wooing, verbally abused an attractive University of Leeds assistant professor, whose derisive name for them stuck.

"A Pict wouldn't take just one," Tad said.

England, green and brown, arranged itself around the young American girl. Her father looked at her and smiled, even as he observed, "The pilfering, if that's what it was, well, people want souvenirs. They think it's all right—what's one coin? But check for it in the museum. Small objects like to hide."

Ginny Garner saw the two men watching her. Her smile acknowledged their homage.

"I'm glad you'll be in Cambridge this fall, Tad." Robert Garner placed his hand lightly on Tad's good shoulder. "Ginny's twenty-two, a grown woman, she can take care of herself. But an American girl with a well-known father and wealthy grandparents, she's a natural target for certain types. I'll feel better knowing you'll be there for her . . ."

Tad took a deep breath. He understood his assignment—to guard, protect. He touched with a faint stroke of fingertips the small lump in his left front pocket.

The professor's daughter smiled again as they came up. "Hi, Tad. How are you?"

Tad drew, slowly, involuntarily, to attention.

Virginia Garner was lithe and healthy and wholesome, her brown hair shining, her brown eyes clear, her skin flawless. To Tad, she had always seemed, as she did now in sandals and a summer dress, simply, exquisitely clean. She seemed utterly whole.

They had met when she was seventeen. He had come to understand that she was what he had fought for, had nearly died for in Afghanistan. Had he told her so, she would simply have nodded, as if that went without saying. She believed herself fated to live a large life. Eventually she had persuaded him to admit his own sense of being driven by destiny.

"Send me an email every week or so," the professor said, "a progress report, and your reading of the situation with the protests."

Recon, Tad thought. Infiltration.

"And let me know if there are any problems at the B&B. It's not on the University Housing Authority's approved list, but students stayed there before and recommended it. The landlady, Mrs. Ball, is said to be attentive, and she gave us a very good rate."

Professor Garner extended his hand. "I hope you find time to enjoy Cambridge, Tad. It's a great town to be a student in."

As the two men shook hands, Ginny Garner smiled. "If you want to have coffee or a drink sometime, Tad, you've got my cell number. I'll be at Hathaway House, or working at Clare College."

Tad assumed the invitation was a gesture, good manners.

He watched as father and daughter settled into the sleek silver automobile. It raised dust as it rolled toward the motorway. Soon it was gone from sight.

ALONE AGAIN, Tad patrolled. After five summers at the dig, he knew every stone and tuft of grass and design of the wind in the dust. Since mustering out of the army, he had lived in a succession of rented rooms and shared houses near the UCLA campus, in none of these spending as much time as he had at the ruins of the Roman fort. The site was as close to a home as he had. Yet he would not miss the place. He would miss only the weight of a trowel in his hand, the caress of damp earth in his fingers. But there would be, if all went as Professor Garner proposed, other digs for Tad Fellows. Until then, there was Horatio.

They had found him in the eighth year of Garner's excavation. They found the stone footings and wooden beams and iron bolts of an ancient bridge over a bog at what had once been the edge of the fen. Then they found the haft and bits of corroded blade of a gladius, a Roman short sword. Finally, they found the beautifully preserved body of a Roman soldier, his flesh stained the deep coffee-brown of the peat, his tunic and strap armor mostly unaffected by the ages. They did not find a shield, but at some distance they found his helmet. Next to it they found his severed head, still fleshed, a Briton's arrow through his eye socket into his skull.

The exuberant archeologists named the bog man Horatio.

Tad had not been part of the team that made the discovery. He had been working at what had been the fort smithy, where over the following days he continued carefully to remove dirt, to record and chart and photograph finds of oddments of iron and steel, brick and wood. But each noon he would walk to the bridge site and watch the unearthing. The soldier's helmet eventually was removed to the lab, eventually too his head and bits of sword. Day by day more of the decapitated form was exposed, as if the legionnaire were emerging slowly from his grave.

Tad realized the archeological value of the find, yet the unearthing disturbed him, seemed disrespectful, nearly a desecration. Horatio was not an artifact. He was a soldier who had died in battle. He deserved ceremony, honor, a military funeral such as Tad would have wished for himself.

No one else seemed to feel so. Oglers of every sort swarmed the site, until Professor Garner, although he enjoyed the media fuss and the academic envy, at last protested. Amid such a mob, forensic technicians with their swabs and calipers and humming machines could not properly do their jobs—the integrity of their data was threatened, the scientific value of the find imperiled. The English Heritage people agreed. The site was secured.

Work continued. Horatio finally was freed. He and the small section of peat that still clung to him were lifted by a crane onto a flatbed truck, covered and tied down, and in a procession fit for royalty conveyed to the museum in Cambridge, where scientists continued to extricate the bog man from the bog. Builders fashioned a wood-and-glass, climate-controlled case, into which a carefully cleaned Horatio was placed. The case was settled securely on a plinth in a small room off the entryway. With considerable ceremony, the room was opened to the public.

Then came the announcement that the bog man, by the media dubbed the Last Centurion, would be moved from Cambridge to America. The mummy was of course the property of Her Majesty's Government but would be loaned long-term to a Southern California museum, which would build for it and a selection of other materials from Professor Garner's dig a special wing.

And for Tad Fellows, who like Horatio had fought a fierce enemy in a foreign land, a future began to take shape.

SOME HOURS LATER, light seemingly without a source lingered in the Cambridge evening, softening the stone of medieval buildings, casting long shadows down narrow medieval streets. Tad Fellows did not notice. After the loading of the lorry and the drive through snarled traffic into the city, he had seen the cargo safely parked in a garage, then set off for the B&B that would be his residence for the next few months. His duffel bag slung over his good shoulder, he dodged lone bicyclists and pods of students as he made his way past the closing shops and the busy cafés and pubs of a college town preparing for darkness. Soon he was beyond the city center, on a road lined with shops vending second-hand clothing and cheap electronics and food and drink. A few turns took him into an area of narrow, ill-lit streets where patches of scraggly lawn fronted worn brick-and-clapboard row houses. Set apart, a large, gabled Victorian bore a sign identifying it as his destination.

A woman answered his knock. Backlit by a lamp in the antechamber, she was a shadow scented with cigarette smoke and hibiscus. From behind her came the lilt of Caribbean music.

"Yes, then." Her voice was rich and raspy, her accent local. "You'd be Fellows, Professor Bob's assistant."

When he didn't respond, she turned back inside. Tad followed. On one side of the foyer, an archway opened into a small dining room. On the other side was a parlor dominated by a sofa, above the back of which hovered a shaved skull striped with a green Mohawk. Ahead, two doors led to the rear of the house and a staircase.

"I'm Mrs. Ball," the woman said, slipping behind a small desk that guarded a closed door. "I thought you'd be tweedy, a scholar. Older, too."

Tad set down his duffel. Reggae rhythms danced behind the door. "Yes, then. My mistake." Mrs. Ball elevated a carefully plucked and penciled eyebrow. "You do speak?"

"Yes," he said.

She looked him over boldly. Then, as if he passed muster, but barely, she told him of the routines—breakfast time, parlor use, cleaning, and linen changes.

"The bath is down the hall. You share it with another gentleman. Clean up after yourself, please."

She gave him his keys and the wi-fi password. "No smoking. Government regulations. No overnight guests, or stomping up and down the stairs at all hours. My regulations."

The music stopped. When Tad said nothing, she went on. "I've seen Professor Bob on the telly. Will he be around, then?"

Mrs. Ball was in her mid-forties, thin but not stringy, worn but not worn out. She had on sleek slacks and a pastel blouse that offered ample décolletage, pearls at her throat and ears, and carefully applied makeup.

"No."

"Hit with the ladies, I hear. Ugly buggers like that are, sometimes." She smiled, as if in private amusement. "Maybe you'll find a way to introduce me."

When he didn't speak, her gaze steadied. "The hat, the pin—you were in the army?"

"Yes."

"My husband was killed in your first Mr. Bush's oil war. Fat lot of good his dying did."

She looked at him, seemed to dare him to respond. When he remained silent, she added, "Never cared much for Americans. Presumptuous lot, most of them."

Tad thought she might be trying to provoke him. He didn't know why.

She smiled her private smile. "Neither here nor there when it comes to your comfort, of course."

Tad hoisted his duffel, wincing against its weight. Mrs. Ball noticed. "Got a pain, then?"

Tad's shrug was nearly imperceptible.

"What's the hat?" A young man, he of the green Mohawk, stepped out of the parlor. Tattoos advanced darkly up his left arm and under his teeshirt, emerging at his throat and curling in a filigree across his forehead. He sneered, "Yank pansy hat."

"You've got your tenner for fags and a pint, Chan," Mrs. Ball said evenly. "Go on, then."

The young man paused as if searching for words. He found only those he'd already used. "Pansy hat." He sauntered out.

"The nephew," Mrs. Ball said. "You'll see him about. He does chores and plays on my sympathies. And Mr. Mobuku you'll meet eventually—he looks after things when I step out."

Tad moved toward the stairway.

"Yes, then," Mrs. Ball said after him.

Tad climbed to his room, a small rectangle once a servant's quarters. A gable window overlooked the street. Two small cheap prints of Pre-Raphaelite maidens graced the walls. Bed and bureau, desk and chair and lamp, bedside table and clock radio, all might have been in any one of the rooms he had lived in over the last seven years.

He unpacked his few belongings. From a protective bundle of sweatshirts he removed and placed on the desk his small laptop in its carrying case. His blue blazer he stuck on a hanger in the closet beside his only dress shirt, blue chambray, and a blue-and-gold striped tie—all purchased at Ginny Garner's insistence and worn only to the parties that her father hosted each fall for department faculty and graduate students. The rest of his clothes, more of what he was wearing, he folded neatly into the bureau. He slipped a laundry bag onto a hook on the closet door and slid a folder filled with personal papers into the desk drawer. On the bedside table he put his tattered copy of *Meditations.*

He removed his boonie hat. With his sleeve he brushed at dust dulling the dark finish of the CIB pin, a small rectangle showing a service rifle within a wreath of oak leaves. He placed his hat carefully beside the book.

He checked his email, finding only a solicitation from the UCLA Alumni Association. In the army, Tad had learned to communicate via computer, but as a civilian he had no use for any of the gadgets that other students constantly fiddled with. Whom would he text? What would he tweet? He had never owned a cell phone.

Tad then took up his toiletries kit and stepped into the hallway. Beneath the door of the other bedroom, a line of light shone, the gap allowing the escape of a soft tap-tap of computer keys. In the bathroom, Tad washed his hands and face. Back in his room, he stood for a while at the window.

Night had fallen. The street was poorly lit in pale yellow from a nearby lamp. He studied shadows.

Tad Fellows often stood alone, watching, even—perhaps especially —when he was among other people.

From boyhood he had known that he was different, separate. His middle-aged parents seemed bewildered by him, unable to account for his presence in their lives, so for as long as he could remember he had felt alien, misplaced. Sometimes, as a boy, he felt as if he were on a street corner hailing passing buses that never stopped for him, and he tried to absorb and nullify rejection, thrive on solitude, learn not to care. As a teenager, he often felt physically unreal, no more actual than the small photograph on his school identity card. Unnoticed, untouched by the world, he felt connected to no one, part of nothing.

He did not feel separate in the army. In the army, he fit. Regimentation and rules gave him guidance. Commanded to discipline and obedience, learning techniques and tactics, he was content. His hands knew what to do with weapons and gear. The protocols and procedures of war were obvious to him, inevitable. And, part of a unit within units—fire team, squad, platoon, company, brigade, regiment, army, America—he had a place. In Afghanistan he proved himself a good soldier, at the same time that he developed a kind of stoic patriotism. He was an American, and America, with its power and authority in the world, was a force to which he, in his own strictly controlled way, was being of service. He did not question the proposition that America was the greatest nation in the world, as Rome once had been the greatest empire. He believed that he had a special obligation to make certain that his country maintained that distinction.

His platoon mates at first viewed him warily, took his silences and dogged devotion to duty as signs of mental inadequacy or psychological aberration, until long hours of training persuaded them that he would always be where he was supposed to be, doing what he was supposed to be doing. They called him "Clam," for his taciturnity, or sometimes, noting his baleful expression when especially intent, "Whacko," but they came, eventually, to depend on him. They came to include him. With them he visited bars, although he drank little, and brothels, where he found sex to be mostly an easing of tension and a voiding of fluids.

Gone to war, doing a soldier's duty—guarding, patrolling, fighting, killing—he felt himself fulfilled, connected, complete.

A long battle in an Afghanistan wadi took place during his first tour of duty. Three platoon members, good soldiers, were killed, their deaths to Tad confirmation of the eminence of America—how great his country must be, that worthy men would die for it. He fought as he had been trained to, and he killed, which gave him the satisfaction of a job well done.

One afternoon during his second tour, manning a checkpoint at the edge of Kandahar, he noticed, in the line of Afghan men and women with their smudged papers and whining complaints, a shadow. A burqa-clad figure shuffled toward them. Other similarly shrouded women advanced haltingly as well, but this one was to Tad somehow different. He watched as, still some distance from the Americans, she dipped her head, shifted her shoulders. With a shudder he recognized her as a form from a darkness like a dream. Involuntarily, he raised a hand. Only the shadow woman stopped creeping forward. She raised her head, and inside the slit in the black cloth, her eyes shone. Her hard brown hand reached inside the black garment, and Tad knew she had a bomb, even as he realized that his squad leader's back was turned. Hurling himself sideways, he knocked the sergeant to the ground as the force of the blast blew him back and splattered shrapnel into his left side.

He came to briefly in a field hospital, again on a hospital plane, and then for good in a recovery unit in Germany. On a tray beside his bed was a piece of shrapnel the doctors had dug out of his shoulder.

Eventually, under a compulsion he couldn't account for, he saved the bit of metal in a small chamois bag.

The army gave him medals and thanked him for his service. He mailed the medals to his mother. They arrived in America the day he received notice that she had died earlier that week.

Discharged, Tad for the first time was actually alone and homeless. His father had died a few months before Tad enlisted, and his mother had sold their market and upstairs apartment. He had no obligations. He had no one to look out for. He was part of nothing except America. With the benefit from an insurance policy his mother had kept in force, along with what was left of the money from the sale of the business and a small disability allotment, he did not need to work. But he was lost. Then he found himself listening to Professor Robert Garner talk about Rome and archeology and England.

Now he stood at the window and watched.

Then from his left front pocket Tad removed the chamois pouch, the nap now worn smooth, greasy black in spots. Sitting at the desk, he took from the pouch a small piece of twisted metal, a shilling, a peach pit, a clothes peg with one broken leg, a lipstick cap, and a small triangle of flaked obsidian. He lined these up in a careful row. He looked at them. He touched the shiny black stone, lightly, with his fingertips, as if making sure that it was actually there. With a knuckle he nudged the gold lipstick cap as a child might to determine if the thing before him was alive or dead.

After a while, he put the items back in the pouch. Rising, he put the pouch back in his pocket. He again stood for a while at the window. Then he closed the drapes, undressed, and got into bed. He took up Marcus Aurelius.

An army doctor in Frankfurt had given him this copy of *Meditations*. Tad had read Marcus in high school, finding in the Stoic attitude a compatible moral uprightness, but now the Roman emperor's aphorisms and adages struck him personally, powerfully. Words written nearly two millennia earlier seemed to speak out of Tad's own experience. The consolations Marcus offered were earned, real.

Tad opened the worn paperback at random and began to read: ". . . your actions are significant, but the circumstances in which they take place have no significance . . ."

He read slowly, silently, his lips moving in a rhythm as regular as a ritual chant or a martial drum or the beat of his heart.

EARLY THE NEXT MORNING, in Mrs. Ball's breakfast room, Tad Fellows sat alone at a table looking onto a small garden, where, from behind a vine-woven trellis, cigarette smoke intermittently puffed up like an uncertain signal. He had found laid out on a sideboard, beside urns of coffee and hot water for tea, a variety of cereals, blueberry muffins, bread for toast, ham, cheese, yogurt, and fruit. He made a substantial meal, would need little more that day.

"Mr. Fellows, I presume." A large man about Tad's age stood in the doorway. He wore wire-rimmed spectacles, a rumpled three-piece brown suit, and a bright white shirt without a tie. He was well fed, soft, with sleek dark good looks and an easy smile. "Mick Curtain. We share a bathroom. May I join you?"

In a few moments, he was sitting across the table, sipping coffee and pinching and eating tiny pieces of a muffin. He began to talk, casually, as one might of the weather, about himself.

He'd lived at Mrs. Ball's for several years, her only long-term lodger—the B&B was convenient to the city center and public transportation, Mrs. Ball reduced his rate, and he was too lazy to move to a flat he'd have to clean himself. A working-class lad from Hull, he'd gone to Oxford on scholarship, then come to Cambridge to read law, but financial exigency had forced him into freelance journalism. He'd had pieces in the glossies and the major newspapers, and he was writing a book about the new British underclass—disaffected youth, lost and angry, tattooed and drunken, violent, doomed.

"I grew up with them, and I joke about nearly becoming one myself," he said, brushing at muffin crumbs on his vest. "But the truth is, they scared me to death."

Mick made his living, he admitted, in the tabloids, keeping England up to date on Cambridgeshire contributions to the national cesspool of sleaze, scandal, and corruption, or rumors thereof. He had become a connoisseur of human frailty and ferocity—a confession he offered Tad with a drawl that suggested mild, amused cynicism.

As he spoke, he altered, subtly and for ironic effect, his accent, now Oxbridge posh, now barely intelligible cockney screech, as if probing, seeking responses and thus information. Tad watched, listened, but said nothing.

Mick's inquiry became more direct. "And you're working for Professor Bob, the telly archeologist?"

He knew about Horatio and the plan to take the bog man to America; he didn't know from whom and for what considerations official approval of the move had been obtained. "A pretty pence, in cash or kind, no doubt?"

Tad ate his ham and cheese and toast.

"Word is that Professor Bob's in-laws made it happen, they and their millions, pressuring English officeholders, letting contracts or promising projects, dispensing perks, that sort of thing."

Tad had no idea how the transfer had come to be authorized. He didn't really care.

Mick tried again. "Are you acquainted with Professor Stuckey?"

"No."

"Good luck there." The cock of his eyebrow angled after the camaraderie of males standing fast before the endless assault of female foolishness.

Tad did not seem to recognize the appeal.

Mick, unfazed, grinned. "You know she opposes moving the mummy to America. Theft, she calls it, and in a loud, angry voice. She can seem a harpy, but she's not a hypocrite—she'll keep all English artifacts in England, yes, but she's also involved in the effort to return the Elgin Marbles to Greece. As far as imperialism goes, she's as hard on the British of the past as she is on the Americans of the present."

Tad said nothing.

"You can expect her to be unpleasant—she is when dealing with people who don't wholeheartedly accept her arguments. She'll offer you little or no assistance."

Tad listened without concern. Professor Stuckey would be and do what she would be and do.

According to Mick Curtain, Professor Stuckey's opposition to the plan to move Horatio to America was also urged by her professional circumstances. Her election to the post of museum director had rankled a coterie of male dons of the bones-and-stones sort. They disparaged her work, which they complained had shifted from the inquiries of science to the imperatives of ideology, and they distrusted her gender, which, despite the achievements of several generations of feminists, lacked, they allowed themselves to believe, vigor and rigor and real seriousness. She had come into the position as a compromise between warring factions in her department; academic gossip proposed that both camps presumed that she would be unable to handle the job, her failure opening the position to their favored candidate. The Horatio issue was her first real challenge. The success of her directorship hung on its resolution.

"So she's under a lot of pressure," Mick offered. "What with her causes and her teaching and writing and now the bog man, she's spread pretty thin, and temperamentally she's— Have you read her book, the one about America?"

"Yes," Tad said.

"She gives your country a working over. And your boss, Professor

Bob. He done her wrong, in a hotel bedroom in Washington, DC, as I recall."

A disheveled couple came in and, with the flat accents of the American Midwest, began carping about the breakfast offerings. In the garden, Mrs. Ball rose from behind the barrier of vines and stepped inside, smiled past the couple's complaint, ignored Mick's invitation to join them, and passed into the kitchen. The couple, unmollified, nevertheless began to serve themselves.

Mick returned to his efforts. "Sylvia Stuckey is one problem. Another is Rupert Quarles—Sir Rupert, master of Waterby Hall, as soon as his father the baronet dies. He's also an MP. He's made moving the Last Centurion a political issue, part of Westminster and Whitehall and Downing Street being the haunt of stooges of Washington, England for the English, rah, rah. He comes off as nearly a John Bull caricature, but by design. He's no fool, Quarles."

Over the top of his spectacles, Mick watched Tad Fellows peel and eat a banana.

"So, corruption, money, sex, ambition—might there be a story in all this?"

Tad didn't know. He didn't care. He finished his breakfast.

"Your hat's seen better days," Mick said. "Afghanistan?"

"Yes."

"Prince Harry's War. Not very popular around here, I'm afraid. The war, I mean. Nor in your country anymore, I gather."

Tad finished his coffee.

Mick tried once more. "You're here to get the Last Centurion ready to go to the States, is that right?"

"Specialists will handle Horatio. I'm collecting data for my thesis, along with cataloguing this summer's finds and arranging records and notes for Professor Garner's book on the dig."

"Ah, sentences. He talks about his work, this grave American." Mick grinned. "So how long will that take?"

"A few months."

"What does it entail?"

In other circumstances, Tad might have told him. But this morning he had things to do.

"Work," he said, rising.

"I'm off to it as well," Mick said. "But I'd like to continue this largely one-sided conversation sometime, perhaps over a pint. I sense story, Mr. Fellows. And once I get on the trail of a story, I'll not be put off it."

TAD KNOCKED for several minutes at the museum door. Finally a portly, middle-aged security officer ambled out of the dim entry hall, impassively pointed a finger at the sign listing opening and closing times, turned, and retreated into the shadows. Tad could only wait.

For forty-five minutes he sat on the stone steps, watching the morning city stir. Cars and buses passed, and uniformed school children, young women alone or in pairs off to work, and groups of backpacking university students. A laundromat across the street was open, and a travel agency and an Oxfam outlet. In a corner sandwich shop, dark figures moved.

As Tad sat waiting, he scanned the scene as a soldier would. Several stores might serve as points of ambush. A number of the doors along the street were set within small entryways that would allow effective fields of fire. Down a narrow alley a dumpster angled against a wall would provide cover. With a sniper on the skyline protecting their rear, a well-trained, carefully positioned fire team could hold off an assault in force.

The morning was clear and bright and warm. Even as his hip bones grew sore against the stone, Tad felt the sun loosen his shoulder. When the door behind him clacked open, he rose almost reluctantly.

The security officer, Jackson by his nameplate, told him that Professor Stuckey usually didn't arrive until midmorning; her administrative assistant, Miss Eversly, would be there any minute and would let him wait for the director in her outer office.

Tad understood protocol, believed in the idea of a chain of command: he should see the director before doing anything else. But time spent waiting was time wasted. Discipline was crucial, but some situations encouraged initiative. This he took to be one of them.

Jackson was going off duty, but he agreed to tell one of his security replacements to let Tad know when Dr. Stuckey got in. Then he led the young American down to the basement and a long hallway, past a door behind which, Jackson said, he could find fuse boxes, the building's electrical system being rather touchy. They passed the forensics lab, where two summers before Tad had watched conservators clean Horatio, and proceeded down the hall to a large, dimly lit room and the materials unearthed over the last summer of Professor Garner's dig.

The air was damp and gritty, smelled of dust and mold and, faintly, sewage. Flimsy metal shelving sagged under the weight of boxes, and a long metal table was strewn with notebooks and charts and drawings. Several cardboard cartons on the floor were dark with wet, which came from a backed-up toilet that stood against a wall. In one corner, under a small begrimed window that looked out at the ankles of passersby, was a workspace—heavy institutional desk and swivel chair, phone and computer, and dented file cabinet.

Troubled by the disorder, Tad immediately set to work.

After lifting the damp-bottomed cartons onto shelves to dry, he unclogged the toilet and swabbed the floor. He examined the materials, which he was satisfied to see the conservators had carefully packaged and labeled. He was starting to arrange the finds by date of discovery when the daytime security man came in and announced the arrival of the lorry. Tad followed him up a stairway to a heavy door opened onto a dock that overlooked a U-shaped parking area. Beyond the parking lot and across a muddy lane, a smooth grassy area spread to the edge of the River Cam.

The sky was high and blue and empty. For a moment in the sudden expanse Tad felt vulnerable, exposed to ambush from the gray windows.

The movers unloading the boxes cheerfully refused to haul them into the building: "Them's the regs, mate."

Tad found a dolly and began to wheel cartons down to the storage room. The movers finished, demanded his signature on a form, and drove off. The security man, joined now by another, watched him work. Neither offered assistance. Tad didn't mind. Sweating, smudged with damp dust, faintly rank with the smell of sewage seeped into his boots, he did his job.

He'd moved most of the boxes to the basement when, stepping again into the sunshine, he discovered the security men gone. At the same time, he became aware that he was still being watched. A partially draped window on the second floor framed a female figure blurred by a sheen of sunlight on the glass.

He didn't know how long she had been there. Again, he felt open to attack. He stood very still, looking up at the shape. Suddenly it withdrew.

Fifteen minutes later, hands and face washed, grime brushed from his clothes, Tad stood before Miss Eversly, the director's small gray administrative assistant. Dr. Stuckey had been in her office for an hour, she said, but had left to attend meetings and would not return until late afternoon.

He went back to work. By noon he had emptied the loading dock and stored the tools and equipment neatly along a back wall and filed away the last site reports and notes. By midafternoon, he had worked his way through the cabinet, sorting the paper records from the ten-year dig—site journals, strata drawings, photographs, and location maps, as well as the printouts from various measuring machines.

Other charts and graphs, as well as a diagrammatic context database, would be in the computer, which at first he couldn't get running. Determining finally that the machine was not getting power, he went into the utility room and found—along with the central air controls, the main light switches, and the hand lever for the security system—a box of new fuses from which he replaced one that had burnt out. He had just brought the computer to blinking life when the phone squawked. Dr. Stuckey had returned, a gray voice informed him, and would see him now.

Ten minutes later Miss Eversly bade him take a seat. He sat.

A half hour later he still sat. So did Miss Eversly, after some slow shuffling about the office, in her gray dress and cardigan and goggle glasses like a great snail. As the minutes passed, she began to shift uneasily in her seat under the somber gaze of the young American so motionless he seemed hardly to breathe. A flush crept up her throat. Finally she rose, gave the door to the inner office a single soft rap, and slipped behind it. She reappeared, inviting Tad to enter. She gave him a small, apologetic smile as he stepped past her.

Professor Sylvia Stuckey sat at a large desk, the inlaid wooden surface of which was, but for a black landline telephone and a pale green cell phone, as bare as her folded hands. Behind her a long table was strewn with precariously stacked files and papers. Other accoutrements of administration—file cabinets, machines, trays, and slots— were situated about the airy room. Books filled the wall into which the door was cut. On the other walls, oil landscapes hung between tall windows that let in the waning afternoon light.

The director gave him a long, empty look but no greeting.

From his pocket Tad took papers authorizing his agency, which he placed on the desk.

"Remove your hat, please." She spoke tonelessly, wearily.

He removed his hat.

"I don't need to see your credentials, Mr. Fellows," the director said, her words measured, uninflected. "I know who you are and what your project is. If you don't know how I feel about what you have come here to do, you should. I do not welcome you. I have no intention of helping you and Bob Garner rob the people of Britain. Why are you taking up my time?"

"Professional courtesy," Tad said.

She opened her laced fingers, then folded her hands as if having captured a living truth. When she spoke, irritation edged her voice. "Some hours overdue."

Tad knew that nothing would be gained by mentioning the guard's promise. And he might easily seem to have flouted or challenged her authority. "I'm sorry."

"I sincerely doubt that," she said.

He brushed his fingers over the lump made by the pouch in his pocket.

"You've acted as if the museum were your personal property. You don't seem to appreciate that you are a guest of the people of Britain, who fund this institution."

Tad said nothing.

She paled, her irritation swelling toward affront. "Abusing me with bad manners and an artificial apology isn't enough, I see. You have to add a taciturn machismo."

He regarded her, her clasped hands, her pale brow, her weary gaze.

"It's all too much," she said, angry now. "Americans are always too much."

Tad remained silent. The expanse of the desktop spread between them like a no-man's land.

She opened and refolded her hands, as if confining her emotion. She adjusted her expression and tone. "You will conduct your activities in our building according to our regulations and requirements. Is that clear?"

"Yes," Tad said.

"Whatever you may need in order to do your work you'll have to provide yourself. We don't have the resources to waste on those engaged in the theft of artifacts belonging to the English people."

"Keys?"

"No keys. You will enter and exit like any other visitor. When the building is closed, you will not be in it. Evenings, Sundays, you will not be here."

He picked up his papers and slipped them into his pocket.

Perhaps because he was about to depart, she looked at him for the first time as if he might be of consequence. "Do you—surely you know, Mr. Fellows, that a so-called 'long-term loan' is tantamount to a permanent move."

"Yes," he said.

"Do you see that you are the accomplice of Bob Garner in cultural larceny?"

"Yes," he said.

She looked at him now with actual interest. "What else do you see, Mr. Fellows?"

He saw the tension in the trim body under her olive jacket, under her pale yellow blouse. He saw the fashionably tousled brown hair at odds with the face free of cosmetics; the large, intelligent brown eyes, watery, streaked in the corners with tiny red capillaries; the regular features, slightly puffed; and the full-lipped mouth sagged by weariness into a grimace. He saw a woman in early middle age, conventionally attractive, who would soon either shrivel into a crone or swell into a late ripeness. He saw that as a foe she would plan meticulously but attack with an abandon that might destroy not only her enemy but also herself. He saw resolution.

"Boudica."

She stared at him. "What an astounding thing to say."

Tad did not reply.

"Are you attempting to flatter me, Mr. Fellows?"

"No."

"You know, I assume, that I have written about her."

Boudica was a Briton tribal queen who, betrayed and widowed and tortured by the occupying Romans, led an uprising that produced several major victories before finally failing. The queen herself was thought to have committed suicide rather than be taken captive. She was a figure of courage and will and zeal.

"Yes," he said.

She gave him a new, a different regard. Then finally she said, "Well, I feel flattered. And I certainly will resist your efforts on behalf of America as fiercely as she did the incursion of the legions of Rome."

Tad said nothing.

"Now if you'll excuse me," Professor Stuckey said curtly, "I have the people's work to do."

Turning her chair around to the table stacked with papers, she gave Tad her back.

After leaving the director's office, Tad returned to the main floor. Signs led him to the museum's newest exhibit.

The dark, oddly twisted human figure seemed to float in the center of the room. The illusion was created by lighting, which left most of the space dim, hid the carved mahogany plinth on which rested the climate-controlled enclosure, softened the wooden frame of the glass cube, and cast a golden glow that seemed impossibly to emanate from the still and shriveled heart of the mummy.

Stepping into the room, Tad activated lights that, as he moved around the dark form, illuminated wall panels of elegant calligraphy interspersed with photographs that created a context for the discovery. Tad ignored these, instead studying the mummy.

Horatio was smaller than Tad remembered him. His knees were drawn up fetus-like, while his torso twisted at a severe angle—one arm, fingers fisted, was flung outward, while the other, hand open, embraced his chest. The conflicting energies in the pose had inspired imaginative flights in visitors and journalists, but Tad saw in the alignment of the body only one more configuration of death.

Conservators had done beautiful work. The skin was smooth and supple, the shreds of tunic carefully cleaned; the leather of the sandals and strap armor was, but for the odd spot of deterioration, strong and still serviceable. The helmet had been placed at Horatio's right knee. What remained of the sword lay on a piece of dark plaster into which had been carefully scratched the outline of the complete blade.

Horatio's head, adorned with strings and tufts of reddish hair, had been found several meters from the body, which had led wags to speculate that the Picts had used it for a football. Now it lay beside the mummy's foot, pinned by the arrow through the eye socket. The violence of the image contrasted with the expression on the dead soldier's face—he had met his destiny, his doom.

In the presence of the Roman legionnaire, Tad felt returned, back where he belonged. At the same time, the display disturbed him. Horatio deserved better.

WHEN THE MUSEUM CLOSED, Tad took a wandering walk back to the B&B. On a side street of scruffy shops and a corner market much like that his parents had owned in South Pasadena, he came upon a small bakery and tearoom, the window of which displayed an appealing tray of tarts filled with fat red cherries. Just as he was about to enter, a young woman, blonde and pleasantly round, offered him a pleasantly round smile as she clicked the door lock. He walked on, to downtown, and then returned to Mrs. Ball's as darkness descended.

In his room, he wrote Professor Garner a brief email. His accommodations more than suited his needs. He had met with Professor Stuckey, he said, but offered no details. All, he suggested, went well.

He took a shower. Then for a while he stood, as he had the night before, at the window, looking out. In the lamp-lit street below, nothing moved, but as Tad watched, everything slowly changed. Objects took on a vivid clarity. Edges sharpened, surfaces shone. In the yellowish light, sidewalk cracks seemed to widen and stains on the street to hover above the pavement. Shadows deepened. Lights in windows flared. In his temples, pain began to pulse.

He got his aspirin bottle. He hadn't had a bad headache for several months, and this one would not be severe either—he had had headaches since his wounding, knew their colors and contours, knew when the throb would merely nag and when, swollen to scream, it would drive him into himself. This one he would be able to walk off.

He swallowed the aspirin. Then he went out into the night.

On Mill Road he stopped at a fish-and-chips shop. Food would help him hold back the pain that shuffled and muttered impatiently just beyond a wavering gray boundary behind his eyes. Eating fried cod and potatoes, he walked.

Tad had begun walking as a boy, moving through nighttime neighborhoods seeking security, confirming constancy, accounting for change. Now he patrolled, an army veteran finding a small satisfaction in military motions.

He had been in Cambridge several times, so he knew the general layout of the center of the city, which he skirted until he came to the Cam. The river shone darkly, seemed unmoving in the dimness of the walkway lights. Pedestrians strolled and bikers sped by, students and shop clerks hastening homeward or enjoying the warmth that lingered in the night. Lights from nearby hotels and streets and businesses were blocked out, here and there, by masses of old stone. Tad reconnoitered, fixing in his memory the location of bridges and cross streets, the shape of green spaces, and the configurations of shadows. The pain in his head ebbed until it seemed but a memory of ache.

Leaving the river, he walked past more college buildings and commercial offices into a neighborhood leafed by plane trees and scented faintly by rose bushes that attended large expensive old homes and new expensive apartment buildings. From the entrance to one of these a canopy extended. Tad passed beneath it, walked another block, then crossed the street and stepped into a deep shadow cast by a thick-boled tree nearly bumped up against a rock wall. Slipping between tree and wall, he became shadow himself. He had a clear view of the apartment house canopy, on the front of which were printed the words Hathaway House.

Now and then the lights of a slowly moving vehicle yellowed the night. A taxi idled up the street, a lorry growled softly past, a white van crept by twice, as if lost. Sometimes a dark human shape moved along the sidewalk. Eventually all was still as Tad Fellows guarded.

THE NEXT DAY, SATURDAY, Tad prepared a work plan. After cataloguing the items unearthed that summer, he would pack up most of them for the move to the warehouse across town where, under the authority of the English Heritage, the artifacts from the previous years' diggings were stored. From the metal pieces he would collect data for his thesis before packing these as well. Then he would collate all the records of the ten-year excavation, so that Professor Garner could easily access the data and images and graphs he might want to use in the book he would write on the project.

Tad looked forward to working with, to touching, to holding the scraps of metal, now cleaned and appraised by conservators. These finds—bent nails, brads, malformed bits of hardware, broken tools, pieces of blade, ruined spearheads—always felt familiar in his hand. Found at various locations and depths, the metals indicated that the outpost had almost from the beginning depended for weapons on repair rather than resupply. That at least was his dissertation thesis, no large idea, and, like most ideas, of no real interest to him, but professionally arrived at and solid enough to satisfy his PhD committee.

The rest of his task, dealing with paper and computer files, would be time-consuming and involve work with his head rather than with his hands, but not difficult. Tad considered the job as concluding the ten-year dig. He would be tidying up, much as he had at the actual site after everyone had left.

Sunday, the museum closed, he walked the crowded Cambridge streets, to all appearances merely one more tourist inquiring into alleys and exploring shop windows while students lolled on The Backs or punted on the river or texted on park benches and enjoyed the last days of summer. In the city center he calculated avenues of retreat. He scouted the terrain of green spaces. He did not see Ginny Garner, but at midday, passing a café patio near the Arts Theatre, he observed Professor Stuckey bent over a wine glass in earnest conversation with a bald, bullet-headed, wide-shouldered man who seemed about to burst his green corduroy suit. Neither noticed Tad.

The following morning, summoned, he again stood, hat in hand, before the museum director. She squinted, as if the sight of him gave her pain. Her hand trembled faintly as she placed two keys on the desk between them.

"I'm making an exception to institutional policy, Mr. Fellows. This is a political decision, in the spirit of international cooperation and shared scientific inquiry. You may come and go as you please, so long as you inform security of your presence."

Tad assumed that she wanted something from him. He didn't wonder what that might be. He picked up the keys.

She folded her hands as if to contain their quiver. "If you don't mind my asking—what is your reward for your efforts here?"

Tad told her. "A job."

"And Bob Garner, what does he get out of it?"

Tad said nothing.

This silence she didn't seem to mind, or even to notice. She sat back in her chair, frowning against the pain that flickered in her eyes.

"I shouldn't think at this stage in his career he'd be after another position, although his colleagues passing him over, twice, for an endowed chair must have done injury to his ambitions. And it can't be financial—his wife left him well off, and his daughter will get millions. As for renown, he's famous enough to satisfy even a vanity as voracious as his own, what with the television programs and the coffee table books and all the Professor Bob nonsense. What does he gain, then?"

The little speech seemed to drain her. She paled. An eyelid twitched. Men in Tad's platoon had exhibited similar symptoms after a weekend debauch.

"You won't say, of course." She nodded at the hat in his hand. "Loyalty is the supreme virtue, isn't it, Mr. Fellows? That's what your army teaches young men so that they'll go out and impose the American will on the world, killing and dying to do it."

"Yes," Tad said.

His answer seemed momentarily to stun her. Then, carefully, she said, "I'm speaking of the loyalty that eliminates the need to make human, difficult, morally responsible decisions."

"Yes," he said again.

The twitch of her eyelid became a jerk. "'What is the American—this new man?' You remember that Crèvecoeur asked that centuries ago. The world has been asking it since. Is it you, Mr. Fellows?"

Tad didn't understand the question.

For a moment they regarded one another. Then she said, "Is there anything about you that I should know?"

"No," he said.

"You are . . . not like others, quite, are you, Mr. Fellows?"

"No," he said.

"No," she said as if to herself, "you wouldn't be. Bob Garner would see to that. I—I must ask, why do you insist on wearing that stupid hat?"

"It makes me whole."

"Doesn't it—Do you understand why some people might think that it's a way to flaunt your Americaness? To invoke the might of the American military? That it constitutes a boast, and a threat?"

"No."

"But you must—" She bit off the thought.

Tad waited, but she lapsed into silence. She no longer seemed to attend to his presence. He turned and was at the door when she spoke again.

"All unwittingly, I'm sure, Mr. Fellows, you gave me a valuable gift the other day. I hadn't thought of Boudica in years."

A smile struggled with the grimace on her pale mouth. "But I do often feel as she must have, her husband murdered, her daughters raped, she herself flogged mercilessly but surviving to lead a revolt that inflicted severe losses against occupying imperialist Rome. Of course, she was finally defeated and took her own life. Is that what you were suggesting?"

"No," he said.

"I've suffered many defeats, Mr. Fellows, but I won't lose the battle to keep the mummy, and I won't do myself in, personally or professionally."

Tad said nothing.

She sat back again in her chair. "In any case, you've given me a boost. I'm beset on several fronts, and I wear down. Remembering her helps."

Tad understood being beset, wearing down. He felt a small spasm of sympathy.

TAD FELLOWS since childhood had sought clear and systematic demarcations. Things belonged in their proper place. He remembered

—one of his few memories of boyhood—the satisfaction he garnered when, stocking shelves or displaying produce in his parents' corner market, he imposed order. Now, driven by an inner urge to organize, he arranged both the site materials and his days. He worked in the museum basement cataloguing materials, numbering each item, preparing a detailed description, and recording these in a computerized inventory. When he needed a break, he wandered through the museum's collection of Iron Age, Roman, and medieval artifacts, or he stopped in to see Horatio. The mummy soon came to be for him a comrade long fallen into unconsciousness but still undeniably there. He sometimes felt the urge to salute.

Tad also came regularly to slip out in late afternoon for a snack, usually the only food he consumed after breakfast, and to make inquiries, through which he learned Ginny Garner's class schedule, her preferred library table, and her favorite coffee shop. He soon recognized by sight the few young men and women with whom she had taken up. He saw her every few days. She did not see him.

One afternoon, returning to the museum by a different route, he came upon a coin shop, in the window of which several Roman denarii lay on a cloth of dark velvet. One of them was a Marcus Aurelius 194. He had not yet found the coin missing from the votive hoard, and momentarily he considered buying this one—a rough conversion from pounds gave him a price of just over one hundred dollars—and putting it with the others from the site. But although that would make a whole, would stop a gap, it would also violate the principles of his profession, corrupting evidence, if ever so slightly. Not that anyone need know, or that many would especially care. They would no doubt think Tad's scruple more precious than the coin. Nevertheless, he passed on.

August slipped by and September arrived as Tad finished cataloging the materials excavated that summer. Others in Cambridge were also concerned with those artifacts, especially with the mummified Roman soldier they called the Last Centurion. Tad emailed Professor

Garner that meetings had been held, arguments articulated, and fly-ers posted, all invariably tagged with the names of Sylvia Stuckey or Rupert Quarles, all invariably stained with anti-American sentiment. Tad heard that a social-media campaign to keep Horatio in England had developed. Broadsides had English bureaucrats collaborat-ing with invaders from across the sea. Graffiti presented Uncle Sam gleefully buggering John Bull. While most people in Cambridge went about their business, on a few pleasant afternoons small demonstra-tions formed in campus quads and spilled out onto nearby streets or spread over the green space along the river. None of this activity seemed to Tad especially threatening. The two demonstrations that he had happened upon appeared almost playful, students feigning out-rage, with excited shouts and enthusiastic chants and hand-drawn signs protesting the removal of Horatio to America. Tad saw in these rallies high spirits but little organization and actual purpose. Never-theless, he gave the students a wide berth.

Professor Garner, responding, queried carefully about the student activities and Sylvia Stuckey's involvement in them. He asked few questions about Tad's progress, and these perfunctory. Tad felt alone behind enemy lines.

Evenings, if Tad was not at the museum, he worked on his laptop in his room at Mrs. Ball's. He went for late walks, establishing perim-eters, scouting positions of ambush and escape. Often he passed the museum, large and silent and dark, and occasionally the bakery and tearoom where the round young woman had smiled at him. Beside the bakery entrance, another door led to a stairway that climbed to a flat above. One night from across the street Tad saw her there, the round young woman, pressed back against the wall by a Pict, a young man thick and squat and in the chill night bare-chested but for an open denim waistcoat, his chest and arms and face dark with tattoos, his hair dyed blue and gelled into spikes. He had his hands on her. Nei-ther noticed Tad's passing.

Other nights—once a week, sometimes twice—he walked off headaches. The throbbing was manageable. It was also portentous. Sensitized by long experience to the slightest disruption at his nerve ends, his system tracked with an almost seismographic accuracy every twinge and crackle of pain. These suggested now in their regularity that a major event, as the doctors called them, was building.

Tad Fellows had begun to have headaches his first semester at UCLA. They were infrequent, but powerful and strange. The pain usually attacked near the end of his day. As he lay on his bed, or sat at his desk, he would grow aware that his surroundings had taken on a throbbing clarity. Beneath his skull a brightness bloomed into torment. Sometimes the pain temporarily paralyzed him. Then, curled into himself, he teetered over an inner abyss, and he thought that he was dying. More often, however, he took aspirin and, waiting for it to work, he stumbled out into the night where, walking, fitting his pace to the rhythmic pulsations in his head, he made the pain part of the vast and shadowed darkness.

When consulted, VA doctors proposed that he was suffering residual effects of the Afghanistan bombing, that the force of the blast may have effected a deep bruising, perhaps even created lesions in the brain. They also noted the army doctors' diagnosis of PTSD, suggesting that Tad's mild OCD and his sense of displacement, as well as his headaches, were part of an expansive syndrome resulting from the physical and psychic damage done by the bomb.

Tad did not tell the doctors what had happened one night, as he walked.

Balancing the pain against the dark, he had moved along now-familiar streets around the UCLA campus, past storefronts and apartment entries, older homes and bungalows, bougainvillea and vines and rose bushes and fruit trees. Traffic murmured in the distance, and lawn sprinklers clicked softly; the glow of city lights grayed the black sky and dimmed the stars and spread shadows. Tad found his progress unaccountably slowed, as if the night, chilling, had gathered to resist him. Wholly occupied by pain, he walked into a different darkness.

Shadows shaped themselves strangely, trembled and stirred, became as real and threatening as creatures driven by fear and rage out of an ancient concealment. Throaty sounds whispered or growled or hissed, promising violence. The commonplace was now grotesque. Everything was as it had been and nothing was as it should be, and all opposed him. But he was not afraid, no—he was vital, alive in a different dimension of himself. He had become what he really was. The ache in his head was an exultation. He commanded the darkness.

Then the night broke into pieces: layered shadows and geometries of light, alleyways and fences of obscure intent, other presences in dark rooms, sounds of life and love and sleep.

Until he was once again in his room, his headache faded, and the experience among the shadows only a stain of remembering. He did not know where he had been or what he had done.

He knew, vaguely, that he had entered other lives. He had entered too a place in himself where, were he not very careful, were he to stay for any length of time, he could be forever lost.

He discovered then that he carried with him a peach. He had no memory of picking it. He placed it on his desk, where it sat for weeks, drying, shriveling. Finally he peeled off the desiccated flesh, washed and dried the pit, and placed it in the small chamois bag that held a piece of shrapnel removed from his shoulder.

About all this he told no one. What, exactly, had he to tell? And whom?

HE USUALLY BREAKFASTED with Mick Curtain while Mrs. Ball smoked in the garden. Sometimes she passed through on her way back to the kitchen and her apartment, and Mick, with a smile and an expansive gesture that seemed to present to her his big soft body, always encouraged her to take coffee with them. Usually she didn't, but once in a while she would sit, briefly, and indulge Mick in his pseudo-seduction and enquire after Tad's comfort and the progress of his work and word of Professor Garner's return.

Before a week had passed, Tad knew from Mick Curtain that Mrs. Ball was the younger daughter of a Cambridge chiropractor and his masseuse wife who had had their home and offices in what was now the B&B. At seventeen she fled to London, as had her sister before her. She was widowed, she claimed, at twenty-five, when her husband was killed in Iraq. Some years later, she returned to nurse her mother through her last cancer-riddled days and to secure title to the family home. She had money, the source of which was mysterious, enough to refurbish the place, after which she began to rent rooms. She liked the steady income, as well as the independence and authority that came with being a landlady.

Mrs. Ball had been handsome, and her figure and carriage still attracted long looks. She had had a few flings, but to no lasting effect and always on her own terms. She vacationed at Christmas in Jamaica, which she loved, and when low would don a flowery dress and listen to CDs of reggae music. When she was gone to the islands, or to London, or when she stepped out to the pub or pictures, she called in a retired Nigerian accountant named Manfred Mobuku to put out breakfasts and work the desk.

Mick Curtain, fifteen years her junior, she mildly abused as a lazy, slovenly, woman-spoiled, perpetual adolescent who couldn't even learn to wear a tie. Mick responded with a repertoire of ogles and leers. Were he ever actually to seduce her, he told Tad with a grin, he would have to find other digs. That's why his efforts were so obvious and feeble and fun.

Over Tad Fellows Mrs. Ball openly puzzled. Once she said, "So it was the war then?"

He didn't mind the question, but he let his silence serve as an answer.

Mrs. Ball normally would have had two or three other semi-permanent guests, Mick said, university students or those in Cambridge doing research for a semester, but she had been dropped from the Approved Residence List of the University Housing Authority because of an accusation of racism, which actually had been just a reservation mix-up. Mick suspected that she hoped to have the opportunity to persuade Professor Bob to help her get back on the list.

At breakfast, temporary guests eager to begin the day might come in, but most rose later, so often the two men had the room to themselves. As Tad ate, Mick sipped coffee and brushed muffin crumbs from his vest and slid his spectacles lower on his nose and talked about Cambridge and England and the UK, about America and war, money and politics, sex and academia, about young Englishmen and class and violence, and as he talked he ran through his repertoire of accents and tones from quiet seriousness to buffered cynicism to ironic umbrage, he probed and he scratched and he peeked, and gradually he discovered that after a five-hour battle in an Afghanistan wadi, Tad Fellows, with four others in his platoon, had been cited for valor; that Tad was proud only of his Combat Infantryman Badge, earned by soldiers who had come under enemy fire; and that because of his injured shoulder he couldn't raise his left elbow more than an inch or two. And he heard how Tad, after his discharge, had spent a lost month wandering the UCLA campus, where he was enrolled in a business program designed for returning veterans, until on a whim he walked into a public lecture by Professor Robert Garner and discovered that he might make a life out of his long obsession with Rome.

On most subjects Tad remained silent, or nearly so. But he would talk about the army and archeology and Rome and Professor Garner. More and more, he would talk to Mick, although he knew the journalist was gathering material. So that one Friday night, when Mick persuaded him to take a pint of best bitter at the local, the Blue Boar, over beer Tad described his experience seeing the film *Spartacus*.

He was nine years old, watching the movie on television. He was immediately caught up, not by the plight of the slaves and the heroics of their revolt but instead by the pure power of Rome. In the opening scenes, showing slaves working a quarry like brute beasts, he recognized something about himself, although he could not have said what. When the story shifted to the gladiatorial training camp, he saw men being made killers for the pleasure of other men. And he watched, awed, as the immense force of the empire embodied itself in the legions and their precisely fitted, highly drilled efficiency.

The Roman army was a machine of men, each armed and armored individual an impersonal, independent component with his own function contributing to the success of the whole. Each soldier, nothing in himself, was linked, ultimately, to all. Tad, rapt, watched the legions march through their formations. He admired the economy of their movements, felt their lethal force. A solitary boy, quiet and watchful, he had found in his young life no place where he might fit, no model for what he might be. His parents seemed vague presences, shapeless and insubstantial. The atmosphere in his home discouraged expressions of emotion, which he learned early on to master, and affection, which he learned to do without. In the legionnaires he saw men who lost their isolation in the good of the whole, whose individual feelings, whose private pain, didn't matter, in a sense didn't exist. He saw what he wished he might become: a soldier, dutiful, disciplined, fitted and locked into place, a force in the inevitable advance of destiny.

He bought a poster advertising the film, tacked it to his wall, and, lying on his bed, looked beyond the toothy grimace and deeply dimpled chin of Kirk Douglas to count the small faceless figures in the background cohorts, fighting men with their armor and weapons, soldiers lined up in neat rows that blurred into an undifferentiated white blob like death. His kin, he felt they were, his ancestors.

Seeking more information, in the school library he found Macaulay's *Lays* and a Classic Comic version of Virgil's *Aeneid* and a collection of Roman legends and a child's book of brief biographies of heroes and leaders. From these he took guidance. He approved of Roman virtues, finding in them a psychological security. Later, in high school, he discovered and felt comfortable with the martial code of Scipio and Marcus, the moral rigor and pragmatic attitudes of Cicero and Seneca. Long before he enlisted in the army, he had reduced life to a series of imperatives—honor and obey parents and the authorities and the gods; do with enthusiasm those tasks assigned by fate; confront difficulties with courage and bold manliness; ever be honest, trustworthy, and reliable. In all this he was largely successful, although few people noticed because few people noticed him at all. He didn't mind.

As Tad offered a quick sketch, a sort of line drawing of all this, Mick Curtain, silent for once, listened carefully. He was not certain that he understood. "So at nine years old you rooted for the Romans rather than Spartacus?"

"I admired Spartacus, and Boudica when I read of her. They were brave, good fighters, but they couldn't win."

"And from then on you wanted to be a soldier," Mick said. "And now at bedtime you read Marcus Aurelius? *Meditations*—that long brooding on death."

"On duty," Tad said.

"On doom," Mick countered. "And the virtues, all part of the aristocratic code. Every man knows his place. Ours is not to reason why. Don't make waves. Power to the powerful."

"Yes."

"Ultimately, that's what it's all about. Power. That's the appeal, is that it?"

"Restrained power," Tad said. "Shaped power. Grace."

"Men shaped into a tool that leaves carnage in its wake. A tool that serves despotism."

Tad lifted his glass, still nearly full. "The most effective tool ever made was the Roman short sword."

The Blue Boar was crowded, the clientele an assortment of older men and women of discouraged mien and cheap attire, middle-aged workers working hard on their drinks, and a small unruly gathering of young men, oddly coifed and elaborately inked, roughhousing at darts.

"The subject of the book I'm working on," Mick said, "disaffected British youth. Children of the punk age, progeny of football hooligans."

"Picts," Tad said.

Mick grinned. "Is that a classical archeologists' joke? Modern youth as barbarians beyond the wall? Enemies at the gates of civilization? The pooh-flingers of our time? I like it."

The pub was old, low-ceilinged, with dark wood posts and paneling and once-white plaster walls stained slick with decades of smoke from now-forbidden cigarettes. Although it was early evening, the air was already unpleasant, heavy with the sharp odor of stale beer and a chemical scent that did not mask the reek of unwashed bodies. From a sound system, unintelligible music strained against the din of voices less and less sober. Most of the drinkers lived in dilapidated council housing nearby, Mick said, on the edge of the welfare state, one generation defeated and hopeless, another trapped and hopeless, a third hopeless and angry. All resented academics, who controlled, and students, who overran their city. They resented Americans too, who controlled and overran the world.

"Three for three with me," Tad said.

"Don't fret," Mick grinned. "They're too beaten down to do much more than scowl at your hat. You might have a touch of trouble if Billy Knox were here, though. He, now, is a true barbarian."

This Billy Knox, it happened, featured in the book Mick was writing. He lived in his capable body, on his impulses. Quick with his fists or a quip, angry and violent and often funny, he thought himself an instrument of mayhem, wholly given over to disrupting respectable lives. His great ambition was to kill someone. Eventually, he knew, he would be killed himself, or crippled, or imprisoned for good. Till then, he would laugh and booze and fight and fuck and steal and ravage.

Tad understood. As Marcus had counseled, Billy Knox embraced the life he had been given. Tad too. "You like him."

"I know him," Mick said. "He's a throwback, almost a 1950s existential antihero. He has a certain . . . appeal. When I'm writing, he keeps trying to take over the book."

"About England," Tad said.

Mick seemed not to have heard. "He works, seasonally, on the Waterby Estate, and does other jobs, from time to time, for Rupert Quarles—sabotage of one sort or another, some say. There's a rumor that they're half-brothers, that Billy's really the old baronet's bastard. Ridiculous, no doubt, but the two men . . . get along."

Tad nodded. The army too made such odd alliances.

"They've always understood each other perfectly in this country, those at the top and at the bottom." Mick lifted his glass. "Speaking of the bottom . . ."

Mrs. Ball's nephew, Chan Hackett, had come in, his hand clamped on the round bare forearm of the young woman from the bakery tearoom. He boisterously greeted his mates. She looked around the pub, as if for rescue. Her gaze passed over Tad, as most gazes did.

The pub was still filling up when Mick announced that he had to be off to a meeting with a source, one of a string of spies and gossips and informants stretching from St. Andrews to Brighton. He implied that most were female.

As they passed along the bar, a woman middle aged and heavily made up lifted a thick leg in a dark stocking to block Mick's advance. When Mick halted, Tad eased around him, making his way past the Picts toward the now-propped-open door. Then he caught the wide-eyed warning of the girl from the tearoom, and he sensed movement behind him.

"What's the hat?"

Instinctively Tad ducked, twisting away from the swiping hand, but too late. Chan Hackett dangled the boonie hat from a finger, grinning nastily.

"Arse wipe, that's what." He was younger than his years, Tad realized, with the slack jaw of the dull-witted. He waved the hat, soliciting his comrades' approval.

The others were several, and mean, and their mutters and snorting laughter hung in the pub din like a growl, but they were after excitement and casual cruelty rather than combat. Were they all to come at him at once, Tad would go down and suffer, but he saw that they were not so eager to let blood and break bones as to risk their own. They would taunt and feint but attack only if they had a clear advantage or were shamed into it.

They had the courage of numbers and a few pints. He had experience and one hand that could grasp and another hand that could assault.

He rubbed his fingertips slowly over his pocket, feeling the points and edges of the items in his chamois pouch. The best defense, Marcus had told him, was not to become like your enemy.

"Don't be giving me no psycho look, Yank. You don't scare nobody."

Time slowed. Tad marked targets, measured commitment, set himself. He didn't know what might be behind him, but he didn't really care. He would damage as many as he could.

"Fucking weirdo." Chan's grin spread, as if appealing for agreement, but his friends were no longer laughing. They were all watching Tad, who had gone very still.

"What? You got nothing to say, Yank?"

"Give me my hat," Tad said quietly.

"An' if I don't?" But uncertainty crimped the corners of his eyes. "What'll you do? There's all of us, ain't there."

Tad said nothing.

Chan's grin faded. "Fucking weirdo."

"Ah, Chandler, my man." Mick Curtain eased into the scene.

Chan scowled. "Fuck off, wanker."

"Messing with your aunt's guest, are you? She's not going to take kindly to that."

"You'd be the one to tell her, though, wouldn't you." Chan seemed now to have forgotten Tad. He glared at Mick Curtain with undisguised hatred.

"Not for a bit of fun," Mick said.

"Bit of fun, yeah," the young man repeated, as if he'd just discovered something of real value. "Having a little fun's all."

"Any more than that, the word will get back to her. You don't want to upset Mrs. B., all she does for you?"

Mick took hold of the brim of the boonie hat, waited a brief moment for Chan to let go, and then handed it to Tad. "I'm late. Let's vamoose, as you Yanks say."

"Yeah," Chan said. "Fucking vamoose, you both. And stay away from my auntie, tosser."

Tad put on his boonie hat. He nodded to the girl from the bakery tearoom. In a moment he stood with Mick on the sidewalk, where a few smokers had gathered, their faces washed red by the neon pub sign.

"You looked like you were getting ready to kill somebody."

"Kill?" Tad frowned. "No."

"They thought so," Mick said. "I gave him an out, but this isn't over. He's a sneaky little twit, and he'd love to impress Billy Knox. You'll have to be on the lookout."

"He doesn't like you," Tad said.

"He's got a brain the size of a cherry pip," Mick said. "He thinks I tell Mrs. Ball not to give him money. As if anybody could tell her to do anything. He thinks I want her body and her pocketbook. Thinks the same of you, I'd guess, now. Take care."

Tad watched Mick move off. Then he crossed the street, walked half a block, and slid into the shadow of an entryway to a closed Boots store. He waited, watching, as if at an outpost near an enemy camp, noting the pub entrance, the smokers by the door, the shadows on the street, the few pedestrians, a police car and a white van and a rubbish truck. He could not have said what he was watching for. When he had watched long enough, he left.

BACK IN HIS ROOM, Tad tried to work, but he was restive and unable to concentrate. Although he'd had only a pint of beer, and not all of that, the alcohol, along with the surge of adrenaline from his confrontation with the Picts, left him edgy.

He read Marcus: "I do my duty; other things do not disturb me, for they are either inanimate or irrational, or else they wander in ignorance of their road."

He took out his chamois pouch and emptied its contents onto the desk and laid out the items in a straight line and touched them. Then he put them back.

He went out to walk.

As he made his way through darkened neighborhoods, which he was coming to know well, Tad thought about what he had told Mick Curtain about himself. He wasn't sure why he had done so. Mick was digging for stories, and Tad had no wish to become one. Still, he had given away nothing of importance.

What was important was that he walked medieval streets in a foreign country, the air brittle with chill.

That he moved past a darkened museum, scanning the street for threats.

That he stood in shadow between a tree and a rock wall and

stared up at a dark window that he knew looked into Ginny Garner's apartment.

That he was there, soldiering.

THE FOLLOWING MONDAY AFTERNOON Tad made his way to the bakery tearoom, the window of which now displayed iced scones and brownies dusted with sugar. Stepping inside, he seemed to recognize the worn linoleum, the scratched tables and chairs, the limp tablecloths, and the old display case with peeling oak veneer. The shabbiness spoke of the same marginality on which his parents' market had floated for years. An obese woman stood in the bakery doorway, smiling his mother's smile, at once hopeful and discouraged. The middle-aged women who occupied three tables laden with pots of tea and plates of assorted cakes reminded Tad of the customers who fingered produce as if seeking offerings to be sacrificed to a fearsome deity.

The blonde young waitress sat him at a table near the window. Raising her order pad, she exposed a gray-green bruise on her forearm. "I'm glad you got your hat back."

"Oh," Tad said. He took off his boonie hat and placed it on a chair.

"No, no, I didn't mean you should—" Patches of pink appeared in her cheeks. "I just meant, the business in the pub, you know."

"I forget I have it on," he said.

"It looks right on you, somehow." Her blush spread. "So, what would you like?"

He ordered and then from across the room watched her prepare tea and a cherry tart. He liked watching her. She was round, face and features, breasts and hips; her limbs were plump and firm—clearly the daughter of the large woman who still stood in the door to the kitchen, she was not heavy so much as filled, complete. A thick knot at the nape of her neck bound her hair. A pink uniform-like dress both clothed and contained her. Her skin was the rich pale white upon which faint emotion and small exertion play with pastel color. When she served him, he took note of her nametag—Rosalie.

"You're an American," she said, lingering. "You were in the war? Is that where you hurt your arm?" Almost apologetically she added quickly, "In the pub, I saw you couldn't . . . well, you favored it, didn't you?"

He wasn't sure which question to answer. It turned out not to matter, for others immediately followed.

"I—what's it like, America? Is it like in the movies?"

"Yes," Tad said, "and no."

"Some people around here don't care for America," she said, her smile indicating that she was not among these. "The war, and all the franchise places. I mean, you can imagine what Starbucks does to our custom. But I always wanted to go there. A person can be somebody else there."

Tad understood what she said if not why she was saying it.

"I love that Yanks think they're better than they are. We're just the opposite." She smiled again. "I—you were in the military. Do you have tattoos?"

"No," he said.

"No," she repeated. "Good." Then, for some reason coloring again, she fled.

He ate his cherry tart and drank his tea, dawdling over the second, cooler cup. By the time he finished, he was the only remaining customer. Rosalie had begun to gather unsold pastries from the display case. From the bakery doorway, her mother watched him, now warily, as if his presence were somehow suspect.

At the register, returning his change, Rosalie said suddenly, "In the pub, you were right to stand up to Chan. But I'm glad you didn't hurt him. He's . . . slow, and without Billy Knox and his gang at his back, he's mostly talk anyway."

Tad nodded at the bruise on her arm. "Talk?"

"Oh, that doesn't mean anything," she said. Then, flushed, she went on, "I mean, I've that kind of skin, haven't I? Even a love pat leaves a mark on me."

Tad didn't know what a love pat might be.

"That's why I don't understand about tattoos. Bruises fade and disappear, but ink and needles, they're for good. You can't ever change."

No one can ever change, Tad knew.

Rosalie looked into his silence. She frowned, pinked. "He's not my boyfriend, Chan, if that's what you're thinking. He's just a neighborhood bloke. I sort of have to go out with him, sometimes. A favor to a friend, like."

Tad remembered how she had been pressed against the wall by the Pict with spiked blue hair.

"I—when they ganged up on you," she said, "you looked almost happy. Like you wanted them all to fight you. Even with your arm. You must have done judo and that in the army? Could you beat them all?"

"No," he said.

"Yes," she said. Then she looked at him.

After a moment, he said, "The tart was good."

"Mum makes them fresh every day," she said.

"I'll be back," he said.

That night, arranging the objects from his chamois pouch in a straight line on the desk, Tad sensed that something was absent, and he felt, faintly, loss. Sleeping, he dreamed that Rosalie brought him a bag of cherries from his parents' market. In the bag he found the missing Roman coin, its edges roughed out of round, its surface stained by what he thought was juice from the red fruit but which turned out to be blood.

TAD RETURNED TO THE TEAROOM two days later and then through September with some regularity. He enjoyed the pastries.

He enjoyed too watching Rosalie Cush. She was pleased to see and to serve him, to speak with him, and as his visits became regular, sometimes, when the shop was otherwise empty, to ignore the glare from her mother and sit with him and describe her unhappiness.

She was twenty-two. Since leaving school at sixteen, she had waited on teashop patrons, supplementing the pittance her mother paid her by sewing. Her great dream was somehow to find a position as a seamstress, eventually as a costume designer. She had skill of eye and fingers, worked needle and her old portable Singer as a sculptor might a mallet and chisel, making her own clothes, altering the garments of her mother's friends, and creating outfits for amateur theatrical troupes. But in Cambridge there were few calls for her talents, she couldn't afford to go out on her own, and her mother wouldn't free her from her obligations in the bakery. She could only work and sew and hope, watch her weight, fight off the sexual predations of local men and slumming students, and endure her parents' reminders that she needed to get herself settled.

Rosalie did not wish to get settled. She wished to get out, to get started on a real, different life, one of her own making. Her great fear was that she would end up like her mother, waddling through the day among confections that she couldn't resist and through evenings suffering the snarls of a domineering dolt of a husband who drove cab and spent what he earned on wagers and ale. Her deepest desire was to go to America, Land of Opportunity, where she might ultimately put her talents to work in Hollywood.

Rosalie felt herself a character in a soap opera, her role assigned by others, her actions and experiences and emotions dictated by scriptwriters who neither knew nor cared what she really was. She felt imprisoned in Englishness, all the regional and neighborhood and class restrictions. She had long envied the freedom that Americans, at least on television, have to be themselves. She loved American sitcoms like *Friends,* in which independent young people went about their varied, interesting lives restricted by nothing but their own inclinations and abilities. She had grown up a fan of pop stars like Britney Spears, whom from certain angles she resembled, whose life, as she understood it, was a wonderful adventure. And she devoured historical romances, finding in their pulpy pages worlds where young women in difficult circumstances gained their heart's desire. But by now she had seen every *Friends* episode several times, and the bright lights of popular culture had slid past Britney Spears, and Rosalie took this to mean that her own moment was passing. She was intelligent enough to know that the novels she read offered a deeply false vision of both history and romance. They still provided her escape, but they once had offered as well, simply because they existed, a kind of hope, which now was fading.

Tad got all this in essence rather than in detail. He had no experience with this sort of discourse—intimacies filtered through popular culture—but Rosalie Cush was talking to him, which girls had rarely ever done, so he listened. Sometimes he spoke. Once he told her how, in Afghanistan, his platoon's vehicles had raised dust that settled on the walls of a ruined fortress built by the army of Alexander the Great. He told her how, when in his parents' market he sprinkled the produce, watering what had already been harvested, he always felt that the world faced backwards. He told her how, as he had walked late one night, the sound of the River Cam was so much like a human whisper that he stopped and strained to make out the words.

They had much in common, she said, single children working in their parents' businesses and living in flats above. She knew Mrs. Ball, Chan Hackett's aunt, who sometimes bought fruit tarts for weekend breakfasts. She had read pieces by Mick Curtain in the newspaper. She loved America.

Because she asked, playfully, Tad swore never to get tattooed. Because she asked, genuinely interested, he agreed to take her some Saturday afternoon to see Horatio. Because she asked, with a glance he couldn't read, he promised to accompany her to the opening of the play she'd been making costumes for.

Tad was aware that Rosalie wanted something from him. He didn't know what. Then Mrs. Ball told him.

Catching him returning one evening, she invited him into the parlor. The room was furnished in the bare Scandinavian style popular more than a half-century earlier, all but the flat-screen television dominating one wall. Sitting on the uncomfortable-looking sofa was a black man, his skin tinged with blue and his eyes streaked with red capillaries. Mrs. Ball introduced Tad to Manfred Mobuku, who would watch over things while she was in London for a weekend.

The Nigerian rose, shook Tad's hand, and with a musical African accent offered a conventional greeting. Then he departed.

"Yes, then," Mrs. Ball said, settling herself on the sofa. "Everything's all right? No problems? Nothing needs attending to?"

"No," Tad said.

"You go out, sometimes, at night, late." When he said nothing, she smiled wryly. "I'll not enquire further."

She had heard about his fuss with Chan in the Blue Boar. She was glad the to-do hadn't blown up into something serious. Chan was her dead sister's baby, and she loved him, but he wasn't the sharpest tack in the box. She asked about the return of Professor Bob, and hoped that Tad was giving him a good report of her hospitality, and wondered again if he might be able to introduce her to his boss, whose books she had purchased and would love to have signed.

She understood that Tad was now taking afternoon tea at the Cushes' bakery. "What," she smiled, "is the attraction?"

"Cherry tarts."

"Cherry? I shouldn't have thought so." When Tad didn't smile, her own smile shifted apologetically. "I don't mean to be nasty. Rosalie seems a nice young lady. Our Chan has a yen in that direction, but no chance. But you've got more competition than him. Lots of blokes straighten up when Rosalie's about. She's pretty, isn't she? Course she'll puff up into a toad if she isn't careful, but so far she's taking care of herself. Does she like you?"

Tad wasn't sure he understood the question. He had never understood these kinds of things. "I don't know."

"And yourself? Are you serious or just itchy?"

"I don't know."

Mrs. Ball looked at him. "You haven't had a lot of experience with girls, have you?"

"No."

For a long moment she seemed to hang on the edge of a decision. Then she said, "You're a Yank. You'll be going back to America in a couple of months. Rosalie knows that. So maybe she just wants to enjoy your company until you leave. But maybe she's thinking more long-term."

"Oh," Tad said.

"Sometimes a girl feels—she looks around at her friends and her life, and all she sees is a rut leading right to the grave. I did. When I was seventeen, I ran off to London. Rosalie's past twenty. It's coming now-or-never time for her."

Mrs. Ball rose from the couch. "I'm guessing, mind you. I don't really know anything."

He had a question. "Who is the Pict with the spiked blue hair?"

"Pict? I don't know about Picts, but the only lad around here with that 'do is Billy Knox."

Tad went to his room and took out his chamois pouch and made his straight line. He felt a headache coming on. He took an aspirin and picked up *Meditations* and read: "Small is the moment which each man lives, small too the corner of the earth which he inhabits."

He thought about what Mrs. Ball had said. He thought about Rosalie and America. His corner of the earth seemed to have gotten a bit larger, perhaps could accommodate more than one.

ONE MORNING early in October, Professor Stuckey came down to the storeroom. Without speaking, she moved among the shelves, noting his sorting system. Now and then she nodded. She made her way, finally, to the desk where he sat before the computer.

"It's all very competent, Mr. Fellows. Professional. I thought I should check, given that we will eventually take it all over." She nodded again, as if she had just fulfilled a requirement. "You know that, don't you? That Horatio will never leave England?"

Tad looked at her.

Professor Stuckey frowned, frustrated, irritated. "How wonderfully stoic of you."

When he didn't respond, she took a deep breath, after control. "You seem particularly adept at pressing my buttons, as you Americans say, Mr. Fellows. But I didn't come down here to berate you. In fact, I came to ask a favor."

She paused, as if awaiting objection. None coming, she continued, "Bob's daughter, Ginny. She's doing research at Clare, I understand. You must know her reasonably well."

Professor Stuckey, it turned out, in the interest of international and professional harmony, had invited Ginny Garner to an evening drinks party, at which the young woman might make or renew the acquaintance of several Cambridge classicists with whom her father had worked over the years. So far Ginny had not responded. The museum director wished Tad to persuade her to accept. He might come too, if he wished.

"This will be to your advantage as well. Your career will depend on the good opinion of the sort of people who will be present."

Tad had never given thought to a career, as such. He planned only to dig and chart and record. He depended only on Robert Garner to provide him an opportunity to do so.

The director today wore autumnal colors, rust, gold. Now she flushed as if in coordination. "Need I say that you will also want my good opinion?"

Tad had come to see himself as temporarily assigned to the museum. He recognized Professor Stuckey's authority. "I'll ask her," he said. "She'll do as she chooses."

"Might she choose to attend so as to benefit her father? I understand she has considerable charm. She might perceive that using it on crusty old dons could make some of them more receptive to his agenda."

Tad had no response to this.

"I of course oppose his efforts, but a gracious host welcomes the envoys of her enemies. Even Boudica entertained emissaries of the Romans who had betrayed her and her people."

Tad said nothing.

The professor folded her arms under her breasts. "I feel confident of my eventual success, Mr. Fellows. I don't need to be discourteous. In fact, I apologize for being so at our first meeting."

Tad looked at her.

Then Professor Stuckey did something she had not done before in his presence. She smiled openly, warmly, pleased.

"In your next report to Bob Garner—that's why you're here, of course, isn't it? As a spy? But tell him that he can't purchase the honor of the English, not with all his dead wife's money."

IN FACT, Tad had already reported to Professor Garner his sense of a strengthening of Cambridge's opposition to the plan for Horatio's removal. As autumn advanced, student protests had taken on structure and coherence. Social media exchanges organized silent vigils outside college gates. Small parades passed along the river. Bullhorns and expensively printed signs appeared at rallies. The increased and altered activity was duly noted, and editorially encouraged, by journalists both establishment and underground. Their stories invariably featured shots of a bald, bullet-headed, burly man in corduroy suits that seemed only barely to contain him. The man's name was Rupert Quarles.

Mick Curtain was happy to tell Tad, who hadn't asked, why this man was, to a student of human perversity, one of the more fascinating figures in all of Cambridgeshire.

Rupert Quarles was the only son of Sir Wilfred, upon whose death, which lung cancer had made imminent, he would inherit both the baronetcy and Waterby, the estate that generations of Quarles gentry had sucked and smoothed out of the fen. However, as a boy Rupert perceived that he wouldn't be getting much, for Sir Wilfred, an enthusiastic sybarite, had in his pursuit of pleasure allowed the agricultural enterprises of Waterby—cattle and sheep, wheat and barley, fruit—to deteriorate. Buildings and fields and roads and water systems had begun to wear or crumble or rot away; herds and flocks developed weaknesses; and debts, accumulated, had become crushing. At nineteen Rupert left Oxford because, he said, he was bored, returned to Cambridgeshire, and began to rejuvenate the business. He worked long hours. He also browbeat, intimidated, and betrayed. So successful were his initial efforts that his father gave him free rein. Despite a lack of capital, he began to repair and upgrade and modernize. Soon the estate again showed a profit. Only debt payments prevented him from making Waterby into a model operation. Still, after a decade the business was footed soundly enough that he was able to give time to politics, which got him elected, eventually, to Parliament.

Rupert Quarles was of course Tory, but his was a conservatism that seemed antiquated even to others on the English Right. He affected to and perhaps actually did scorn all government. He wore corduroy, which he called Manchester cloth, he led the local fight to continue fox hunting, he insisted on the rights of squires and the deference he deemed due those of his class, and he expressed a nostalgic yearning for an England he had never known, the seat of an Anglo-Saxon empire on which the sun never set. He argued for English military and economic imperialism abroad, unfettered capitalism and the closing of borders to immigrants and the dismantling of the welfare state at home. That England had been unable to reestablish its domination in world affairs he blamed on America. That England was, day by day, becoming less English he blamed on America. That young Englishmen were dying in foreign lands for a cause that would produce for their country no economic advantage he blamed on America. This struck a cord among his constituents, who admired his success, liked his bullying brashness, and took a kind of cultural comfort from his assumption of superiority of place.

"Tony Blair told us we were all middle-class now," Mick said with a grin, which had been present through most of this account. "Rupert Quarles tells us different, and we know he's right. Our betters are always right. Besides, politics, economics, that's nothing to do with the likes of us."

What this had to do with Horatio Tad didn't know.

"He's your real enemy," Mick said. "Sylvia Stuckey is making noises among the gowned, she's organizing volunteers, preparing for a big rally in a week or so. She'll give it numbers, but Quarles is the one who will give it energy."

"How?" Tad asked.

"Who knows?" Mick said. "But he's ambitious, hugely, and Horatio is a perfect issue for him: Up the English."

At thirty-five, Mick said, Rupert Quarles was a solitary figure, his family more and more mere background. His dying father he despised, not for his debauchery but for his weakness before temptation, as well as for his inability to pay for his pleasure. His mother had never been of consequence in his life—beautiful and rather dotty, she now drifted through her days fussing with flowers, tasting tea, painting watercolors of the scene outside her window, and humming the tunes to which she once had danced, belle of the ball. His sister, Rowena, as beautiful as her mother, bred horses, rode dressage, and attended parties to which men were never invited.

Rupert Quarles had no real friends, although he seemed to enjoy the company of the few louts, most notably Billy Knox, whom he employed for odd jobs and heavy labor at the estate. He also enjoyed the company of women of all classes. Physically powerful and rather ill-favored, he was a man of forceful will, difficult for women to resist or dissuade. And of course there was Waterby and his impending title, which attracted the interest of young ladies whom he was pleased to humiliate sexually. For nearly twenty years stories had circulated about seduction and betrayal, broken promises, abortions and regret and woe.

"He wants to be prime minister," Mick said, "but he acts like he's going to be the fucking king."

THE DAY AFTER Professor Stuckey came down to the basement, Tad contrived to meet Ginny Garner as she was leaving the Starbucks she frequented. After they exchanged greetings, and she introduced him to a gaunt young man in a denim suit, an Argentinean sculptor she said, he relayed the museum director's invitation.

"Why would she think I'd want to hang with a gang of classical archeologists?" Ginny made a face. "What could be more deadly dull? Besides, Tad, you turn into a stick at those things. You're the world's worst schmoozer."

"She wants to meet you," he said.

"Why? I—" Her mouth shaped itself into a moue of surmise. "Oh, is this the one that wrote the book? About my dad?"

"She mentions him."

"That's different," Ginny said. "That ought to be fun."

Thus, two evenings later Tad presented himself at her apartment door. Ginny looked at him and laughed. "Well, either way you'll be half right, Tad."

He wore his one good shirt, his one tie, and his blue blazer. He also wore cargo pants and hiking boots and his boonie hat.

Ginny was in black, skirt and sweater, with a green and scarlet scarf at her throat and small turquoise studs in her earlobes. She looked fresh, scrubbed, whole and wholly contained.

She took up a shawl, lavender cashmere streaked with tones of fire and flora. She grinned. "So let's have a look at this floozy who insulted my pa."

Professor Stuckey had rooms at her college, but the party was being held at her home, a small bungalow off Milton Road. Twilight was dimming as Tad paid the taxi driver. Ginny smiled. "Be sure you list that on your expense sheet. This is all for Horatio, isn't it?"

Sylvia Stuckey met them at the door, took Ginny's hand, and, assuring Tad that she would immediately get back to him, spirited the young woman away to introduce her to those already present—a dozen men and half that many women, four of whom seemed significant others of some sort. Tad found a soft drink and a corner, and, hat in hand, he watched.

Ginny Garner attracted the attention of all. This was to be expected, for she was young and attractive and charming. And she was the daughter of Robert B. Garner, the American telly don who had found the Last Centurion, who had by bringing classical archeology to the public opened channels to funding sources for their professional enterprises. And she was heiress to a fortune of a considerable number of millions. She smiled and sipped white wine and appeared to take as much pleasure in the company of these academics as they took in their sense of themselves. Professor Stuckey hovered at her elbow.

At one point a pale, bent, elderly man approached Tad, introduced himself, and began to speak of Heinrich Schliemann, leading him to several jokes about Achilles and Patroclus, until, at last perceiving that Tad was utterly uncomprehending of his purpose, he drifted off. Sometime later a woman reported to Tad, as if he might be a steward, that the cabernet was rather acidy. No one else noticed him. He observed that, given the human clusters the party created, well-placed grenades would have maximum killing effect.

Finally Ginny said something to her hostess, who with a jerk of the head turned to look across at Tad. She came over. "I'm sorry, Mr. Fellows. I got caught up in—Well, it doesn't matter. Let me take your hat."

"No," Tad said.

"Oh. Well, you would like to meet these people, no doubt."

Tad didn't, especially. He had nothing to say to them. Experience had taught him that they had nothing to say that he wanted to hear. Nevertheless, he allowed himself to be introduced to three men, one who had forgotten that they had met two summers before at the dig, another who would speak only of a book he had written on nutrition and foodstuffs for a marching army, and a third who interrupted an assassination of the character of a university vice chancellor to look at Tad's hat and ask, "I'm sorry. Who did you say you were again?"

Soon Tad was back in his corner. Guests came and went, so that, as darkness bunched up against the window, the makeup of the group slowly changed, the men and women grew younger, less archeological. The conversations changed as well, for the new arrivals were not academics but agents from Professor Stuckey's other life.

Tad by now knew something of Sylvia Stuckey's many activities outside the museum. She would save, she would defend, she would protect. She unhesitatingly threw herself at issues of controversy, and she could never resist the appeals of those representing the causes of anyone or anything abused or threatened. At the university she led the on-going fight for women's rights and equality. She supported national efforts to resist the wash over the British Isles of American popular culture—movies and music and fashion and franchise foods. And she championed endangered species and their habitat and the planet, consequently opposing everything from local building projects to nuclear power plants to the presence of the American military anywhere but in America.

She was reputedly difficult to work with or for. She labored at a pace many found impossible to maintain. She did not delegate well—distrusting others to do what must be done, she grew angry when she had to do everything herself. She was a member of dozens of organizations, yet she was essentially alone.

None of this was of real interest to Tad. Professor Stuckey's causes had nothing to do with him or his job. And now, when board members and social workers and agitators and advocates began to drift in, and the gathering swelled, and the room grew hot and noisy, he caught Ginny Garner's eye. She too was in a corner, smiling over the tense shoulder of Sylvia Stuckey.

Ginny raised an eyebrow. Tad understood. Time to go.

Before he could move, however, there came another arrival.

Rupert Quarles threatened to suck the oxygen from the rooms in a single breath. His laugh fluttered the candle flames. His physical presence, as he greeted the hostess, sent her tottering back a step. "Madame Director."

Party voices diminished as if on a rheostat, so that even Tad in his corner heard Professor Stuckey finally reply, "I'm pleased you could attend, Mr. MP."

"Couldn't miss the chance to meet an American princess." His grin, aimed at Ginny Garner, was not quite a leer.

Sylvia Stuckey smiled. "Who would imagine that a man so busy doing the business of England and her people would have time for such ceremony?"

"Ceremony." Quarles said. "Need it. Why else have royals? Introduce me."

Quarles didn't wait for her to speak. He offered to Ginny Garner a hand better suited to a smith or a gladiator. "Rupert Quarles. Here to help your father, I imagine. Try to smooth the deportation of Horatio."

Ginny took his hand and said sprightly, "My father doesn't need help against the likes of you."

He grinned. "Spirit. One thing you can say for Americans. Got spirit. Their women, anyhow."

She looked at him. "Unhand me, sir."

He laughed, releasing her hand. She laughed as well, softly. Each seemed well pleased. Each seemed alive to something in the other.

Sylvia Stuckey looked on, stunned.

Tad didn't know what was happening. He had never seen Ginny Garner as she was now, bright-eyed and flushed, radiating heat.

Ginny signaled that she was not quite ready to leave. Tad waited in his corner as she, Quarles, and Professor Stuckey conducted a quiet conversation. After some minutes, Quarles separated himself and came over to Tad. "Bodyguard?"

"Escort."

He nodded at the hat Tad held. "Guts, anyway. You and Harry. No brains. Ten minutes after you Yanks are out of there, it'll be Taliban business as usual."

Tad did not disagree. But he didn't say so.

"Couldn't be satisfied to do it on your own. Had to get that twit Blair to drag us into it as well." Quarles paused, noting Tad's silence. "You can be off. I'll take over escort duties for Miss Garner."

"No."

"Fucking Yank twit," he said pleasantly. "All guts, no brains."

Quarles made his way back to Ginny, who, when addressed, looked at Tad and smiled. When he went to her, she said, "Mr. Quarles has offered to drive us back, Tad."

Tad retrieved her shawl. With an elegant gesture she draped it across her shoulders.

"Thank you for coming," Professor Stuckey said.

"No, I need to thank you," Ginny said. "I had a lovely time."

"Oh, good. And perhaps we can continue—"

"I always enjoy discovering what kind of woman would fuck my father."

A WEEK LATER, Tad again had on his tie and blazer, as instructed by Rosalie Cush. "You'll want to look a suitable companion," she'd told him.

She wore a sheath of fawn- and milk-colored silk, which she had designed and stitched herself, with pearls at her throat and ears. When she opened the flat door to his knock, she said, eyes wide, color high, "Please tell me at once how nice I look."

Their relation now swung on such instances of edification. Rosalie, grown aware of Tad's inexperience in most of the basic forms of social intercourse, playfully assumed the instructor's role. "At the theater, help me out of my coat, slowly, so I can show off my frock."

She had by now trained him to compliment her appearance when he stopped in to the tearoom. He assiduously followed her instruction, for his acquiescence ensured that she would continue to talk to him so that he could continue to watch her.

She had introduced him to her mother, after a preliminary caution. "Be sure to mention how tasty you find her tarts." He obeyed. Mrs. Cush continued to regard him with suspicion, however. Mr. Cush, who when not driving his cab was drinking in the Blue Boar, Tad had never met.

Tad accepted Rosalie's tutoring, but he did not dwell deeply on what she told him about herself and her life. He had understood quickly that he was a receptacle into which she could empty her frustrations, that talking to him was purgative. Her smile, as she spoke to him, suggested that she was ridding herself of an inner rot. Parting, she moved with buoyancy, as if less weighted in both spirit and flesh.

"I know sometimes I babble," she had told him. "But it's good for me. You just listen. You don't judge. And you aren't always after me for something."

The evening of the play, they walked to the theater in a fine drizzle. "A gentleman always stays on the outside, near the curb, so his lady doesn't get splashed," Rosalie said, taking his arm.

The weight of her hand, the faint firmness of her clasp, felt right. "Or cut up by the shrapnel of an IED."

The theater was a rather haphazard construction fitted into a narrow, gutted, and converted department store. Wooden bleachers rose precariously in a U-shape around the stage, on which in short order actors cavorted. The cast was mostly students, the piece an unrelieved assault on the politics and proposed sexual habits of Margaret Thatcher and Ronald Reagan. Tad missed many of the allusions and found most of the British idioms obscure, but he didn't mind, as he wasn't paying attention to the plot anyway. Beside him, Rosalie shifted with pleasure, brushing his arm and hip and thigh as she whispered remarks about the hang of a skirt or cut of a jacket. He felt the warmth of her body, the damp of her breath on his cheek. Her scent was a compelling balance of lavender and musk. Her bare arms were white and round. He did not want simply to watch her. He wanted to touch her.

At the intermission, standing in line for the ice cream that Rosalie had told him it was customary to purchase, Tad espied Mick Curtain at the bar. Drink in hand, the big man came over.

"Pretty girl, your date. I've seen her somewhere. Can't think of her name."

Tad shuffled forward in the line.

Confronted by Tad's silence, Mick laughed. "After, cast and crew— ah, yes, she does costumes, doesn't she? Roz? Rosie? So you'll be at the Golden Monarch after, with the rest of the troupe?"

Tad looked back at their seats, as if the sight of Rosalie might answer Mick's question, but she was not there. At the same moment, he heard, the only real sound in the thick murmur of the crowd, a laugh, and he turned to meet the gaze of Ginny Garner. She smiled, then offered a comical leer, and laughed once more, ignoring the two young men who vied for her attention.

Tad raised a hand in greeting.

"That would be the boss's daughter," Mick said. "You won't mind, I know, if I use your name to introduce myself."

Mick grinned. Then he made his way to the bar, approached Ginny, and after a moment's hesitation began to speak. She looked over at Tad and smiled. Mick said something more, and she laughed.

Tad got ice cream and took it to Rosalie, returned from a brief conference with an assistant director. "Mrs. Thatcher is having trouble changing. I may have to rip out a few stitches tomorrow."

"Are you my date?"

"Your date?" Color played on her cheeks. "Would that be all right?"

"Yes," he said.

"Then yes, I'm your date. I— Have you never been on a date before?"

"No."

She smiled her round smile. "You are very strange, Tad Fellows."

The bell rang, the audience found seats, the lights dimmed. In the darkness Tad sat in his strangeness.

Rosalie Cush was not the first female to notice that Tad Fellows was different. Even in childhood, girls had not found him a prospect for whatever they might have had in mind. His grave silence they recognized as something beyond shyness, so they made him exempt from their mating games. This had not troubled him as a boy, but in puberty some young women began to stir him sexually. However, his sense of being alien, separate, overpowered any inclination to couple. Romances, those he had witnessed or watched in films or read about in books, he always found complex and confusing affairs for which he had no instincts whatsoever. So if his classmates would paw one another in hallways, or cuddle or clinch in corners, or race off in cars, or sneak into or out of bedrooms, he could only leave them to it.

His adolescent sexual urges were in any case curiously passive. If he had ever fantasized, it would be not to possess or pleasure another so much as to fade into the entity created in their coming together, much as he would dissolve after death, Marcus Aurelius would later tell him, atoms scattered about the universe.

Then he went into the army, and he killed and he got laid, and the pleasure he took in both was fleeting.

And now he sat in a rough-hewn theater in Cambridge, not really watching the action on the stage, feeling the heat and savoring the scent of the body of the young woman beside him and understanding what he could not have articulated, that he was experiencing for the first time a basic human impulse, a pure desire to connect with another.

The play ended, to what point Tad could not have said. Rosalie was flushed with pleasure. She now averred the effort a success. If he was willing, they might stop for a few minutes at the Golden Monarch, where the company was gathering and she could offer and accept compliments.

Drizzle still dampened the night. The pub, before which hung a sign featuring a mustard-colored moth, was recently redecorated, now all potted plants and mirrors and burnished steel tables. The crowd was mostly young, outfitted in a student dishabille that made Tad's boonie hat and striped tie and hiking boots unexceptional. Many seemed to have gathered only to talk on their cell phones. As Tad and Rosalie stood at the door, seeking a seat, in a corner Mick Curtain rose from a table and waved.

Once Rosalie was introduced and situated, Tad went to the bar for drinks. Then, waiting, he discovered that he was being watched.

At the far corner of the bar, his back to the wall, stood the Pict with blue hair worn in spikes stiffened with gel. Multicolored tattoos covered his arms and shoulders and chest, which his open denim waistcoat exposed. A tattoo on the left side of his face gave him the look of one maimed in battle.

Billy Knox, Tad knew. He did not fit in this place, with these young people. Roughly their age, he seemed of another time, another world. His bare chest and detailed tattoos and blue hair seemed outrageously real, mocking the poses of those huddling over their drinks as they eyed him warily.

He looked powerful, would be quick of fist and foot. He would be armed only with his ire. Tad met his gaze and saw something of himself.

The noise of the crowd fell into fragments, each sound clear, crisp, identifiable. Movement meant. All became an instant. The world pulsed with the throb of his heart.

Then the bartender placed drinks before him. Billy Knox grinned, raised his glass in salute, drank, and made his way through the parting crowd to the door. When he stepped out into the darkness, something like a sigh shivered through the room.

"What was that all about?" Mick asked, once Tad was reseated at the table.

When Tad didn't answer, Rosalie offered, "Billy Knox. He's Chan Hackett's mate. They're still on about the Blue Boar, the hat and all."

"Yes, I know," Mick said. "But what was he doing?"

"Saying hello," Tad said.

"Talk about the play, Tad," Rosalie said quickly. "Please."

"That's more Mick's line," Tad said.

Encouraged, Mick offered a critique of the effort—good performances, fine set, insipid direction, uneven writing. He smiled. "Excellent costumes."

Mick expanded on the subject, evaluating other theatrical offerings in town. Rosalie, through this, occasionally waved or smiled at other celebrants. Then, excusing herself, she visited tables, chatting, laughing. She seemed to know everyone in the pub. She was pink of cheek. She looked happy.

"Hard to see how she'd come to be in the Blue Boar with Chan Hackett, isn't it?" Mick drank. "Almost as hard to see why Knox would be here tonight."

Tad knew why.

"You and he have one thing in common," Mick said.

"Rosalie?"

"Rosa—" For the first time in their acquaintance, Mick Curtain was uncertain. "I— No, no. I just meant that he prowls the streets at night too, in an old white van. Or hunts, that's probably a better word."

"Hunts what?"

Mick shrugged. "Opportunity."

The crowd was beginning to thin, those not dispersed increasing their decibel level as if to compensate for their diminished numbers. Rosalie returned and suggested that they depart. A few minutes later they left an uncharacteristically silent Mick Curtain to brood over his beer.

The drizzle had changed to a thick mist that muffled the sounds of the city. Streetlights shone a pale yellow that did not penetrate the night. Every shadow was an occasion for ambush. Tad found himself searching the mist for a white van.

Rosalie, after her expansive pleasure in the pub, had contracted into a thoughtful quiet. Then, as they neared the bakery, she said, "Billy Knox."

"Yes," Tad said.

She stopped. She placed a pale hand on his arm. "He thinks I belong to him. He's got lots of girls. He thinks he can tell us what to do."

"I saw you with him one night," Tad said.

She scanned his face, frowning, as if it bore a message smudged by the damp. "He's not my boyfriend. He's just a bloke who comes around, you know?"

Tad didn't know, exactly.

"He's always been there, in school, in the neighborhood, getting uglier with each tattoo. He makes people do things. He makes me go to the pub with Chan sometimes, for a joke. Billy, he's like a stain you can't scrub off. He's—"

This had come in a rush. She choked it off, turning away from him.

"He doesn't matter," Tad said.

They walked on. As they neared the bakery, Rosalie once more took his arm, her grip firmer, fast. "Most Americans aren't like you, are they?"

"No," he said.

"Did you— Did the war do it? Are you all right, really?"

For a moment he didn't answer. Then he said, "I'm not sure."

She stopped. They stood in the damp dim night. Behind her the bakery display window was empty. "I'm taking a great chance with you," she said.

"Yes."

"You won't betray me?"

"No."

"No," she said. "What do you want from me?"

"I want to touch you," he said

Her smile faded. "Touch me? I don't—"

Slowly he lifted his hand and drew the backs of his fingers across her cheek. Then he softly pressed two fingertips to her temple, feeling the pulsation beneath the skin. He touched her as he touched, at night, the objects in his chamois bag.

She closed her eyes and was touched.

"Like that," he said.

She opened her eyes. After a moment she said, "Do you want to kiss me?"

"I don't know much about kissing girls," he said.

"You don't— Oh, you're not gay, are you?"

"Gay? No, I'm not gay," he said.

"Well then," she said, and she smiled.

THE NEXT NIGHT, the wind, which had sprung up at midday, blew through the streets of Cambridge. Tad didn't like the wind. Assailing leaves and weak hinges and loose papers, it moved and confused the shadows, created alien noises to mask the usual sounds and silences of the city. Tad felt himself in familiar territory made strange, dangerous.

His head ached. The wind was cold, scraped the skin of his face and the backs of his hands. It pierced the layers of sweatshirt he wore in lieu of a jacket. It tugged at his hat, which he had to reseat regularly. In the narrow streets it swirled and stuttered, battering at his balance. It hissed in his ears, whispering a warning he could not quite construe.

He was not alone. Isolated figures, the derelict and the dutiful, the restless or the ambitious, tradesmen and trysters, were always about, slumping on a bench, unloading a lorry or delivery van, emerging from or disappearing down an alleyway. Police patrol cars slowed as they approached him. Motorcycles grumbled past. Once an old white van nosed out into an intersection, stopped, stayed for a long moment, and then with a screech of tires sped away.

Tad walked and felt watched. He walked, and he knew that winter was coming. He walked, cold, edgy, wary, straining to advance through the shadows.

He made his rounds, patrolled the perimeter. He stood in the shadow of tree and wall and watched the window of Ginny Garner's apartment at Hathaway House. He circled the museum, alert for light or movement, for a presence or an absence that might suggest a threat to Horatio. He passed, slowly, the bakery tearoom and the flat above it.

He stood watch.

**O**NCE CELEBRATED BY HISTORIANS as a mission to bestow the benefits of civilization on a barbarian horde, the Roman invasion and occupation of Britannia were now properly understood to demonstrate the manifold evils of imperialism. They came, they savaged and looted, and they departed, leaving behind constructions that would collapse and sink under the earth, as well as DNA to make slightly more complex the genetic mix of the people who saw them go. These were fewer, so many having been cruelly slaughtered. Of course, the invaders had suffered their own losses, entire legions having been put to ruin, their famous tactics often ineffectual against the depredations of the local tribes, their vaunted martial values of no assistance in combating wild, tattooed men defending their own land and families and freedom and led by such fierce figures as Boudica. The story was one of history's many cautionary tales. Imperialism, political or economic or cultural, be it organized on the banks of the Tiber or the Thames or the Potomac, serves the interests of neither the empire nor the people whom the empire would bend to its will.

So at least said the calligraphy on the wall panels in the museum room dedicated to the Last Centurion.

Tad had saved Horatio for the end. He had shown Rosalie his workspace, then taken her on a tour of rooms containing Iron Age artifacts, gleanings from recovered Roman farmsteads and manors and markets, and collected objects and implements from medieval Cambridgeshire.

Rosalie had been attentive but unimpressed. "It's just that we grow up with all this," she said. "Every other week, it seems, somebody finds some old farm or house. We just sort of take it for granted."

In Horatio's room, she had read the commentary, now and then venturing an observation—the reference to Boudica reminded her of the statue of the tribal queen she'd seen in London—or a question to which Tad responded with easy if terse authority. Finally she asked, waving at the wall, "All this, is it true, then?"

"Archeologists don't talk about truth," Tad said. "We have theories, stories."

"Well, yes," she said, "but don't you really, finally, want to know?" She lifted a hand toward Horatio, as if she would touch him. "Who was he? Why was he at that bridge? What happened to him?"

"We collect data," Tad said. "Facts. Museums are rooms full of data. Horatio is a collection of facts. Where he was found is a fact. What he was doing there is a mystery. Any accounting for his presence is a hypothesis impossible to test. It's just a story."

He had offered each statement as if paying out coins. Rosalie smiled, clearly pleased at having drawn them from him.

"There isn't a final explanation?"

"We can't explain the past," he said. "We can only be it, sometimes."

"Be it?" Rosalie didn't trouble to hide her confusion. "You mean like history repeats itself, that sort of thing?"

Tad didn't mean that. But neither did he know quite how to phrase what he did mean. "Those people, the Romans, the Picts, they're not us, even if, deep down, we're them."

"I don't think I understand," Rosalie said.

"I don't think I do either," he said.

Rosalie drifted over to look at Horatio. The angles of the body argued. The head, even assaulted by the arrow, seemed peacefully to sleep.

"I left school when I was sixteen, but I'm smart. You know I'm smart, don't you?" Rosalie might have addressed the mummy.

"Yes," Tad said.

"Yes," she said, in confirmation. After a moment, as if reassured, she turned to examine Horatio. "He's beautiful. But why . . . is he a black? Romans weren't, were they?"

"The peat stained him," Tad said. He described the tanning effect of the acidic bog water. Then he added, "And he wasn't an ethnic Roman. Most legionnaires weren't, except the officers. His DNA says that Horatio, or his grandparents, came from Hungary. He wasn't a centurion either."

As he was speaking, a small family had entered, young parents bearing backpacks and clutching museum brochures, their two children small and wide-eyed. The mother tugged her daughter and son to respectful silence and, taking Tad for a docent, asked him what a centurion was. Pleased with his straightforward answer, she led him through a series of simple questions, responses to which Tad addressed to the children. The boy and girl seemed immediately to trust him.

The young father asked about the helmet.

"That's how we know he wasn't really a centurion," Tad said. "The centurion's helmet has a crest. Horatio was just a soldier."

"Why did they chop off . . . ?"

"Beheading enemies was a common Celtic practice, a final insult."

"Like the poem we read in school, about the green knight," the father said.

The mother smiled, patting the shoulders of her children as if to congratulate them on a chore successfully completed. They moved off.

Rosalie smiled. "I've wondered how you could be a professor, the way you hardly ever said anything."

He had, with a word here, a phrase there, informed her of his prospects—a PhD, a job. "I won't teach. I'll work in a museum, maintaining materials, setting up displays, and I'll dig when I can."

"Sometimes, won't you have to talk to people?"

"I like to talk about artifacts."

"Do you like to talk about anything else?" Her smile was playful.

"Digging. Rome." He paused. Then he said, "Usually when people want me to talk, I don't have anything to say. When I do, they don't listen."

"I'll listen, Tad." She smiled. "From now on I'll give you topics, like they did to us in school. You'll have to talk about them. I'll only grade you on effort, though."

"All right," he said.

She took in his expression and laughed. "You look so serious!"

"I am serious," he said.

"But not today." Rosalie took his arm. The touch of her hand, the connection, felt right. "Today is our holiday."

The plan for the day had come together with the spontaneous ease often mistaken for providence. They would, this early November Saturday, visit the museum, where Tad would show her around and introduce her to Horatio. In the afternoon they would look on at the rally protesting the mummy's removal, in the evening see a film about a squad of British soldiers in Iraq.

Attending the rally was Tad's suggestion. He did not tell Rosalie, because there was no reason to, that two days earlier, for once by chance meeting Ginny Garner on the street, he learned that she was planning to be at the rally herself. He had cautioned that she might be thought by some to be a logical target of the protestors' invective. She had dismissed his concern with a laugh, at which he had determined to be there, too.

Rosalie had proposed the movie. Over the few weeks they had been talking, she had sometimes quietly, tentatively inquired into his experience in Afghanistan. He spoke of war as he did everything else, succinctly, matter-of-factly. He answered her questions but told her no stories. He described what he had done as a soldier but said nothing about how he felt doing what a soldier does. One afternoon, as he sat over his tea and a cherry tart, she asked about PTSD: did he know any soldiers so diagnosed? Only himself, he told her.

As far as the film was concerned, to Tad war movies were just war movies. Most he'd seen were too focused on the personal, missed the powerful compulsion that drove the action; they treated the soldier characters as if their emotional lives had relevance in circumstances governed by inscrutable, implacable forces. They discounted destiny. Not like *Spartacus*, where all either served the interests of Rome or died.

"So you won't get upset, reliving your war?" Rosalie had asked him.

He said no. He knew that she didn't entirely believe him. Like Professor Garner and others, she suspected that his psyche held horrors that diverted, stunted, or otherwise altered his responses to life and to people. To her. But he had been different, separate, shut off long before he went to Afghanistan.

The tour of his workspace had visibly disappointed her—boxes, a computer, charts and photos and drawings. Her smile strained over the few coins. He did not tell her that one was missing. The other exhibits exacted from her only polite nods.

On the other hand, she delighted in the sheer physical fact of Horatio. Her great disappointment was that she could not touch him. She studied his body, the bare limbs, the torso under his tunic and armor, as if mentally measuring him for a new outfit. She examined his face, his smooth skin and stubble of beard and reddish tufts of hair, his slightly parted lips and closed eyelids.

"The Romans," she said, "they didn't tattoo themselves, did they?"

"That was a barbarian practice."

"It still is," she said, not smiling.

Tad drew her attention to the outline of the gladius. He illustrated how it would be used, thrusting out and up. He praised its suitability in the close-quarter combat in which Horatio would have been engaged. "It's exactly the proper length and weight."

"Its shape," Rosalie said, "It's shaped like a—" She stopped, reddening.

Tad waited, but she didn't continue. Then he said, "It's the perfect weapon for its purpose."

TAD AND ROSALIE left the museum and walked toward the river and the protestors who, after marching in a large circle, were crossing the bridge to gather on The Backs to listen to speakers. The day was bright, the sky high and clear—a well-positioned artillery spotter might see advancing armor and troops for miles. The chilly breeze tugged recalcitrant leaves from the trees and spun them down onto the river to drift and settle in clumps along the banks or, sodden, eventually to sink.

The wind stirred Rosalie's blonde hair, spread washes of pale pink and red over her cheeks. She had made up, lightly, her eyes and mouth, Tad noticed, and she wore a familiar faint scent and a white bulky knitted sweater that suggested the heft of her breasts and fashionably faded jeans that shaped her hips and a trim green jacket with padded shoulders that put her whole body into balance. Tad was simultaneously pleased by two thoughts—she was sexually appealing and she had made herself so for him.

He had taken pleasure in their kissing in the mist the night of the play, but he had not kissed her since. He was satisfied, as he listened to her, and spoke to her, to enjoy her pure presence. He liked the way she brushed against him, or took his arm, or placed her fingertips briefly on his wrist, his hand, and on occasion he had touched her face as a child might, making certain that she was really and still there.

He saw her at the tearoom every few days, under her mother's glowering gaze. Mrs. Cush did not approve of their friendship, fearing, Rosalie said, that he would spirit her away to America. She said this with a smile that argued with her gaze.

Evenings, Tad sometimes walked her home from the theater, where she was consulting and planning and beginning work on costumes for a Christmas Panto. Or they went to the movies. Or they walked, and she talked about costumes and how difficult it was to have to work around an actor's tattoo, about films, about America. She occupied a space beside him that he hadn't known had been vacant. He didn't think about kissing her again. He was content to be with her.

She took his arm and leaned into him. "You've forgotten your coat. You'll freeze."

Tad hadn't forgotten his coat. He didn't have a coat. He'd lost his field jacket, along with his Class A uniform, in one of his many moves of residence. But until now he hadn't needed much more than a hoodie, Los Angeles winters being what they were.

Hearing which, Rosalie assumed her tutorial pose. "You're not in California anymore. In Cambridge, only a fool would try to go past September without a warm coat. After the rally, we march you down to Marks and Spencer."

They walked on. Then Rosalie gave his arm a squeeze. "You were wonderful with the children."

Tad didn't understand what she meant.

Eventually they encountered the protesters, ambling more than marching, a loose and genial crowd completing their circuit through the inner city and college environs. Tad and Rosalie walked with them for a distance, she huddled against his side as if to share her warmth, until they rose up onto the bridge. Halfway across, Tad stopped. From there he commanded a view of the approaching marchers, strung out around the corner of a college building; and of the River Cam, on which punters lazily poled and ducks nodded at drifting leaves; and of the crowd bunching up in a grassy bowl before a raised platform. On this stand he saw two portly men, sashed as city officials, as well as Sylvia Stuckey, Rupert Quarles, a woman Rosalie said was Rowena Quarles, and, between brother and sister, astonishingly, Ginny Garner.

For a moment Tad thought that Ginny, fifty yards away, had seen and recognized him. He started to wave when she abruptly turned away. He watched as, with Rowena Quarles, she stepped down to the grass.

Beside him, Rosalie's breathing changed. "That's her, isn't it? The daughter? Professor Bob's daughter?"

"Ginny," he said.

"She's very . . ." But Rosalie could not finish her sentence.

The section of The Backs blocked off for the rally clearly wouldn't accommodate all the protesters—half again more than the two thousand expected, Tad guessed. Local media had all week announced the event, characterizing the rally as either a patriotic exercise or a raging against the machine, which they were now prepared to record. To that end, television cameramen jostled for position, and reporters—Tad could see Mick Curtain's head bobbing above the throng like a ball on the water—scribbled in notepads as the swell of demonstrators spilled over into an avenue of lime trees and pressed up against the river's edge and backed slowly toward the bridge. They crunched closer together, increasing the effect of a mortar round.

The mood of the marchers was mixed. Some seemed serious, nearly grim. Others chatted casually on cell phones. Some of the signs, both hand drawn and commercially printed, bore the image of Horatio; others pulled Uncle Sam's beard or castigated American imperialism and British complicity. The chants that broke out and died for no clear reason were simple, even simple-minded. Many sloganeers were students, others their teachers. There were townies too—the still-spry elderly out for an air, some professional and working men and women, a few young families, and larking teenagers hunched into the quickening wind. There was a scattering of hooligans, beer cans at the ready. Among these was Billy Knox.

Tad had followed Ginny Garner's descent from the speakers' platform and was tracking her progress through the crowd when the sudden clench of Rosalie's hand on his arm told him that his position had come under threat.

"Not enough the Yank gimp shames our Chan in front of his mates," Billy Knox said, suddenly there. His smile mocked. The tattoo—of a creature all claw and fang—darkening half his face made him seem a demented harlequin. "Now he's sniffing after his girl."

"I'm not his—"

"Shut it," Knox said with soft, smiling savagery. "We'll get to you."

Rosalie made a strange moaning sound. She pressed herself against Tad's arm.

They were four, Knox and Chan Hackett and two others whose bright blue eyes and weak chins made them brothers. Tad was backed against the bridge balustrade, trapped, caught wandering in the desert where Americans died.

Knox moved forward, the tattoos on his muscular arms and chest shifting like leaves drifting over submerged and hidden danger. Exactly Tad's height, he was thirty pounds heavier. He was not afraid and would be merciless.

"Now," Chan said, panting with excitement. "Now."

Protesters straggled by. On the river, punters floated toward the bridge. At the edge of the crowd, a pair of bored policemen observed.

Alert to Tad's awareness, Knox said, "Coppers'll be no help, Yank."

"Now," Chan said.

Now, Tad assented. He settled into himself, grew at once older and fresh, fierce and at peace. Now.

Billy Knox studied him, grinning. "You too, Yank? You too?"

From the speakers' platform came the scratchy screech of a woman testing the microphone—Professor Stuckey, Tad realized, which for some reason made the situation suddenly absurd.

The sky was very blue. The wind blustered and died, whipped and waned. The crowd in the grassy swale surged and sighed. The River Cam made a sound like breathing.

"Leave him alone, Billy," Rosalie said then, nearly whimpering.

"Shut up, you fucking cow." This from Chan, shuffling, panting. "Now, Billy."

"He's a killer, our gimp Yank," Knox said, apparently pleased. "He's ready to kill us, all for a smile from our sweet fat Rosie and a fucking hat."

Tad felt Rosalie lurch against him, as if she'd been struck.

"Now."

"You want a hat?" Rosalie's cry came low and throbbing, like a sob. "Is that what you want?"

Knox laughed.

"You'd thump somebody over a hat?" Rosalie, despairing, snatched the boonie hat from Tad's head and hurled it at the tattooed face. "Here. Here's the bloody hat. Now go away. Just . . . go away!"

The hat had fallen to the stone of the bridge. Tad knew to make no move to retrieve it.

Knox bent and picked up the hat and ran a thick finger over the CIB. Then on the same finger he twirled the hat for a moment before tossing it to Chan. "What'll you do with it, laddie?"

"Piss in it," Chan said gleefully, catching it. "Shit in it. Wipe my arse with it."

When one of the brothers laughed, Chan flicked the hat to him. "What you gonna do, Rodney?"

The three young men tossed the hat back and forth, repeating obscenities. Tad didn't move. Rosalie followed the flight of the hat as if mesmerized. On the gusty wind came Professor Stuckey's exhortations to umbrage.

Billy Knox watched Tad. Then suddenly he grabbed the hat as it waffled past him, and with a snap of his wrist he sent it sailing out over the river. For a long moment the hat hung, quivering in the wind, finally with a kind of sigh settling onto the dark water, where it floated among the yellow leaves like the ducks that slid and swung in the placid current.

"Off to the fucking North Sea," shouted Chan, even as the hat, sucking up water, began to sink. Soon the brim had disappeared. The crown became a cap. Then, as the lump of cloth started into a small bend in the river, as the sun glinted off the Combat Infantryman Badge, with what almost seemed a purposeful dive the boonie hat dipped and disappeared.

Tad had seen none of this. He had not taken his eyes off Billy Knox, the blue hair, the tattoos, the gaze in which he recognized a comrade, a brother, himself.

"There," Rosalie said. "You've had your fun. Now go away and leave us alone."

Knox grinned.

"Please, Billy."

There was in her plea a softness, a familiarity, even an intimacy, which turned Tad away from Billy Knox, to look at her.

The blow came out of a peripheral blur like a dust storm and struck his temple with a blinding flash of bright white light, and then another fist battered his bad shoulder and slammed him into the stone balustrade and hard fingers dug into his leg and lifted and he was upended and he fell, free, and finally he hit the water and he sank into the cold darkness.

Forces fought to control and to kill him. Physics, he bizarrely thought without thinking. He fought, too, even as he accepted his destiny, his doom, if such this was—death by water, food for creatures of the deep, salt for the sea.

He surfaced as if dropping into a dream—blue sky, willows trailing in the river, hoots of laughter.

For a very long while, or so it seemed, he struggled, thrashing one-armed against the small river, the drift and suck of the water, the cold that numbed his muscles but not his pain. He did not so much swim as with a single hand claw his way slowly toward the trees and the mud of the bank. For a longer while, he clung to a slimy tree root, spent, waiting for someone to pull him from the swirl to safety.

Back on the bridge, Rosalie's round face hung above the balustrade like a sign on which the message had been weathered to blankness.


TAD TOLD THE POLICE that he had been tossed into the river by an acquaintance in a fit of exuberant horseplay. Rosalie concurred. When the constable heard the name Billy Knox, she scoffed her incredulity at Tad's account, but she wrote her report without comment. She eyed the knot, already purple, near Tad's eyebrow. "Are you all right?"

"Yes," he said, but he wasn't. He wasn't sure who he was.

In the police car, the heater blasted warm air, but Tad, wrapped in a thick blanket, continued to shiver with cold. Rosalie sat beside him, pale, her torso hunched and limbs clenched together as if to make herself small. "I'm sorry," she repeated, whispering, often to herself. "I'm sorry."

Over the hum of the heater he could hear the sound of speeches from the rally, human voices amplified into meaninglessness. His head hurt, and his shoulder, and his back, and his lungs. He couldn't get control over his shivering.

He had made mistakes. He had allowed himself to be distracted. Stay alert, stay alive—but he hadn't. And he'd lost his hat.

He closed his eyes.

Rosalie touched his wrist. Cautiously, like a team of sappers infiltrating a perimeter, her fingers felt their way to his hand, where they settled, softly.

When her hand tightened briefly on his, he opened his eyes. He didn't know where he was. He didn't know who he was or why he was so cold and why he hurt. There were people on a bridge. One was Ginny Garner. As though she might guide him back to a familiar world, Tad watched her move down the bridge and along the walk. She turned a corner and was gone. His head hurt, and he did not understand.

The constable drove them back to Mrs. Ball's. Tad's shivering had become deep hard shudders. He didn't know why Rosalie was helping him to the door. Then all was shadow. Faces—Mrs. Ball's, Manfred Mobuku's—were configurations of fog. Forms filled his room. Voices hollowed holes in the gray. He was handled, helpless, a leaf in the current. He was in the river again, cold, buffeted by nothing, nothing...

He dipped a galvanized sprinkling can to water lettuce, peppers, radishes, celery.

He stood in a shadowed alley, rank with the rot overflowing a dumpster, foul with human decay, where men drank and slept and pissed themselves, and he looked down at a crumple of blood and rags, and in his hand he cupped a piece of obsidian.

From a doorway he stared into a dim room where a body, splayed on a bed, breathed in, breathed out.

He waited on a Pasadena street corner, and on the opposite corner people gathered for no apparent reason, and hailed him, encouraging him to cross the street, but the traffic light would not go green.

He sank slowly into water, warm, smooth and weighty and firm like pudding, fragrant with lavender and musk, and he was not afraid.

He watched as she crept toward him, a woman from the shadows, shapeless, her eyes bright in the slit in her black burqa, and as her dark hand began to move, he thrust his swollen hard phallus up and out, a gladius from which she backed away, and she became part of the night, her eyes still bright, black.

Rosalie awoke him, her smell, her warmth.

But it was Mrs. Ball who stood at foot of the bed. "Yes, then. You're back."

He had collapsed just inside the door, she told him. She and Manfred Mobuku and Rosalie Cush had helped him up to his room and into bed. By the time the doctor arrived, Tad had slid deeply into sleep. His temperature was low, but otherwise his vital signs were strong. The doctor asked about the incident. He asked about Tad's scars and a history of concussions. He said that Tad had suffered a hard blow to the head but otherwise, except for a few scrapes, he was undamaged, at least physically. That was Saturday. It was now Monday, midmorning.

"Rosalie?"

"She was here all day yesterday."

"I smell her," Tad said, confused.

"You were shivering. She got in bed with you. To keep you warm." She smiled then, a warm, human smile, the first, really, that he'd seen from her. "Doctor's orders. Or at least doctor's suggestion."

Tad slowly sat up. His headache was faint, a rumor of pain. His body was stiff, his shoulder and back sore. He was about to swing his feet onto the floor when he realized that he was naked.

"Concussions," Mrs. Ball said. "Have you had them?"

VA doctors had asked him that question seven years earlier, when his headaches had begun. Not that he could remember, he'd told them.

"I've got to go to work."

"Billy Knox knocked you barmy," she scoffed. "No work today, bucko. You'll be lucky to manage getting dressed. While you're at it, I'll lay out something to eat."

At the door, she stopped. "Rosalie told me what happened. I'm sorry our Chan—well, he's easily led, isn't he? It's too bad about Billy Knox, though. He's not the sort you want after you."

Tad remembered then what had distracted him on the bridge, what had caused him to take his eyes from his enemy. "What is he to Rosalie?"

"Chan? Nothing, really. She goes to the pub with him sometimes because Billy Knox makes her. It's a joke of some sort."

"Not Chan. Billy Knox."

Mrs. Ball hesitated. "She's not in love with him, if that's what you're asking."

He didn't know, quite, what he was asking. He didn't know either what he was feeling.

"He has girls, Billy," she said carefully. "He has ways of making them do what he wants—menace, threats, sex. He frightens them, but . . . there's an attraction. But I don't really know, do I?"

THE SUN WAS SINKING, the blue sky going gray, when Rosalie came. She had his clothes, washed and dried and neatly folded into a shopping bag, which she set carefully on his chair. "How are you?"

"I'm fine," he said. Rising, showering, dressing, he'd been wobbly. He felt somewhat stronger after eating, but not enough to engage the world. He'd spent the day dozing, and reading random sentences of Marcus Aurelius—"Every man carries his appointed fate with him, and it carries him along"—and arranging and rearranging on the desktop the contents of his chamois pouch.

Rosalie reached out and gently drew her fingertip over the bruise, now black and dark purple and green and a sickly yellow, on his temple. "I'm so sorry."

He looked at her.

A single teardrop, clear, pure, spilled over her eyelid and started down her cheek, where it collapsed into a wet smear. "I'm so sorry," she repeated.

He sat on the edge of the bed. He felt a powerful urge to say something, to tell her something. But he didn't know what, and he wouldn't have known how.

After a hesitant moment, she sat beside him, warm, fragrant.

"Your hat. I don't know why I threw it at him. I— We could get another, the army surplus store has them. Or Oxfam, sometimes."

"No," he said.

"Half the folks of Cambridge have noticed that hat," she said softly, not quite smiling. "Now no one will recognize you."

He feared that he might not recognize himself.

Tad didn't know why the boonie hat had become part of who he was. He'd worn several different army-issue covers in Afghanistan. But he'd had on the boonie hat when he stepped off the plane, back in America, and he'd attached the CIB when he received his discharge papers, and he wore the hat and had come to feel incomplete without it.

They sat silently. Then she said, "I didn't know who to call. Professor Stuckey has no reason to care, from what you've told me, and Professor Garner's not here. I thought maybe his daughter, but I didn't know how to get in touch with her."

When he didn't respond, she elaborated, "I mean, the way you were watching her, at the rally, I just thought maybe the two of you had—"

"No," he said.

She released his hand to smooth her pleated skirt over her round thighs. "I know you don't— I mean, I know you aren't the sort to fall in love or anything, are you? But I thought you might . . . want her. You know, even your Marcus Aurelius there felt desire, didn't he?"

Tad didn't know what to say. He found Ginny Garner not desirable but complete and clean. He didn't want to possess her. He wanted only to protect her.

He rose and went to the desk. They were laid out in a straight line— the shrapnel, the peach pit, the broken clothes peg and lipstick cap and shilling and bit of obsidian.

"It's all right," Rosalie said to his back. "If you . . . wanted her, I mean. I'd understand."

The peach pit was a hair out of line. He touched it with his fingertip.

"I only want to do my duty," he said. "To embrace it, like Marcus says."

"Duty?" Rosalie furrowed her forehead in faint dismay. "What duty?"

"She's what I'm here for."

"Here in Cambridge, you mean?"

He heard Rosalie rise from the bed and move to stand behind him.

She didn't touch him with her hand or her body but he could feel her presence nevertheless. Her scent seemed to allow another aspect to his existence.

"I'm trying to understand, Tad."

He nudged the broken clothespin out of line and then nudged it back. He couldn't really explain.

"When she was seventeen, she came on the dig. A local thug followed her into a grove of trees and attacked her. I was there, and I stopped him. It was..."

Tad turned to face her. The trail of the tear down her cheek had dried into a soft shining, like a sunlit desert river.

"I wasn't doing anything there, in the trees. That's the thing. I was just there, as if I had to be. It was . . . intended, fated. Everything in my life, growing up in that little market and fighting in Afghanistan and stumbling into her father's lecture at UCLA, all of it led me to that copse. It was destined. She was the reason for everything."

He had never thought about his commitment to Ginny Garner in these terms, never tried to explain his certainty. Now he felt frustrated by his inability to put something so pure and simple into pure and simple words.

Rosalie stood very still. He could feel her breathing. "And now? What is she now? To you?"

"If she needs me, I'm there," he said.

"But otherwise? If she doesn't need you, you'll just go on with your life?"

Tad wasn't sure that he understood. "Yes."

"I mean, you're in the same city with her but you hardly ever see her, do you?"

Rosalie didn't know about his nights standing watch. But in fact he did not often actually see Ginny as he stood across the street from her window, in the shadows. "No."

"So it isn't really . . . personal? What you feel for her?"

"Personal? You mean— No, no," he said, "it's not personal. It's not . . . personal."

Rosalie looked at him. Something happened in her face, around her eyes, her mouth. "What about me, Tad? Do you feel anything personal for me?"

"I—"

"I know you liked kissing me," she said. "Didn't you."

He watched her.

"Say it, Tad. You liked kissing me, didn't you?"

*Liked* wasn't the right word, but he hadn't a better one. "Yes," he said.

"But you haven't done it again. You haven't tried to do anything else, either."

"No," he said.

"I thought maybe the war, your wounds, you know, that maybe you couldn't—But then when I was hugging you, warming you, you, well, got excited, so I know you're just like any other bloke that way."

He thought of the whores his army buddies had led him to. Friction and spasm and spurt. "Yes."

"And you want me. I know you do."

He didn't speak.

She smiled then, for the first time since she had arrived. "I know you want me. But you've got to ask, Tad. Even when a girl cares for you, she needs to know she's . . . wanted."

Tad said nothing.

Rosalie moved, pressed her body gently, carefully against his. They stood silently, each aware of the stirring of his genitals.

"See?" she said.

He still didn't speak.

She raised her face. "You have to say it, Tad."

He said, because he must, "I want you."

And she smiled.

Time changed then, as it had on occasion in combat. Motion

slowed. The world impressed itself on his awareness. He became a taut quivering receptor, registering and sorting and classifying sensations. His body became a body engaged in a body's business. Life used him, and paid him in pleasure.

Rosalie, naked, was all bow and arc and circle, warm and moist, fit for filling. She tutored him, patiently, as if inducting him into mysteries—signs, shibboleths, codes.

He became other. Yet he remained as he was, as he had learned to be as a boy, detached. Even at the most intense of moments, he watched.

Then she watched him. She leaned on one arm, looked down at him. "You liked that, didn't you?"

"Yes," he said.

"And you like me, don't you? At least a little?"

He looked up into her smile. He thought she might be playing, but he wasn't sure. "Yes."

"If I needed you, would you be there?"

"Yes," he said.

"If I asked you, would you take me with you to America when you go?"

"Yes," he said. And if she was playing, he was not. This too, he knew, was part of a great design.

"Yes," he said again, promising.

THE WEATHER TURNED. Cold rain fell in fits as a gale blew off the North Sea. Then a heavy fog spread from the fen. After that came more wind and showers of ice pellets and finally small dry flakes of snow. Departed, the storm left the mid-November air sharp with cold, the city briefly white under an inch of snow that melted in the sunlight and froze to black ice that night. In the light of neon and streetlamp, frost glittered dully. The river steamed in the cold. Sounds seemed brittle, as if they might snap. Tad, walking well after midnight, stepped carefully.

His head ached. Tonight aspirin had had no effect, and walking wasn't helping very much either. He felt, in his pain, distant, threatened, at the edge of a darkness in himself.

At least he was warm in his new sweater and anorak. Rosalie had taken him shopping. The afternoon they'd spent in his room she had looked into his clothes closet and despaired at its great gaps. Learning that his blazer and shirt had been purchased at Ginny Garner's insistence, she grew resolute. Tad Fellows, prospective PhD, must be properly attired. So a few days later at Marks and Spencer they bought him another jacket, tan corduroy with leather patches at the elbows, and three pair of dress slacks, brown and black and tan, and a shirt, only one, cream with thin pale blue stripes, which she would use as a pattern to make him several more, and two new ties. They bought turtlenecks and sweaters and underwear and socks and shoes, black wingtips. They bought him a Clare College windbreaker and a wool anorak. Rosalie wanted to buy him an Australian brush hat, but he said no. As they shopped she fretted about cost, until finally he told her that he wasn't sure how much money he had, his checks from the VA and the university going directly into his account with his other money, but he rarely spent anything except on food and lodging, so he knew he had enough to buy whatever she thought he needed.

They browsed in the central market and the coin shop and the Regent Street mall and an antique store where Rosalie admired old brooches and pins and cameos. Back at Mrs. Ball's, to satisfy Rosalie's concerns he went online and checked his bank account—he had a balance of slightly more than eighty-two thousand dollars. Hearing this, Rosalie grew quiet.

Now, warm in the cold night, Tad walked to the rhythm of the throb in his head. Once a police car stopped at a corner, the officers watching him make his way along the sidewalk. His pace regulated by his pain, he came to march toward trance, toward a world he knew well but could not remember.

At Hathaway House, Ginny Garner's window was dark. The street was empty, and the sidewalk, and the night.

Above the bakery tearoom, the glass panes wore rims of white. No one was pressed against the wall of the entryway. The shop seemed not merely closed but abandoned.

In the museum atrium, pale nightlights thinned the darkness. Nothing that Tad could see was wrong. Nevertheless, he stopped, because something was not right.

Now fully in the present, he listened—night sounds, the creaks and sighs of a cold city. He climbed the stairs to the glass doors and peered in at shadow, grayed at the edge of the light but undisturbed.

Tad fought his headache, thinking. The night security man, the portly Jackson, could be anywhere in the building, making his rounds, or, more likely at two-thirty in the morning, dozing. The team of cleaners would have departed by midnight. He considered going in—he had a key, after all—but decided instead to reconnoiter the perimeter. He didn't know why, but something was not right.

Something was not right. Such was a certainty familiar to every soldier ever to stand guard. Because in the darkness, in an alien land, many things might be not right. Always, one of them was that the enemy was about.

Most of the time, the enemy was not actually about. Most of the time.

Alert, his cheeks and chin and ears burning gently in the cold, Tad made his way down the block and around toward the rear of the museum, watching the line of rooftops against the city-lit sky, scanning the dark emptiness spreading toward the river, studying shadows, plumbing city-sounds for any indication of another presence.

Peering past the corner of the building, he saw immediately what was not right—a small white van was backed up to the museum loading dock. Tad felt suddenly alone, exposed and without support. His fingers curled to grip the weapon that he did not have.

He watched until he was convinced that the vehicle was unoccupied. Then he slipped forward through the shadows. The odor of warm oil, the faint tick of cooling metal, insisted that the van had only recently arrived.

One of the museum's loading doors had been jimmied and left open a few inches. That should have set off the alarm system but hadn't. Had the shriek, harsh and brief, of ripping wood and metal sounded his own inner alarm? Or the cough of an engine, dying?

Tad slid inside. The warm air suggested that the door had not been ajar for long. Whatever was happening was only beginning. Burglary, he guessed. The museum owned all sorts of small, portable items that would fetch a price in specialized markets—weaponry, utensils and flatware, porcelain and pottery, to say nothing of coins, many worth much more than a one-hundred-dollar Marcus Aurelius 194.

As if to clear a space in which to sort through the information from his senses, Tad's headache retreated. He listened to the building, took in its heavy hush. He noted differences in the darkness. He smelled cleaning compound, wax, and, faintly, ammonia. Finally he started quietly down a long hallway toward the front of the building and the stairway to the upper floors.

The odor of ammonia grew stronger. Even as he realized that he smelled urine, he stubbed his boot against, unmistakably, flesh. He froze, sensing the shape of the body sprawled out before him. Kneeling, he felt for and found a pulse. Jackson, the security man, it would be. He heard the faint susurrus of the man's respiration, and at the same time, ringing down the hallway, the sharp screech of tortured wood.

Tad knew then where they were and what they wanted.

He crouched in the darkness, uncertain. He had to this point been patrolling. Suddenly he was amid the enemy, without his team, his squad. He had no tactics to which he might resort, no one with whom he might coordinate an action. His training had not prepared him for this situation. In war he had been but an integer in a calculus of combat. Now, alone, he could only improvise.

The invaders were intent on removing Horatio, not violating him. Otherwise they would have done their vandalizing and been on their way out already.

To keep from damaging the mummy, they would have to take the whole case, which with its climate-control technology was heavy, would require three or four men to urge it onto a truck or dolly of some kind.

They would need to move slowly, take great care.

They would cross the atrium, where the ambient light would expose any ambush he set for them. He might have an advantage in the dark hallway, but he might not, and in either case there was a real risk that Horatio might be abused in the conflict.

The security man carried no weapon. He did have a large flashlight, which might do effective work, but not enough if the enemy were several.

Tad did not know what to do.

Then he did.

Taking Jackson's flashlight, he found his way back to the door and descended the stairs to his own workspace, where he picked up the phone and called the police.

He had difficulty making the sleepy desk sergeant understand the nature and accept the legitimacy of his information. Then he was told that officers would arrive in three minutes. Tad was to stay where he was, to do nothing.

He put down the phone and sat in the dark room and waited. Three minutes passed. Five minutes. Eight. Ten. Twelve.

He could wait no longer. He had no idea how far into their

dismantling the thieves were. They could even now be rolling Horatio down the dark hallway toward the door and the panel truck and the night. He couldn't take that chance.

He went to the utility room and threw emergency switches to turn on the lights of every hallway and common area in the building.

When he was halfway up the stairs, he heard footsteps running down the hall. By the time he got to the back door, three figures were climbing into the white van. One of them was wearing a helmet crested like that of a centurion. But of course it was actually a Mohawk hairdo.

He found Horatio in his case, which was loaded onto a small hand truck, just outside his display room. The mummy was undamaged. A constriction like a grip on Tad's heart eased.

Tad returned to Jackson, who greeted him with a moan. He helped the security man sit up and was kneeling at his side, checking the bloody gash at the back of his head, when the police finally arrived, brandishing weapons much like those Tad and his squad had carried in Afghanistan, like the soldiers armored in vests and adrenaline. After a frenetic few seconds, Tad was down on the hallway floor, his shoulder wrenched and aching, his hands cuffed behind him. So he stayed until a Detective Chief Inspector appeared, checked Tad's ID, and listened to what he had to say and told an officer to help him up and remove the handcuffs.

At the police station, the same DCI gave him coffee and alternated with a sergeant asking, over and over, the same questions. Where was his passport? Where was he staying in Cambridge? What was he doing in England? Was he a student then? But he was not enrolled in any of the Cambridge colleges? What was his position or job or function at the museum? Was his work related to the mummy? How? How long had he been doing it? How did he come to be passing by the museum at two-thirty in the morning? What kind of headaches did he suffer? How long had he had this condition and had he seen local doctors and had medication been prescribed for it? What, exactly, hadn't seemed right? Why hadn't he used his key to go inside? Why had he gone inside when he discovered the jimmied door and knew that a crime was in progress? How had he known, in the darkness, where the intruders were and what they were doing? Why had he turned on the lights and allowed them to escape? How had he known where to find the power switches? Did he know how to turn off the security system? What could he tell them about the van other than that it was white? Was he sure he couldn't identify any of the three men he saw fleeing?

Tad answered the questions truthfully. He told the detective about the Mohawk hairdo. The detective said that there were lots of those about and did not ask him if he knew anyone who wore his hair that way.

The detective agreed that Tad had interrupted an act of theft rather than of vandalism. But who would steal a mummy? Why? What value had it? To whom?

Tad did not speculate about these matters, referring the detective to Professor Stuckey.

The detective clearly found Tad's story unsatisfactory, partly because of its details, partly because of its gaps, but also because of Tad's manner—at once exact and at ease, he answered questions as if placing measures of dirt onto a sifting screen.

At one point the sergeant asked Tad detailed questions about the security system and who might have had access to it. Tad, who knew nothing about the technology, could tell him only that the utility room was never locked and the basement area rarely patrolled, so that anyone who knew where the switches were could easily get to them. The DCI, skimming a report form, then asked about his swim in the Cam. Tad repeated what he had said at the time, to which both officers expressed skepticism. They seemed to think that being involved in two incidents in a short period of time somehow was significant. Finally, after having Tad write out and sign a statement, they released him.

A BIT LATER, at breakfast, Mick Curtain, to whom Tad offered an abbreviated account of the night's events, asked questions similar to those of the police. Tad gave him similar answers.

"The white van," Mick said. "Billy Knox."

"I didn't actually see him," Tad said. "The DCI said half the vans in Cambridge are white."

Mick mused. Then he excused himself. He returned with a camera and a command. "Smile."

"What are you doing?" Tad said.

The camera flashed. Mick grinned. "Making you a hero."

By midmorning, all the local media had the story. Throughout the day, print and radio journalists phoned him at the museum after information, which he gave, and elaboration, which he did not. As he had with the police, he referred angled inquiries to Professor Stuckey. Late in the afternoon, just as he was about to go out for tea and a tart and Rosalie's round smile, the director called and asked him to meet her in Horatio's room, where a television newswoman from a BBC affiliate was waiting to interview them.

The mummy was in his case, the case back on its plinth. The wiring for the climate controls was reconnected. But for the gouges left by a pry bar, all was as it had been.

The reporter was clearly disappointed to find herself in a scene of so little actual destruction. Brightly bow-lipped and deeply rouged, a small pink fleur-de-lis tattooed on her inner wrist, she spoke like a doll that intones a rush of scratchy recorded words when a string is pulled. On camera, after establishing the basic facts, she led Tad through a sequence of questions laced with insinuation: surely the burglary and assault were connected to the protest against the move of the Last

Centurion to America; surely America, with its armies and drones and Levi's and fast-food franchises and hip-hop, had demonstrated its disdain for the cultures and the sovereignty of other nations; surely an American graduate student working in the museum would have access to the security system; surely his presence on the scene was so unlikely as to raise suspicion. Tad replied with single words or phrases, which were followed by silences he allowed to lengthen. Appealed to, Professor Stuckey managed to give credibility to the reporter's intimations even as, on behalf of the English people, she thanked Tad for having saved a national treasure, which, she felt obliged to point out, he was engaged in an attempt to steal administratively, being an agent of Professor Robert Garner, who headed the effort to remove Horatio to America. Tad, encouraged to reply to this charge, said nothing. To the question of who would steal the mummy of a Roman soldier, he also remained silent, even as Professor Stuckey smiled an answer. "Perhaps a patriot."

That evening, in the Golden Monarch with Rosalie, Tad watched the interview on the television. Ten minutes had been snipped and shaped into two, a transcription of reality made into a minifilm cast with, he thought, less than able actors. The reporter was played as the intrepid British ingénue, all innocence and pluck. Tad was the taciturn American bully. The characterization disturbed him. He knew himself a cog, a machined nub of metal whose sole purpose was to turn and to mesh. The young man on the screen Tad could not recognize. He seemed not so much military and disciplined and stoic as repressed.

Rosalie, who had taken an almost personal affront to the reporter's tattoo, was delighted. "That's lovely, isn't it, the way you won't let her force you to say any more than you want to say."

"I wasn't—"

"All that stuff about America—she read that in some book. They're always like that, wanting to make something when nothing's there. That's what they do for a living, make up stories."

So too archeologists, Tad thought, but he remained silent.

Rosalie smiled. "I know you were only being you, looking out for everybody, when you went into the museum. Still," her eyes shone, perhaps from the white wine she'd sipped, "you were very brave."

Tad didn't think so. He didn't think in those terms. He had done what there was to do.

He said the same thing the next morning, as over breakfast Mick Curtain read to him from the article he'd sold the newspaper. Mick had told a different story, stressing the violence—the ripped-open doorway, the bloodied security guard—and valor: against three miscreants a lone hero, effectively one-armed, weaponless, outthinking the villains. He managed to imply that the would-be robbers had fled before Tad's indomitable presence. He offered Tad as a man of both intellect and action, a decorated veteran of the Afghan war become classical archeologist, an American turning his military training to the defense of England and her interests. "I managed to get in everything but the whip."

"Whip?" Tad didn't understand.

"The model," Mick grinned, "is Indiana Jones."

Tad looked at the black-and-white photograph that accompanied the article. His eyes empty, his expression blank, he was in the still image much closer to what he thought he was.

Along with his report of the burglary, Mick had sold the newspaper sidebar pieces on the Horatio controversy, including sketches of the principal antagonists: Professors Garner and Stuckey and MP Quarles. Here he took a different tone, hinting through his style at the Mock Epic. He would have his readers consider whether the question of where the mummy of a Roman soldier ought to be displayed was important enough to bloody a head over.

"What would happen, Tad, if Horatio just stayed here?"

Tad had never considered the question.

THAT NIGHT he received an email from Professor Garner, who congratulated him on his defense of Horatio, which he had learned of from his daughter. He urged continued vigilance. Those ultimately responsible for the attempted theft would not be deterred by failure. He felt in the affair the hand of Sylvia Stuckey, who could so little value a prize like the mummy as to risk destroying it, and he lamented that academic politics could place in her position a person who hadn't turned a trowel in dirt since she was a graduate student. Soon her opposition to the move would be irrelevant, however, as fundraising went well. He also said that he planned to be in Cambridge in December, when he had agreed to give a lecture at the museum. However, the purpose of his trip was not primarily professional. Rather, he wished to spend the holidays with his daughter, who looked forward to experiencing an English Christmas. There would be many festive occasions, social and professional, to which he would see that Tad received invitations. It was time, he jested, that the young man developed the skill most indispensable to the classical archeologist—schmoozing.

The next morning Ginny Garner called, congratulating him on his heroics and inviting him for coffee.

Tad had not seen her since the rally. Actually, he had not seen her often even before that. Not long after Professor Stuckey's party, Ginny had altered her routine. She slept late, lunched long, shopped casually, or she spent the afternoon riding horses at a stable west of the city, and she allowed young men to enjoy her company at restaurants and theaters and clubs. This at least was Tad's sense of it. But he too had changed his routine, for Rosalie now took up time he once had dedicated to shadowing Ginny. He did not often seek out the American girl, and when he did he often did not find her. He still walked to and watched at Hathaway House, but this, like so much of his behavior, had taken on the regularity of ritual. If Ginny was in her apartment, he saw no more than a silhouette passing before her window. Most nights, darkness told him that she was not there.

He came to understand that she was no longer actively pursuing her studies. She was playing, having a good time. This did not especially concern Tad, for as her father had said, Ginny could take care of herself. If she needed him, she would call.

Now he looked forward to their meeting. Tad was, he realized, tired—work, at which he spent long, solitary, intense hours, was wearing him down. He had finished the cataloging and taken as much data from this summer's metal find as he could; now he was sorting and arranging records, matching notes and records to images and graphs, a slow, tedious task. And intimacies of the sort he shared with Rosalie carried, he was discovering, their own demands and burdens. But Ginny's presence always, somehow, revitalized him.

When they met five years before, he had thought Ginny Garner utterly unsoiled. He thought so still. Without physical smudge or blemish, she must also be, he sensed, incorruptible of conscience. She embodied all that young American men, fighting as he once had in far-off lands, believed that they were dying to preserve. She was not pure, nor innocent, nor always nice, but she was forthright. She would do what she would do because she was what she was. She would age but never decline. She seemed, like America, inviolable.

In the Starbucks on Market Street, her presence altered alignments, gapped conversations, redirected gazes. She smiled over her latte. "You're famous, Tad. Everybody's looking at you."

"No," he said, "at you."

This was true. Among the student crowd, her serene confidence even more than her stylish attire made her different, as a royal differs from her subjects. But it was also true that he had set to whispering a group of students at a back table.

"You'll just have to accept it. You're a hero."

"The television—"

"What a wench. And Sylvia Stuckey didn't help much, did she? We'll have to plot an appropriate revenge." She smiled again. "So who is she, Tad?"

Ginny, it turned out, had seen him at the rally. She had also noticed that he was not alone.

"Her name is Rosalie. Rosalie Cush," he said. "She's a friend."

"A friend you're sleeping with?"

Watching Ginny's smile deepen, he knew his relationship with Rosalie now to be real in a way that it had not been before. Ginny Garner, allowing it, made it so. At the same time, he realized that his allegiance had shifted, or at least expanded—Rosalie too was now due his fidelity.

"I'm happy you've found somebody."

They sipped their coffee. Ginny asked him about Rosalie, her family, her work, her ambitions. She asked for details of his saving Horatio. She told him what her father had, that they were spending the holidays in England. "We'll do something while he's here," she said, "the four of us."

It was a measure of the change in Tad and in his life that he did not know whether she was serious or simply polite.

Then Ginny smiled. "I want you to stop following me, Tad."

He was startled but not disturbed.

She offered an emphatic silence. Then she said, "I know it's not your idea. My father must have put you up to it, asked you to watch over daddy's little girl. I appreciate his concern, but it's unnecessary. And it's embarrassing. Some people even think you're stalking me, the way you're always around at night outside my apartment building. I have to explain it to people, people who don't understand how you and I . . ."

She didn't finish her thought. She didn't need to, probably couldn't.

How explain their mutual trust? How describe what they were to one another?

"I imagine you promised him. Gave him your word."

"Yes," he said.

"Now I'm going to create a dilemma for you, Tad. I'm going to ask you to violate that promise and make another to me."

"All right."

Now she was the startled one. "You'll stop? I have your word?"

"Yes."

For a moment she frowned. Then she smile. "Well, that was easy. How come?"

After a moment, he said, "I can only do my duty as I see it."

"That's from Marcus Aurelius, I bet." She smiled again. "What would you do without him?"

Later, as Tad walked back to the museum, he came to wonder how Ginny knew he had been guarding her. He felt sure that she had not seen him. But someone must have observed him walking the dark streets of the city, standing silent between the tree and the rock wall. Someone.

ROSALIE WAS FASCINATED by Ginny Garner. She thought her a character like those whose amorous adventures she followed in historical romances, a lovely American heiress who ought, if the author of her story properly understood the conventions of the genre, to be pursued and fought over by hot-blooded aristocrats. That Ginny and Tad would be friends was a quirk of democracy, which often threw together the little and the great. To Rosalie, this was encouraging. In America, anything indeed was possible. Nothing need remain as it was.

Rosalie believed, or more exactly yearned for assurance, that everything could change. Tad believed that, but for superficial scruff, nothing ever changed. But he did not say so.

He did try to tell her about Ginny.

Robert Garner was in his late thirties, advancing in his career at UCLA, and ten years into a deliberately childless marriage when, the first day of a new semester, he discovered, in a front-row seat for his Introduction to Classical Archeology class, one Tiffany Schumacher, pretty, rich, spoiled, willful, and, soon, mad about him.

The inevitable ensued. His divorce was amicable, the betrayed wife getting nearly everything. Bob Garner didn't mind, for he quickly married Tiffany, whose grandfather had made ball bearings for the military and whose father had made deals with politicians, the efforts of each resulting in a fortune now metastasizing. Professor Garner lost no time in making a daughter, whose birth secured for the ambitious academic the stamp of Schumacher acceptance. Two years later, rather tipsy after a long lunch with her father, Tiffany Schumacher Garner caught her heel in the gap of an elevator door and fell, freakishly breaking her neck. The widower, grief-stricken, nevertheless assured his guilt-ridden father-in-law that young Virginia would always be available to him. The toddler, the only child of an only child of an only child, would be wealthy.

Tad Fellows met Ginny Garner when she, at seventeen, had already become what she always would be—lovely, soft- and well-spoken, amiable and never condescending. She was intelligent but had no interest in ideas. She was curious and imaginative but only about the effect of actions and events on herself. She had a small talent for drawing and a decorator's sense of color and fabric and layout, and she sometimes fancied herself a recluse on a Pacific beach, painting gorgeous seascapes, or the mistress and patron of a handsome and virile Picasso type, or the CEO of her grandfather's financial empire. She loved to ride her horse. She was eager only to do, to live.

She had told Tad all this over the summer they spent with her father, digging at the site north of Cambridge. She also told him that what she was doing, really, was waiting, for what she could not say.

But like Tad himself, she believed that she had been designated by fate for . . . something.

Until such time as her destiny declared itself, however, she looked upon the world with equanimity. Educated in good but not elitist private schools, she knew what social conventions and parental expectations demanded, but she actually understood, about herself, about life, little. She especially did not understand about values and virtues, about right and wrong—that is, she knew what they were, she just didn't quite see why they were important. She was utterly, casually, good-naturedly amoral.

She talked to Tad because he was weird and because she knew that he didn't want to fuck her. She told him she had lost (how inappropriate the predication!) her virginity to a groom in her grandfather's stable at Big Bear Lake the previous summer. She told him that the young man whose attack on her Tad had thwarted might have had what he wanted had he only understood that it must be her choice.

Over the years since, Tad had come to know that Ginny had dabbled sexually—with young men, mostly, but also, for a time, with her Mills College roommate's sister.

She had done some drugs but was too satisfied with herself and her life to get into anything serious. She felt no need to alter her perception of the world, which suited her quite well as it was.

About life, about human enterprises small or great, about the questions that had so plagued the human spirit for so long, she had no interest, for there was only her, Ginny Garner, and the world in orbit around her.

Meeting Tad Fellows, Ginny Garner had thought him one more digger geek. Over that summer, however, she came to see that he was not like others. He came from a world bare and constricted. He thought himself a tool. He had killed. He had headaches and amnesia, and he did unaccountable things.

She and he were alike, she once said, in that neither thought very much about others, he because it did not occur to him to do so, she because she rarely could be troubled to.

She thought him deformed, twisted and bent like a plant pulled out of shape by the sun. He thought her a sword, the clean hard sharp edge of power.

Each believed in destiny, she because of who she was, he because of what he was.

Rosalie did not know quite what to make of all this. Tad did not know quite what to make of what Mick Curtain had to add to it.

Shortly after she arrived in Cambridge, he knew, Ginny had begun trekking to a stable at the western edge of the city, where for an hour or two she rode a rented horse along trails through the countryside. Now, Mick said, she was still riding, but on the horse and the estate of Rupert Quarles.

"She rides with him? The two of them?"

Rosalie leaned over her wine glass. They were in the Golden Monarch, where, to commemorate the Thanksgiving being celebrated in America, she and Tad had taken a meal of turkey and giblets. Mick had joined them for a drink. They had talked about holidays and the impending arrival of Professor Garner. His daughter's name came up.

"Two of them, yes. But not him."

"Her? The sister, Rowena?" Rosalie paused. "But isn't she ..."

"She certainly is." Mick, enjoying the moment, let the silence spread. Finally he added, "But what's going on is not Rowena Quarles and Ginny Garner. What's going on is so sexually and politically convoluted that they all might be back in imperial Rome."

Mick had only a theory, it turned out. Ginny Garner was spending much of her time at the Quarles estate, riding horses with Rowena Quarles and sometimes staying the night at Waterby. Rowena was lesbian, so certain ideas suggested themselves to certain people. However, Mick said, Ms. Quarles was a beard, so to speak. If young Miss Garner was disporting between the sheets with anyone at Waterby, it was with the next baronet. Some might think that she would wish to hide her relationship with Rupert Quarles from her father, but in fact she was with Rowena's help concealing it from Rupert's political allies and foes—his anti-American railings might lose force if it got out that he was dallying with a rich young Yankee. As far as Professor Garner went, he knew all about his daughter's affair, for he had suggested it. Because—ta-dah!—Ginny was his agent, engaged in attempting to discover the plans the MP had for Horatio and trying to persuade him to join the American cause.

"Much of this is speculation, of course," Mick said with satisfaction.

"All of it," Tad said.

Mick laughed, rising. "Well, we know she rides with Rowena Quarles and has stayed overnight once or twice at Waterby. I've just filled in a few blanks."

After Mick had departed, Rosalie, no real drinker, asked for another glass of wine. As she sipped, she talked in her mock tutorial manner about Thanksgiving, which she found a lovely tradition, utterly American even if arising out of the experiences of people technically English. She knew enough about the colonists not to confuse the Pilgrims with the Puritans, the *Mayflower* and its Compact with the *Arabella* and Winthrop's City on a Hill, but she expressed admiration for both groups, intrepid souls daring to cross an ocean and change the world they found even as they were changed by it. Now a bit tipsy, she pronounced America the country where a person could be all she could be.

Tad did not tell her that she had just repeated a recruiting slogan for the United States Army.

She talked about the America that she'd seen in movies and on television. She thought it a vast country where a person could lose, or find, herself. She thought that it offered possibilities limited only by the imagination. She thought it was a land where talent and industry were rewarded, no matter whose. Her eyes shone glassily.

She told him again of her dream—Los Angeles, employment as a seamstress with a costume-design firm, eventually designing herself, seeing her creations on the screen. Couldn't happen in England. Unions. Nepotism. Class—even a seamstress is hired on the basis of her accent. She hated England. Had to get out. Would. "I'll make a wonderful American, won't I?"

That evening she asked him to take her to his bed, where she was especially attentive to his pleasure.

When, in the early hours of the morning, he walked her home, at the entryway to the apartment stairs she clung to him. He remembered seeing her in the same place with Billy Knox. The image prompted him to turn from her to scan, carefully, the street, but he saw no one.

T HE NEXT DAY Rosalie proposed a Sunday trip to Waterby. The bus to the village of the same name went right past the estate. They could get a look at the grounds, take in the local sights, have lunch, and return in time to view a film. Tad had no particular interest in seeing the house and holdings of Rupert Quarles, but under Rosalie's insistent smile he nodded assent.

The weather turned again, bringing biting cold and a hard frost. When Tad picked her up, Rosalie was bundled in a tasseled cap and woolen scarf and quilted coat like a bright-cheeked, chubby child on a nostalgic Christmas card. They had the chilly bus largely to themselves as it growled its way out of the city, past the tech businesses and small shopping malls and residential developments that inexorably advanced on old farms and decaying hamlets. For some distance the highway edged the fen, the drainages and service roads and flat brown fields on which frost still glittered dully in the feeble sunlight. Then the pavement bent in a long curve toward a line of low hills, gray-green, tree-patched.

Rosalie touched Tad's arm. "It's just there."

Stands of timber bordered the grassy expanses that swelled over the gentle climb of the earth. Abutting the spread of intensely worked fields—drained and measured and plowed, to Tad's approving eye meticulously ordered—the park asserted the profligacy of power: rich, valuable soil squandered for show. On a lip of land approached by a tree-lined, graveled drive sat the manor, gray stone, solid and graceful, commanding the barns and stables and sheds placed around it in a respectful arc. The rows of Georgian windows looked out in insistent symmetry.

"It's impressive, isn't it," Rosalie said. "Intimidating, even."

Tad thought that that was probably the point.

"These great houses never change," she went on, "no matter who owns them. Aristocrats and the rich, they're both privileged, aren't they? They live in the same houses and they stay the same and they keep everybody else the same, too."

Marcus had said something similar: that the inferior exist for the sake of the better, and the better for the sake of each other.

"My grandmother worked in a house like this," Rosalie said. "She cleaned. All day she cleaned, and at night she slept in a room the size of my closet, and she believed God intended it so. When the family went bankrupt, she thought the world had come to an end. She found work scrubbing floors at City Hall. Nothing had changed, really. It never does, in this country."

Tad had heard this sort of talk from Rosalie before, but not this bitter tone.

"There's been a Quarles here for centuries. They're nothing to do with the likes of us."

As the bus drew nearer, Tad could see about the place signs of recent labor. Most of the outbuildings had new roofs, repaired stonework, or fresh paint, and a horse stable might have been a new construction. On the side of a large barn, scaffolding hung like a headless insect. The manor, however, had suffered lengthy neglect not yet attended to—angles seemed untrue; small cracks shifted and discolorations stained the stone.

"He's left the house to last. Rupert Quarles, I mean, fixing it up. They say he doesn't have money enough to restore it properly. Now that he's a MP, though, he'll find a way to get it."

The bus ground on past Waterby Manor, which slid behind a screen of trees. Stone and briar fences partially blocked out pastureland. Then came the village—a small square, a few streets crossed by narrow, twisting lanes.

"We're here," Rosalie sang, as if willing her spirits into revival.

They walked about the town—shrubbery overgrowing frame or stone cottages, most ill-kept; an unimpressive Norman church now the property, a sign said, of English Heritage; a market–post office, and a few shops and marginal businesses. There were old trees and two small brooks and a barking dog, several cows and three blanketed horses grazing in the pasture, and nary another soul on the streets. The village was very old but seemed neither worn by time nor abused by history but merely shabby. Tad's archeologist's eye caught nothing of real interest. He didn't know why they had come.

"It isn't the way I remembered it," Rosalie said, discouraged. "My aunt lived here, I used to spend summer weeks with her. I thought it was real England, with the manor and the village, everyone in their place..."

Near the end of a dirt-track lane, Rosalie paused before a small, ruined cottage. The roof, missing a number of slates, sagged, and the few windows were gray with grime; paint peeled to bare wood, while an untended apple tree scratched a wall.

"Billy Knox's house. His and his mum's, till she died."

For no clear reason, a large padlock secured the front door. One of the windows had recently been rebuilt. A power cable slung from a pole to the corner of an eave looked new.

"Does he still own it?"

"Who'd buy it? But he doesn't live in it. He lives . . . around. He just roams." She took his arm. "Why don't we roam to the pub? I'm getting hungry."

In the scruff and tatter of the old village, the Lion and Lamb was an exception announced by the number of vehicles in the parking lot. The exterior was tidily painted, the interior carefully restored, oak and plaster and stone. In the dining room, patrons and their Sunday roasts occupied several tables. A pair of couples sat in the bar. Rosalie and Tad made a third.

They were finishing their tea and sandwiches when the stillness was disrupted by the entrance of a man outfitted as a farmer in Wellingtons and muddy work pants and a multipocketed jacket that he seemed about to burst. His pate gleamed in the low light.

Noticing Tad's attention, Rosalie turned to look. Then she leaned across the booth table. "Isn't that . . . ?"

Rupert Quarles reached the bar just as the barman placed a pint before him. He took a long swallow, turned, and recognized Tad. Instantly, anger flushing his face, he started across the brief space between them.

Tad had no time to rise and use the man's weight and rush against him. He had only a single hand with which to counter the attack, thrusting up, fingers stiff or clawed. He identified points of vulnerability—ribcage, genitals.

Then Quarles checked his advance. He had, Tad saw, finally noticed Rosalie's blonde head.

Slowly now Quarles came up. "Fellows, as I remember."

Tad's hand dropped to his lap to brush at the pouch in his pocket.

"No vote there, but maybe your friend?" Smiling, he extended his hand to Rosalie. "Rupert Quarles. Be a constituent?"

Rosalie stared at the hand, thick-fingered, knobby-knuckled, scarred, enclosing her own. She seemed suddenly uncertain, anxious even, Tad saw. Frightened.

"No," she said. "I mean, yes, but I didn't vote. I—I'm not . . . political."

"Have to change that." Quarles turned to Tad. "Sunday excursion, is it?"

Tad nodded.

"No other reason?" The smile remained even as the voice gathered weight. "Snooping. Stalking."

"It's me," Rosalie said quickly, "I wanted him to see Waterby. His friend, Miss Garner, that is, his professor's daughter, I wanted him to see what she . . ."

Rupert Quarles took a long swallow from his glass. "English ale. One thing you Yanks will never steal. No English grit in your water."

Tad watched him.

"Couldn't see much of the layout from the road," Quarles said then. "Come along. I'll show you a bit more of the place."

"Oh, no," Rosalie said, again flustered. "We couldn't impose—"

"Serve constituents, what I was elected for," Quarles said. "Besides, your young man here can help me unload some pipe. Finish up and we're off."

In the parking lot Quarles led them to a small flatbed lorry on which was lashed down a bundle of PVC pipe. The cab was warm but, with the three of them, crowded, Rupert Quarles occupying space with his force as well as his flesh. He pulled the lorry out onto the highway, almost immediately turning off at the entrance to a long graveled drive bordered by old plane trees in need of pruning.

As they approached the manor house, the deterioration of the building became even more obvious. The stone seemed soft, frangible. Concrete showed signs of rot; windows had warped joints, the roof broken and missing tiles. The grounds were largely unkempt, the lawn grown wild and the shrubbery untended.

"Take a fortune to get it the way it was," Quarles said.

"Won't the government help?" Rosalie asked. "It's English history, isn't it?"

"Government never helps. Takes over." He swung the lorry around the graveled circle before the house and headed back down the drive. Then he pulled onto a muddy service road. "Don't believe in history myself. One thing the Yanks get right. What matters is today. Go for it. Money rules."

He smiled, as if to himself. "That's right, isn't it, Fellows? Americans reduce everything to money. Nothing else to measure things by. History you ignore, as you should. What you miss is tradition. Tradition, that's a different matter. Keeps order. Everybody knows where they belong."

Tad knew Quarles to be addressing him, personally. What the message was, however, he could not say.

Quarles drove into the park, talking, his elisions and tone transforming statements into pronouncements. Pipe late arriving last night. Drop it off now, save hours and pounds. Here attending baronet, who won't do all a courtesy and die. Busy in London, Parliament recess soon, work to do, Horatio an irritant. "Ginny's father, the professor—why's he making all the fuss about the mummy?"

Tad looked out at the parkland. Trees and low hills blocked out the fen fields, the village, the manor. The grass, still gray with frost, stood stiff on the buckled earth. Nothing moved. The scene might always have looked so. It seemed a fine battleground for phalanx and cavalry and tanks.

"Because he can," Tad said.

"Ha!" Quarles's laugh was like a mortar burst. "Right. Right."

Between the two men, Rosalie sat silent. She seemed smaller. She seemed, when Tad looked at her, even more like a child. Suddenly, powerfully, Tad felt compelled to protect her.

They drove out of the park, to the edge of the fields and a low platform on which perched complex pumping machinery. Here Quarles urged Tad out, and they unloaded the plastic piping.

"Do all right for a gimp," Quarles said when they'd finished. "You really ready to fight, back at the inn?"

Tad didn't answer.

Quarles smiled. "Didn't do much good against Billy Knox, when he dumped you in the drink."

Tad looked at him. He had met men like this in the army. Some were leaders. Others were just killers.

"More damage done next time." Quarles weighted his words, as he had in the inn.

Tad again touched the small pouch in his pocket, connecting.

Quarles nodded, as if Tad's silence announced his understanding. "Get in. Something to show you."

He drove back into the parkland, soon taking a branch road little more than ruts that eased up a small slope into a dark grove. There the road, winding among the thick-boled trees, became a trail chewed up by the hooves of horses. At last Quarles drove out into the open, onto a long, bare bench of land that curved around the side of a low hill. Before them, stuck with a few saplings, was a large round mound.

Quarles got out of the lorry, as did Tad and, after a moment, Rosalie.

"So then," Quarles said.

Tad determined that he was to notice something. There was nothing to notice but the mound swelling from the slope. It might cover a geological jut. It might cover human ritual. "A tumulus?"

"That's the question," Quarles said. "Some say so, others not."

"You mean—" Rosalie hadn't spoken for some time. Her voice now came brittle, cracking. "It might be a burial mound. Celts? Iron Age?"

"Nobody knows. Lots of theories."

"It would be easy enough to find out," Tad said.

"Radar, all that, I know," Quarles said. "Used to be, they wanted to dig. The baronets—father, grandfather, the rest—said no. Nobody sticks a shovel into our land."

"A plane with the right equipment could fly over it," Tad said.

"Nobody will," Quarles said easily. "No one invades my property. Or air space."

"Don't you want to know?" Rosalie's voice was clearer. "Mightn't there be something important there?"

"Not to me," Quarles smiled.

"But to England?"

"This part of England, artifacts under every little bump in the ground. An old farmstead every two hundred meters. What's one more pot or coin or bunch of bones?"

Rosalie seemed both cowed and, although she had said much the same to Tad in the museum, dismayed.

Quarles smiled again. "Frivolous pursuit, archeology. History has only one lesson—get and use power. All the rest—sentimentality, excuses. Participate in power or get crushed by it. Right, Yank?"

"Yes," Tad said.

The three stood looking at the mound. Then the quality of the silence changed.

Under his feet the very earth began to move, and tiny tremors so distant, so faint they might actually have been the beating of his heart, until the shudders became sound, rhythmical, a rapid thudding and ancient signal, a call to blood, that drew nearer and grew louder and made the earth seem hollow. Around the side of the hill came racing, two horses, a bay and a black, their sharply configured muscles straining, their eyes wild with exertion, froth at mouth and flanks, and astride each animal a young woman, leaning forward in the saddle, urging more, more . . .

Rowena Quarles, on the black, grinned into the wind, acknowledging no other presence on the hillside as she raced toward and disappeared into the trees.

The bay bore down on the three people beside the lorry. Tad could see the red veins in the animal's eyes, the yellow brutal teeth. Then without breaking stride the horse suddenly angled away from them. Ginny Garner smiled fiercely.

TWO DAYS LATER Rosalie persuaded a former schoolmate to fill in for her at the tearoom, so that she and Tad could go punting on the River Cam. Wisps of mist rose from the water into the cold air. Ice edged the riverbanks and froze the clogs of leaves under the bare trees. No one else was on the river.

Rosalie sat thoughtfully as Tad thrust the pole into the river bottom. She had said little since he picked her up. Something troubled her. Then she told him, "You're my only hope, Tad."

He didn't answer. His attention was fixed on a gray-green lump gathering a thin edge of ice at the riverbank.

"You know that, don't you?"

But it wasn't his boonie hat, only a mass of leaves.

"Yes."

"You won't . . . betray me?"

"Yes," he said. "I mean no."

He thought that Rosalie might be his only hope as well.

NOT LONG AFTER THE ATTEMPT to steal Horatio, Professor Stuckey had called Tad to her office, where she handed him a copy of a letter, the original of which she was sending to Professor Garner, commending Tad's diligence and decisiveness in thwarting the intruders, as well as complimenting his industry and attention to task.

"Ironies compound," she said, frowning as if against bright light. "You save an English national treasure that you're trying to make off

with through political chicanery. And I'm bound by professional eti-
quette to applaud what the police suspect was your botched attempt
at theft."

Tad took the letter but did not look at it. "The police think I was
involved?"

"They suspect a plot, and then a falling-out among thieves," she
said. "If there's a market for the mummy of a Roman soldier, who but
a classical archeologist would know where and whom it might be?"

On the long table behind her, a stack of files for no obvious reason
slowly sagged and slid, several of the manila folders spilling papers
onto the floor.

Professor Stuckey sat back, folding her trembling fingers in her lap.

"Then there are the problems with your story—just happened to be
passing by and all that. You can see how the authorities might think
you likely to have had something to do with it."

He could see that. He could see too from whom they might have
gotten the idea.

He realized then, when she did not react to his silence, that she
might be unwell. She looked at once haggard and bloated. Her skin
was sallow, her eyes red-rimmed. She slumped, nearly sagged in her
chair, not so much ill, he saw now, as weary.

She too was for a long moment silent, until finally she said, "Please
leave my office."

He stopped to visit Horatio. Looking at the outline of the short
sword, he realized at last what Rosalie had seen in its shape and he
understood why she had blushed. The connection between sword and
phallus, which he had never made before, shocked him.

The next day Professor Stuckey came down to his room, offering no
explanation of her presence. She wandered the neatly arranged rows
of boxes, she looked over his shoulder at the graph on the computer
screen, and then she left.

A few days later she came again. Again she said nothing. Tad continued his work.

The next week she stopped in once more. Tad did not ask what she wanted, if anything. He thought, although he could not have said why, that she was resting.

By now Tad knew even more about Professor Stuckey's many obligations, academic and otherwise. The newspapers were always interested in her activities, as was Mick Curtain, who thought her the perfect subject for a Sunday Supplement article—the scholar who would Save the World, that sort of thing. So he had done some digging.

"Her childhood and family history are a matter of public record, unfortunately," Mick told Tad. "Booze and battering, hospital and jail and social services, the whole package. Mother mercifully dies of cancer and leaves ten-year-old Sylvia to stand between her drunken father and her younger brother and sister. Father, blotto, stumbles out of the local into the path of a lorry. The two younger children are placed in care, for which they ultimately blame Sylvia, who blames herself for all of it."

Mick adjusted his glasses. Sympathy dissolved some of his usual cynicism. "Sounds Dickensian, but it goes on all the time in this country."

In every country, Tad thought.

"So this is the load she carries into the world. The first-born who feels somehow responsible for the horrors of her childhood, she's controlling, passive-aggressive, and intensely ambitious—it's textbook stuff, really, her life is predictable. She'll drive herself to professional success, as a kind of defensive maneuver. She'll have few friends and no intimates—what woman could she trust not to abandon her, as her mother did, what man, no matter how agreeable, wouldn't reduce to the figure of her father?"

Tad said nothing.

"I know," Mick said, "pop psychology. But in this case . . ."

Sylvia Stuckey's career too was a matter of record. BA in Classics from Sussex University as a scholarship student, MPhil at Oxford, PhD in Classical Archeology at the University of Leicester, her thesis, a revised version of which was published by Oxford University Press, on the *canabae,* the communities made up of Roman soldiers and their native wives and mistresses, which attached to hinterland forts. In Cambridge, she narrowed her research, moving away from the exclusively archeological as she investigated in records and art and literature the relation of invading male and indigenous female, on which topic she published a number of articles and books, one featuring a chapter on Boudica.

"Her authority on the subject is unchallenged," Mick said. "Her reputation is international. She's a star. Even if her work is poo-pooed by some in the digging community."

Her personal life had been less than stellar. She had formed no attachments, female or male, sexual or otherwise. While a student, she dated rather haphazardly, usually men involved in one or the other of her causes, none for any great length of time. In America at Georgetown, on the last night of a conference, something happened between her and the keynote speaker, UCLA Professor Robert B. Garner. Back in England, she saw for short periods a sequence of suitors, some of whom she slept with, some not, but in any case she shied from any attempt at real familiarity. She began to insist that she was too busy to concern herself with personal relations. Others proposed that she had "trust issues." She was thought now to be celibate. Cambridge *quid nuncs* imagined her lack of a love life to result from some ugly sexual secret or moral failure, but on no evidence.

So she ground through her days, from chore to chore, committee to committee, driven and drained. And if, evenings, she might imbibe a bit too much red wine, she did so for therapy, to relax, to calm and quiet herself, to rest.

There had been talk, lately, about Sylvia Stuckey's drink problem. Mornings she sometimes had difficulty concentrating, seemed not wholly present. She was becoming rather forgetful, so that gray Miss Eversly was constantly reminding her of her schedule. Her features had begun to blur, alcohol watering her gaze and puffing her cheeks and flooding red the wings of her nose, where tiny blue veins mapped her course. She was still an attractive woman, but would not be for long. More and more that seemed to matter to her less and less.

ONE AFTERNOON in the first days of December, Professor Stuckey came to tell Tad that she would be working late that evening; as that was his habit, perhaps they might have dinner. He had no reason not to accept. He didn't wonder what she might want.

She drove them in her tiny, bubble-like automobile to an Italian restaurant on the south edge of the city. Over lasagna and chianti she attempted to draw him out on the subject of Cambridge, the English ethos, and his accommodations, all the while carefully controlling her tone, apparently resolved not to allow his reticence to stoke her irritation into anger. As the level of wine in the carafe lowered, her tongue loosened. Finally she mentioned Ginny Garner, hinting at a liaison between the American heiress and Rupert Quarles. She would have Tad tell her, he perceived, about the relationship. Tad did not know one to exist. When he said so, Professor Stuckey poured more wine and swung into an account of her sojourn in America.

She had gone to America to assess the empire of democratic capitalism. She had found what she had been prepared by her reading and study to find.

American women were desensitized to the scourging laid on their bare backs by American men, many—most—having learned to love the whip.

American men were most cruel in their kindness.

American poor were thought deserving of their condition.

American government and corporations engaged in a sort of mutual pleasuring.

Americans, she said, would maintain a prelapsarian ingenuousness as they corrupted the world.

Americans, she said, believed that the world began in 1776, that everything prior was merely preparation for them and their country. Even those who studied the past did so to justify the present. Look at how Robert Garner, in his television shows and glossy books, managed to convince uncareful thinkers that Roman aggression determined American foreign policy. Rot, utter rot. But there you were. Of course it was homely-cute farmboy charm rather than scholarship and science that accounted for his success. Compelling voice, engaging grin, but mediocre mind, really. Liar. Manipulator. Serial seducer.

Professor Stuckey picked at her meal, quaffed the red wine, and sank rapidly into inebriation. Her anger dissipated, her eyes brightened, her smile warmed as she ticked off the failings of America: ignorance, greed, bullying. The USA was a nation of plastic and cardboard. The essence of American democracy was a dedication to the lowest common denominator.

Tad had heard all this before, these ideas, notions, theories, accusations. They might or might not hold truth.

She at last finished the wine, of which Tad had had but a few swallows. Paying the bill became an adventure as she fumbled in and eventually dropped her purse, the spilled contents of which Tad and a waiter retrieved on hands and knees. She swayed as he helped her on with her coat. She smiled brightly, glassily, as if in coquetry. "Do you drive, Mr. Fellows? I shouldn't, I believe."

Tad had learned to drive in the army. He nodded.

"If you could just get me home," she said. "We can call you a taxi from there."

At her car she paused, confused, as if climbing into the passenger seat required skills beyond her competence. Tad, scrunched behind the wheel, drove carefully, under her direction. The night traffic streamed like a convoy headed for an assault rendezvous. Tad tasted the stringent sourness that came with anticipation of battle.

Beyond the old, inner city, the streets emptied. The few other cars passed like silent sentries. Near Professor Stuckey's home, lights shone in windows, but no shadows moved, indoors or out. Tad turned the car into her drive and stopped.

"Come in, come in," she insisted, as if he had been resisting. "We'll call you a taxi."

Once inside, however, with a flap of her hand she bade him sit as she disappeared down a hallway. She did not immediately return. He heard her bump against a wall. He heard a heavy plastic thump as something hit the floor. He waited.

The room was not as it had been for the party, when tables and sideboards bearing food and drink had surrounded the space and the seats were set out in patterns to urge conversation. Now all was, like his room at Mrs. Ball's, arranged for the convenience of one. Images soothed, quieted—prints of Degas's dancers and a medieval Madonna and a Georgia O'Keefe iris, studies in charcoal of children at play, pastels of quiet seascapes. Books were brightly jacketed. On the sideboard, several bottles of wine and a row of glasses reflected the lamplight. Beside the couch, an end table displayed her publications: off-prints of journal articles; her revised and bound PhD thesis on the *canabae*; two books, *Roman Rape* and *Lucretia's Lament*; a monograph entitled *Fathering Jesus*. And another book, her personal account of the experiences of a young, feminist, English classical archeologist in the US: *Digging Dirt: Sexism, Academics, and America*.

"Have you read my work, Mr. Fellows?" She stood in the doorway, swaddled in a fleecy beige robe, shod in slippers.

"Yes," he said.

"*Digging Dirt,* I expect." She moved to the sideboard, where she eased the cork from a dark bottle. "Everybody's read that. Think it's all gossip. Can't get people to see how . . ."

She was pouring wine into a large brandy snifter. She found it necessary to concentrate on the task. When the glass was nearly full, she took it carefully to the couch. She sat and tugged her robe tightly over her knees and smiled and sipped her wine and began to talk.

To Tad, listening to wine-soaked Sylvia Stuckey was like viewing the site of a recent battle, the ground littered with the commonplace and the horrific. She spoke of the ravaging of indigenous female by imperial male, Briton by Roman, Native American by European. And Sabine women. And Virginia and Lucretia. Was Jesus of Nazareth the result of a rape by a Roman soldier? If the story was not exactly true, did it possess truth? Rape? Had she herself been raped? Sometimes it seemed as if she must have been. Couldn't remember. Robert Garner luring her into his bed with lies? Treachery. Like the slamming doors and drunken roars and broken crockery of her childhood. Horrors. Fear. Always alone. Mother dead, brother and sister lost in the system—her fault? The great paradox of her life—seeking peace, she must engage in conflict. Peace and love. Love. Patriarchal scam. Boudica battled. Dried-up dons belittle her work. Set her up to fail. Gossip. Tired of chasing after funds, fighting department and college and university.

Archeology, Tad knew, tried to recreate civilizations from bits of pottery and bone, seed and scat. So Sylvia Stuckey would construct a life.

Her glass was empty. She stared at Tad in a near stupor. Slowly she raised a finger. "I—one moment."

Struggling to her feet, she weaved toward the bathroom. Tad rose, watching as she disappeared into the hallway. After a considerable time, hearing nothing, he followed.

She was in her bedroom, unconscious, sprawled supine across

her bed. In the parallelogram of dim light from the hall, her legs were splayed in obscene invitation.

To Tad this was familiar, this scene, this room and bed and body, these shadows. Somewhere, sometime, he had stood like this before, stood and looked. He was certain of it, although he could not account for this certainty. But he knew.

He left.

The cold snap had been replaced by a mild, swirling wind. Over the city scudded ragged clouds turned pale pink by the lights below. Tad walked toward them. He did not notice the miles. He did not know, quite, who he was. He knew only that he was in retreat, plodding toward some ultimate redoubt.

THE NEXT DAY, Sylvia Stuckey did not come to work. The following day she appeared, near noon, in Tad's workspace. She trembled, twitched. "Thank you for getting me home the other night," she said. "And I apologize for my . . . inhospitable behavior. I—I shan't be having any wine for a while."

He looked at her.

"I remember talking quite a lot," she said, "although I don't recall exactly what I said. Nothing indiscreet, I hope?"

"No," Tad said.

"You've heard from Professor Garner?"

"Not recently." Tad had emailed Professor Garner regular progress reports, and what little information he came to about resistance to the Horatio move. Recently he'd had no response.

"I've just had an email from him. I suspect you'll get one soon." She paused, her furrowed brow proposing dubiety. "He asked me to do the initial introduction at his lecture. I would in any case, as he's using the lecture hall upstairs. But I'm sure this is some sort of public relations or political ploy."

Tad said nothing.

"As for the actual introduction, he wants you to do it." She paused again. "As I say, this is no doubt part of some larger scheme. Given the great many worthies available for that task, a graduate student—Well, that will stand out on a CV."

"Yes," he said.

"Could it be merely a bald attempt to capitalize on your recent heroics?"

Tad looked at his computer screen. On it, a graph identified artifacts at various depths and locations in the earth. He remembered digging, the weight of a trowel in his hand, the smell of dirt, the silence of the deep past.

Her expression changed, thickened with satisfaction. "But it doesn't matter what he's up to. All your work will be for nothing, Mr. Fellows. Horatio is not going to America. Even now, forces are at work to prevent it. I hope you can prepare for the disappointment."

Tad was not surprised by her remarks. Neither was he troubled. She might be right, or not. In either case he could do nothing about it. He could only persevere. He could only, as Marcus insisted, welcome with love whatever happened to him.

After Professor Stuckey left, he found the email. Professor Garner would arrive in forty-eight hours. The lecture was a week off. Tad would have plenty of time, the professor assured him, to prepare brief remarks of the sort that would at once argue their cause and improve his career prospects.

Tad needed no time at all. What he would say had just come to him, immediately, inevitably.

**A**T BREAKFAST, Mick Curtain, hearing of Robert Garner's imminent arrival, asked Tad to set up an interview with the telly archeologist. Then Mrs. Ball wondered if the professor might be enticed to the house, where he could see how well his colleague was being taken care of. That afternoon, at the teashop, Rosalie smiled her round smile at the news of Tad's participation in the lecture. When he invited her to accompany him, however, she demurred—scholars, professors, she shouldn't be comfortable around them. That evening he walked her home from the theater, where she had been working on Panto costumes. Some were a challenge to design, sumptuous and regal, the show telling an Arthurian story, adulterous love and quests and all that, mixed up with little skits and jokes about local characters and incidents. But farce, of course. Tad would love it. He asked her again to come to the lecture, and this time, her confidence buoyed by her work with the costumes, she agreed. She would even make a new dress for the occasion.

Arriving in England, Professor Garner called Tad at the museum. He was on his way, he said, to Waterby, where he would spend a few days resting up with his daughter, at the invitation of Rowena Quarles. "It'll be an interesting visit, given her brother's anti-American views. I anticipate politics and guile. I'm preparing to be worked on. I plan to do a little arm-twisting myself."

Tad repeated Mick Curtain's request, and that of Mrs. Ball. The professor rather surprisingly acceded. "I'm already up to my eyeballs in academics. An hour in the company of a Brit landlady will be a refreshing change."

Midmorning two days later, Robert Garner pulled his daughter's silver BMW to a stop before the B&B. Tad ushered him into the foyer and introduced him to Mrs. Ball. From behind her smile, she looked the American professor over carefully, his bashful grin, his bold glance as, for his part, he took her in—lips and nails bright bloody red, silk blouse a swirl of tropical colors, slick dark slacks. Smiling, suddenly assured, she offered him a tour of the house. It turned out to be rather lengthy, ending in her apartment, from which Jamaican music bounced as background for her deep-throated laugh. Then she showed him into the breakfast area, where she brewed fresh coffee as Mick Curtain made final checks on his recording devices.

Garner's reasons for agreeing to the interview soon became clear. He was full of enthusiasm for international cooperation among all in archeology, praise for the wisdom of English Heritage officials, and appreciation of the excellent care Professor Stuckey and her staff had bestowed on all the artifacts retrieved from the Horatio site. Drinking coffee and exuding charm, he eased past Mick's questions about protests and rallies, instead congratulating the English on their interest in their history. He confessed himself in sympathy with many of the England-for-the-English objectives of Rupert Quarles, decried globalization, and made a joke about Starbucks, whose coffee, he insisted with a grin, was inferior to that of Mrs. Ball. He got in several references to his upcoming lecture. When Mick's questions became more confrontational, when Mick suggested that the decision to allow Horatio out of the country resulted from bureaucratic flimflam, political horse-trading, or bribery, the professor merely grinned, admitted ignorance of details, expressed certainty that all dealings with English officials had been aboveboard, and again complimented Mrs. Ball on her coffee. Mick aggressively followed up. Robert Garner pleasantly prevaricated.

"Slippery sort, isn't he," Mick said, irony mixed with admiration, once Garner had departed. "He manages to advertise his talk and do PR for his project without my laying a glove on him. But at least Mrs. B. got what she wanted."

"What's that?" Tad said.

"His eye." Mick grinned. "And a personal invitation to his lecture.

Considerate of him to invite us, wasn't it? Or perhaps not so considerate, considering."

Tad looked at him. Mick laughed.

THE EVENING OF THE LECTURE, Tad did not need to be coaxed
into admiring Rosalie. Her dress of beige accented with shades of
orange and apricot set off the blonde softness of her hair and the faint
blush of her skin. He wanted to touch her. He wanted to nibble at her,
taste her.

He knew by now what to say: "You're beautiful."

Her flush made her even more appealing.

On the bus, Rosalie was unusually quiet. Then she said, "I've never
been to a university lecture. They have them all the time, free ones,
anyone can attend, but I— Will he be like he is on television?"

Robert Garner's professional discourse, be he a presence in a hall or
an image on a screen, was easy and informal, strewn with allusions to
history and politics and culture high and low. For this he was by some
of his colleagues disparaged. He had been heard to suggest that their
objection was to not his casual manner but rather his popularity with
all audiences.

"You'll like him," Tad said.

She squeezed his hand but didn't appear convinced.

At the museum, the lecture hall was filling. The university term
having ended, Professor Garner had feared that attendance might be
slight, but already half the seats were taken, and people were drifting
in at a steady rate—academic types, more than a few students, and a
good number of curious or bored townspeople.

Tad found places along an aisle. He helped Rosalie with her coat
and removed his own. When she noticed that he wore only what he
had bought under her instruction, she impulsively kissed his cheek.

They sat quietly. Then she said, "You aren't nervous? I'm nervous enough for both of us. I don't know why. I'm sure— Have you got notes? Or have you memorized your speech?"

"I won't be making a speech," Tad said.

Mick Curtain and Mrs. Ball came in and took seats two rows down from them. Mrs. Ball too was got up sufficiently to attract notice. She made Tad think of a bird, finely feathered, raptorial.

The hall slanted down to a small stage backed by heavy dark curtains, from behind which Professor Stuckey now slipped out. Sighting Tad, she beckoned him forward. As he rose from his seat, Rosalie squeezed his hand again.

"I know you'll do well," she said with ill-concealed concern. He saw then that in fact she feared he would falter. He couldn't think why she believed that a possibility.

Professor Stuckey waited for him behind the curtain. "Are you sure there's nothing special you want me to mention when I introduce you?"

They had had this conversation earlier that day. "No," he repeated.

She pursed her lips, frowning. "I can't pretend to approve of what you are doing downstairs."

"No," he said.

"I could certainly justify any embarrassment I might cause you."

He remained silent.

"I believe what I believe, Mr. Fellows. I act on my convictions. I'm grateful for your kindness the other evening, although I don't really remember how it ended, how I got to my bedroom— But that changes nothing."

"No," he said.

She looked at him. "You're a trusting soul, aren't you?"

Tad didn't quite know what she meant. Apparently Robert Garner, who had just pushed his way past the curtain, did. "And loyal. And brave. Tad has all the virtues of Marcus Aurelius's legionnaires."

Sylvia Stuckey went still, pale. "That would make him a murderer and a rapist and a thief."

"Hello, Sylvia." Garner smiled and extended his hand. "You're looking well."

In fact, Professor Stuckey was looking considerably better than she had a week before. Apparently she had stuck to her resolve to stop drinking. Color came back into her face as she stared at Garner's hand, which she did not take.

Robert Garner with a twist of wrist waved off the rejection. He brushed at his hair and remarked on the crowd, the number of young people attending, and, jokingly, the possibility of his being hooted off the stage by Professor Stuckey's students and Rupert Quarles's minions. Sylvia Stuckey watched him, seemed now oddly satisfied. Tad looked on as the two professors favored each other with false smiles, hers very small.

Then a young man appeared before a bank of switches. Professor Stuckey waved a hand in signal, and as a curtain raised she stepped to a lectern, waited as the lights sank in the hall and the crowd quieted, and began to speak, offering standard greetings, thanking the individuals and entities under whose auspices the evening was organized, and announcing future events at the museum.

After a clearly transitional pause, she smiled thinly, giving her tone an edge that might have been irony, might have been disdain. "Our speaker this evening is one for whom any introduction would be gratuitous, given the fact that for the past thirty years he has labored to be known to all, everywhere."

A restless murmur rose in the dim hall.

"His fame is such that he shines in even the dimmest light. That might be why he wished to be formally presented to you by one of his students," she said in the same tone, which suggested that she found the whole subject distasteful.

"This particular student too needs no introduction, at least not to those concerned with preserving the treasures of our native land. Some of you will recognize his name as that of the young man who saved from robbers the mummified Roman soldier the media refers to as the Last Centurion."

An "ah" of quiet approval stirred the audience.

"Some of you will know that he—the young man, that is—is himself engaged in what many believe to be the theft of that very mummy. So too his mentor."

Those to whom she spoke sank into a helpless silence. They did not know what they were supposed to think.

Then Professor Stuckey smiled. "It may be that one or both will speak to this issue. Ladies and gentlemen, I give you Mr. Tad Fellows."

The applause came scattered and uncertain. Stepping onto the stage, Tad passed Professor Stuckey, who affected not to notice him as she stepped down into the hall and took a seat in the front row.

The room was two-thirds full. Tad found in it Rosalie's round face, her round smile and fretful gaze, and the encouraging visages of Mick and Mrs. Ball. A few rows down, in the center, Ginny Garner sat between the Quarles sister and brother. Ginny met his eye and nodded, as if granting him permission to begin.

He felt the weight of his chamois pouch resting against his leg.

He spoke, enunciating the words carefully, precisely, as if he had selected, considered, and approved each: "Professor Robert Garner changed my life."

He fell silent. His expression suggested that nothing more need be said.

He looked out on the faces floating in the dimness, fading to shadow near the back of the hall. He remembered dark faces enfolded in dusty cloth in the desert sun. He sought out the revealing glint of eye, the telling twitch, but he found only Rosalie's anxious quivering round mouth. She seemed silently to plead.

Murmurs drifted through the hall as some in the audience began to stir uneasily in their seats.

Finally Tad spoke again. "I was just back from Afghanistan, where I'd been killing."

The silence of the room altered.

"I had killed there many times, long ago. I had choked on dust stirred by Alexander's army. I had taken up fighting positions with Moslem and Mongol invaders. I killed for Caliph and Tsar and Queen. All that I did then, I had done before."

He had spoken dispassionately, as if reporting the minutes of a meeting. Now he paused again. No one stirred.

"Which was impossible, of course. Which couldn't be. Everyone insisted. Post Traumatic Syndrome Disorder, the army said."

He went on. "Fate is real. Destiny is inevitable. I don't yet know my destiny, but I know that when I returned to America fate took me to a lecture hall much like this, where Professor Garner spoke of classical archeology. He said that archeology told us, again and again, that everything happened again and again. Archeology told us that human experience occurs in cycles, and life repeats itself, be it the life of a person or of a people. He said that each cycle has the same beginning and events and end, and differs only in the details."

They were listening to him, those in the dimness, fascinated or perplexed or incredulous.

"History is an account of sameness," he said. "All is one. To kill an enemy is to kill all enemies everywhere. To be a soldier is to be all soldiers. To work with Roman artifacts, Professor Garner told us, is to work with Romans."

Tad paused once more, as if mentally checking a list. Had he got it all?

"I left that lecture hall and went into the world of classical archeology, where I had always belonged."

He looked out at the faces, blank or frowning or smiling. Ginny Garner grinned in a sort of savage delight. Rosalie seemed stunned.

He realized then that he hadn't said it right. Perhaps it could not be said correctly, exactly, completely.

"Probably no one will be affected that way this evening. But if anyone could change your lives, it would be our speaker, Professor Robert Garner."

Tad took a small half-step back from the lectern, prompting a polite spatter of weak, uncertain applause. Then the clapping gathered force and rhythm as Robert Garner stepped onto the stage. The professor smiled as he took Tad's hand. "Thank you, Tad. I was moved."

Tad nodded, then made his way down into the hall and up the aisle, past the faces that seemed to bob like damaged floats on the night sea, to Rosalie and her searching, troubled gaze and her whisper: "Are you all right?"

"Me?" he said softly, surprised. "I'm fine."

Professor Garner thanked everyone, including Professor Stuckey and Tad. Then with colonial-boy charm he slid into his speech.

"The lecture Tad referred to I gave while bent under the weighty influence of Herr Jung, whom I'd recently reread. It was universally well received, that lecture, mostly because of the psychological comfort the ideas offered—constancy, closure of a sort, the consolations of the circle."

His smile shifted as his countenance took on the expression of open, honest, innocence. "I knew I'd stumbled onto something important when I got a call inviting me to appear on *Oprah*."

When the laughter subsided, he continued with a grin, "This evening I'd like you to consider a remark of the Big Lebowski of psychology, Herr Freud. We all remember it, to our deep discomfort. Freud said, 'Man is wolf to man'."

His grin grew more boyish. "Although it dismays those in my profession who would rather not think about these things, so says classical archeology."

There were a few titters. Throats scraped. His grin remained fixed.

"What do our excavated sites and recovered texts tell us but that we are the children of creatures pleased to kill, rape, and enslave one another? We uncover fortresses. We analyze poems about battle. We study both the bones of the slaughtered and their war cries. And as we classicists do our work, our own world witnesses the rise of empires that overrun and absorb other cultures before disintegrating under the weight of their own acquisitions. As Professor Stuckey and other scholars have so thoroughly documented, human history is an account of invasions and occupations, of savagery and brutality and carnage. Such is the material record that we have so far unearthed. What we do not have is evidence that we ourselves, civilized to beat the band, are any different. All our efforts to understand our forebearers suggest that over millennia nothing has changed. We are what we always have been. From Homer to Henry James, from Boudica to Tony Blair, the story is much the same."

Rosalie took Tad's hand, squeezed.

"Consider," Professor Garner proposed, "crafty Odysseus . . ."

Rosalie was upset, Tad realized, by what he didn't know. He would reassure, he would comfort her, but he didn't know how.

". . . raider of cities. The first thing he does, after leaving Troy, is attack and destroy Ismarus, slaughtering the Cicone men and enslaving the women and children."

Tad listened. Greeks and Romans. Ravaging and plundering. Tactical dances both beautiful and mindless advancing those responding to the eternal human cry: I want, I want, I want. Occupation and insemination and synthesis in blended blood.

And then Tad was no longer listening. He did not close his eyes, he did not sleep, but he was not present. He was a substance among shadows. He was scouting the darkness beneath his skull, closing in on the enemy.

Rosalie squeezed his hand again, hard.

". . . and so it ends in marriage, as if it's all really been a Jane Austen novel. The invader marries the native, the occupier marries the occupied, and they breed the future as civilization, having absorbed the energies of barbarism, cracks and crumbles and makes way for something not very different. Empires disappear under the earth."

Professor Garner stopped, looked out at his audience, and smiled his boyish smile. "First we murder. Then we mate. Then we vanish."

He stepped back from the lectern and offered a brief bow. He acknowledged the applause, which, his boyish smile suggested, was but his due. He stepped down from the stage to greet the well-wishers and commentators who had begun to gather.

"Where were you?" Rosalie asked Tad.

"I've heard it all before," he said. "And I'm fighting off a headache."

"I— Do you understand it? I mean, most of it was clear enough, but . . . What does it mean, finally?"

"It's just a story," Tad said. "It's all just stories."

"It'll write up nice, though." Mick Curtain stood in the aisle, grinning. "Interesting introduction, Tad."

"You made me think of Prince Harry," Mrs. Ball offered. "In your little speech, I mean." She ran her hands over her hips, smoothing the clinging cloth. "Killing is his job, he said."

Ginny Garner separated herself from the group that clustered around her father. Advancing up the aisle, she smiled at Tad. "It was like a poem, Tad."

Her smile broadened. "You have a new tie. That's a new jacket, too, isn't it?"

"Rosalie picked them out." He introduced the two young women. He introduced Ginny, then, to Mrs. Ball.

"We're assembling for a drink at my apartment," Ginny said, "I hope you all can stop by." Speaking, she examined Mrs. Ball, appearing to find her suitable. Then she turned to smile at Rosalie. "You've turned him out very nicely."

Rosalie, flushed, flustered, could say nothing.

"You and I can discuss the care and feeding of American graduate students."

"I—yes. Thank you," Rosalie managed, her flush deepening.

Rowena Quarles joined Ginny in the aisle. "He's gone off. Phone calls."

Tad understood her to be speaking of her brother. Rupert Quarles's sister looked so little like him they might have been of different species. She was lovely, her features fine and smooth, so that she seemed smaller than she actually was. Her smile was pleasant, her gaze kind. Tad recalled the ferocity of her expression as she rode past him on the straining black horse.

Ginny did not introduce her. Instead, the two women silently started up the aisle.

"I'm going to try to get a quick word with our speaker," Mick said. "Mrs. B.?"

"As I've just received permission to approach, yes, I'll join you." Mrs. Ball laughed her throaty laugh, again smoothing the fabric at her hips. "Cheeky thing, isn't she? But then I suppose she can afford to be."

Tad and Rosalie made their way out of the lecture hall, down the stairs, across the foyer. For a moment he thought to visit Horatio, but a mass of people milled about the glass case. Tad felt a stab of something like anger—the Roman soldier did not deserve to be the object of such gawking; he had died in battle and was owed the honor of a pyre or grave.

Tad ushered Rosalie out into the night. At the top of the entryway steps, she suddenly stopped.

Across the street, Billy Knox leaned against a white van. Under his sleeveless jacket he wore a bright white teeshirt, his only concession to the chill. His blue hair stuck up from his skull like thick thorns. He seemed some cruel instrument of siege and mayhem.

"No," Rosalie said, even before Tad moved. She grabbed at his arm, jerking his shoulder painfully. "Don't, Tad."

"What does he want?" But even as he asked the question, Tad realized that he knew the answer.

Tad also knew what he himself wanted. He wanted a gladius.

"I— Just take me home, will you, please?"

"What about the gathering at Ginny's?"

"I can't . . . I'll not be wanted there."

Across the street, Billy Knox hadn't moved. Rosalie, her head bent submissively, stared at the concrete step in front of her. And Tad finally understood that Rosalie was caught in a trap. He was not certain that he could free her.

"Do you really want to go to America?"

She looked at him in dismay, sudden tears glittering in her eyes.

"In America nobody cares about accents or tattoos."

He could see her distress, see it clench the flesh around her eyes, turn her round mouth into a stiff rippled grimace. He lay his hand on her cheek, smoothed.

"Yes," she said, "all right. I just hope I . . ." But she couldn't tell him what she hoped. She could only take his arm.

They started down the street. Glancing back, he saw that Billy Knox hadn't moved.

The night was chilly but not cold. They decided to walk to Ginny Garner's. Tad hoped that the exercise might ward off the headache gathering in the darkness behind his eyes.

It was a Friday evening, not late, and the old center of the city was busy, buses grinding and growling along the streets, young people ambling down the narrow lanes and alleys or stuffing themselves into restaurant booths. Across the river, lights shone in many windows. Tad walked with Rosalie as if they were simply one more couple.

It struck him then that with Rosalie he might have a chance to have something like a life. He would never be the same as others, he would always be different, but maybe he need not always be as he had been.

He had promised to take her to America. He would keep his promise. At the same time, however, he sensed to certainty that his destiny was to be met here, in this shadowed city.

GINNY GARNER'S flat seemed less a living space than a gallery showing the work of a postmodern sculptor. The main area was open and almost antiseptic, bits of chrome and glass and marble and blonde wood and cream leather, abstract paintings, small pieces of primitive statuary. An odd effect was that the physical movements of Ginny's guests made them seem mannequins posed in a store window.

Rupert Quarles had been called to Waterby, where his father had suffered a serious stroke. Ginny seemed unconcerned about the old man's condition. Mick Curtain had gone off to file his story, she said, but she'd invited the usual assortment of university personages, potential donors, and highbrow hustlers. Tad recognized two academics who had been at Sylvia Stuckey's party and who now, without wives, attended Mrs. Ball.

"Get yourself something to drink, Tad," Ginny said. "I want to get the lowdown on you from Rosalie."

"You'll have to stand in line," said her father, who had just come up. Not waiting to be introduced, he said, "You're Rosalie. What a becoming dress! Tad says you make magic with a needle and thread."

Rosalie, coloring prettily, allowed herself to be eased toward the drinks buffet. Ginny laughed. "You may not see her the rest of the night."

He asked for an aspirin.

She led him to a bathroom. "No one knows quite what to make of your introduction, Tad. The prevailing opinion is that it must have been some sort of performance art."

He took two pills. "It didn't come out quite right."

"On the contrary," she said, "It was perfect."

Back among the gathered, Tad saw Rosalie still engaged by Robert Garner. She was flushed, speaking, and seemed to be enjoying his attention. Rowena Quarles and Mrs. Ball each centered a circle of men. Professor Stuckey stood at the window, alone, a glass of clear liquid in hand, looking out into the night. Tad found a soft drink and joined her at the window.

"Club soda," she said, raising her glass. After taking a sip, she asked, "Your friend is a student?"

"No," he said. "She works in her mother's tearoom. And she's a seamstress."

"A local girl."

"Yes. Rosalie Cush is her name."

"A conquest. I shouldn't have thought you were the type. Tell me, Mr. Fellows," she paused, seemed to examine him, "that 'I am all soldiers' nonsense—does it assuage your guilt?"

"Guilt?"

"Guilt, Mr. Fellows. For murder and rape and general savagery." When he said nothing, she went on calmly, "I knew you were wrapped up in an emotional straightjacket, a perfect stooge for Robert Garner. I didn't know that you were totally corrupt. I wonder why, killer that you say you are, you haven't killed anyone here yet."

Tad looked out the window, into the darkness. "There's someone out there who wants to kill me."

"And paranoid." She flushed, suddenly exasperated. "You're so transparent, Mr. Fellows. So pathetic."

"He has blue hair," Tad said. "His name is Billy Knox."

"I know Billy Knox." Rowena Quarles had come up to stand at his shoulder. "He does jobs for Rupert. He was born in Waterby. Local gossip has him our brother."

She smiled at Tad. Then she turned to Professor Stuckey, spoke her name, and watched as the museum director seemed to bend into a subservient bow, muttered phatic phrases, excused herself, turned, and departed. Tad and Rowena Quarles watched her cross the room to the drinks buffet, where she stood, unmoving, silent.

Miss Quarles smiled at Tad. "I wanted us to talk. Ginny speaks so highly of you. She hasn't many friends, but she says you are among them."

"Yes," he said.

"But how, exactly? What is the nature of your relationship?"

She smiled pleasantly. Rowena Quarles had no reason not to be agreeable, but Tad thought that her open air and soft glances were real. "I know you won't mind my asking."

"I have her back."

"That's a military phrase, is it not? It means that you protect her against enemies whose presence or intent she's unaware of?" She sipped at her drink, studying him almost apologetically over the rim of her glass. "Do you find yourself inclined to protect her against me and my brother?"

Tad looked at her. "I think you might be the ones who need protection, Miss Quarles."

"You may be right, Mr. Fellows." Rowena Quarles smiled again. "Now tell me why Billy Knox wants to kill you."

"Because I'm here," he said. "Is he really your brother?"

"No one knows for sure," she said, shrugging faintly. "Country people —whenever there's an illegitimate birth, everyone looks to the lord. In this case, rumor feeds on my father's sexual history. But DNA testing has never been done, mostly because nobody really cares, least of all Billy Knox."

"Long ago people would have suspected a soldier." Tad looked out the window, into the darkness. Rowena Quarles, he was discovering, was easy to talk to. "A Roman occupier was commonly thought the father of Jesus, at the time. Professor Stuckey wrote a book on the subject."

"Professor Stuckey rides many hobbyhorses, doesn't she? But about Ginny." Her smile and gaze softened. "I appreciate that you've placed her under your protection. But you have no other designs, I take it? No intention of impeding her progress?"

Tad wasn't quite sure what she meant. His headache surged.

An old man, the same pale, bent don who had approached him at Professor Stuckey's party, interrupted them. Tad now discerned, in his talk of Greek athletic events, his erotic purpose.

Miss Quarles slipped away, as did, soon, Tad, to bob from one conversation to another. Others seemed to accept his presence among them as a matter of course. Rosalie, again under Ginny's urging hand, also was drifting from group to group. The two young women ended together in a corner. Rosalie laughed, a high soft shriek of pleasure that Tad had not heard from her before. A brace of elderly dons advanced upon them.

Professor Garner came to stand with Tad, again at the window. Tad, he said, had with his introduction initiated himself into the professional ranks. "They're even a bit intimidated."

"I didn't get it right," he said.

"They don't know that. They think you're quite brilliant. Sylvia Stuckey is annoyed that they find you so interesting, but she hasn't been able to persuade them otherwise. She gave up and left."

Tad thought that it was time for him to leave as well. The aspirin confronted but would not long ward off the pain building in his head. It would be bad.

He found Rosalie. "You can stay, if you want. Professor Garner will see you home, I'm sure."

"No, no," she said. "I'm ready to go. It's all been . . ." Again she couldn't complete her thought.

Ginny seemed genuinely sorry that they were leaving. As they rode the elevator down, Rosalie said, "She's nothing like I thought she'd be. And her dad, the professor, he's just a regular bloke."

As they stepped into the night, she took his arm. "I'm glad you made me come, Tad. I . . . had a good time."

At the corner they caught a bus. Riding across town, Rosalie was full of questions about the various people she'd met. Tad could give her limited information about the guests, their titles, positions, and achievements, if any. About Rowena Quarles Rosalie, it turned out, knew more than he did—a dressage rider, quietly lesbian, her odd mother's companion.

Rosalie had felt the force of Professor Stuckey's animosity toward Tad. "I don't understand. Did you do something to her? Are you a threat to her?"

"I work for Professor Garner," Tad said, "and I'm American."

The bus stopped two blocks from the tearoom. As they walked down the quiet streets, Tad grew aware that the night illuminations had begun to change. Objects took on outlines. The pain in the back of his head advanced.

He forced himself to continue slowly to the stairway, up to Rosalie's door.

She had been silent as they walked. Now she asked, "The lecture, what the professor said about endings. Did he mean us? Are you going to marry me?"

"I'm going to take you to America," he said through gritted teeth. "I promised. Is that what you want, to get married?"

"I don't know," she said. "I . . . sometimes it all seems like, what you said, like an old story with the same ending, over and over."

"Yes," he said.

"But even so, that doesn't mean we can't be happy, does it? I can be happy with you, Tad. You . . . leave me be. I—I'm happy now. Can you tell?"

For a moment, she disappeared in a bright flash of pain. His voice, when he spoke, was a grunt. "Yes."

She seemed about to say more, but instead kissed his cheek, briefly pressed her body against his. "Good night, Tad. Thank you."

Tad stood before her closed door for some time, resisting the pain.

He descended the stairs. He half expected Billy Knox to be waiting for him at the bottom, but the landing and sidewalk and street were empty. He forced himself to walk.

F AT WET SNOWFLAKES fell thickly, slowly, in the gray dawn light. Snow whitened the banks of the River Cam, outlined narrowboats tied to pilings, drifted down onto and disappeared in the dark water. On the tarmac path that edged Jesus Green, snow lay two inches deep and trackless. On a bench in the snow sat Tad Fellows.

Melted snow trickled from his hair down his temples and neck. His coat felt wet and heavy, he was cold, and his muscles were stiff. He had been on the bench for a long time—at least, the absence of footprints argued, since the snow began.

He felt no real pain, although his shoulder ached faintly and his thighs were strangely sore, his quadriceps and hamstrings.

His skull felt hollow, emptied.

He had had a headache, he remembered, and he had gone back to himself, he knew, again. He did not know how long he had been gone or what he had done.

One day he would go into himself and not come out. But not now. Not today. Not yet.

Now images flickered in his memory—a shadowed alley, a bright white glare, a patch of light cast on an elaborately pillowed bed, a small, clean, empty room.

His right hand was clenched into a fist. He let his fingers fall open. In his palm lay a coin—a Roman denarius, Marcus Aurelius 194.

The light was changing, the gray going pearly. From the road beyond the river came the shush of tires churning snow to slush. Down the path strode an elderly man, like an alien being in fuzzy red earmuffs and a bright green scarf, tethered to a pair of Jack Russell terriers that jumped and snapped at the snowflakes.

Tad rose, took out his pouch, placed the coin carefully inside it, and slipped the pouch back into his pocket. Then he started off across the green.

At Mrs. Ball's he discovered that he was wearing the same clothes he'd worn to the lecture and party. In the shower he inspected his body for abrasions or bruises but found neither. The soreness in his thighs eased under the stream of hot water.

At breakfast, Mr. Mobuku fussed about in the kitchen, and a couple, American by their drawl, ate and worried about getting around in the snow.

Mick Curtain drank coffee and picked apart a muffin. Over his spectacles he gave Tad a knowing look. "Missed you yesterday. Get lucky, as you Yanks have it?"

So he had lost, or found, a day. He scooped cereal. He was very hungry.

"Did you like my piece on the telly don?" Mick smiled.

"I didn't see it."

"An oversight easily rectified," Mick said. From the empty chair beside him he lifted a copy of the local newspaper, open and folded to a picture of Robert Garner.

Tad skimmed the review. Professor Garner had charmed, cheerfully offering his audience a vision of violence. Humans are innately killers of their own kind, greedy, grasping, murderous creatures set on invasion, conquest, and occupation, all Id under thin layers of civilization (best line of the evening: "If you want to see humanity raw, attend a birthday party full of seven-year-old boys"). Classical archeology, a digging through the sediment of vanished societies to record the inhumanity of humans in every instance of their history, offers only footnotes to Freud.

The argument was interesting, the reviewer allowed, even entertaining, if perhaps based more on whimsy than on deduction. Others in the field, Professor Sylvia Stuckey for one, found it all very American, derivative and logocentric and unsound—"Freud indeed! He needs to read Foucault." However, few in the audience took offense at being called murderous brutes, perhaps because few took the charge seriously. Most expressed their pleasure in Professor Garner's performance, the informed geniality of which seemed itself to refute his propositions.

On the same page was a portion of Mick's interview with the American professor. Tad didn't bother to read it.

"So," Mick smiled as Tad put down the paper. "Have I harmed or helped him?"

"I don't know," Tad said.

"Well, can you tell me what's up with the Garners and Rupert and Rowena Quarles?"

"I don't know," he repeated.

"Professor Garner enjoys the hospitality of an MP who adamantly opposes his project—the MP a baronet now, his daddy having croaked last night. His daughter enjoys the company of that man's lesbian sister. You find nothing in all this to exercise your curiosity, not to say your concern?"

"No."

"Something's going on, Tad. Don't you want to know what it is?"

"What could I do about it?"

"There's that," Mick said. "Still . . . and how does Sylvia Stuckey fit in all this?"

Tad finished his coffee.

"I know. You don't care," Mick grinned. "You probably also don't care that Mrs. Ball was particularly cheerful yesterday morning. One assumes that she was happy enough with the professor's performance to set up a repeat engagement, given that last evening Mr. Mobuku was at the desk and this morning he's handling breakfast. She hasn't yet returned."

For the first time that morning, Tad thought of Rosalie. She had told him she was happy. He didn't know what being happy felt like.

Back in his room, Tad took out his chamois pouch and lined up its contents on his desk. The coin fit.

He didn't know where he got it, but that didn't matter. He would put the coin back where it belonged, with the others in the cache. He would tell everyone merely that he had found it, which was, in a way, the truth.

He put the objects back in the pouch and the pouch in his pocket. He was aware of the slight added weight of the coin against his thigh. It felt right.

His headache had been severe but had passed. He was prepared to follow Marcus, who urged one "after the most violent headaches to return to one's customary tasks with renewed vigor." Marcus knew about headaches.

The snow had stopped, the sky had cleared, and the temperature had fallen, as if in a new, different, somehow dangerous day. Walking to the museum, Tad was alert, apprehensive. He had patrolled snowy streets and alleys before, feeling this same tension. He felt now, too, the absence of a weapon, a rifle, a sword. He was aware, vaguely, that he was no longer certain what was real.

Once in his basement room, amid the order he had wrought, he began to relax. The materials from the summer's dig were catalogued and carefully packed in sturdy containers, ready to be sealed and sent off to the warehouse. The data for his thesis were compiled in a form appropriate for presentation to his PhD committee. And many of the records and images, both digital and paper, from the ten-year dig were collated and cross-referenced and would be easily accessible to Professor Garner when he composed his narrative of the excavation. It was all competently, professionally done, Tad knew. But now, assessing his achievement, he was confronted by a fact that he had somehow not noticed—he had much left to do.

Tad had said that he would be finished with the documentation by the beginning of the spring semester, so that he and Professor Garner, back at UCLA could produce a manuscript ready for a publisher by summer or early autumn. He had fallen behind. How that had happened he didn't know.

It was now a few days before Christmas. He would return to America in a month or so. He had to work faster, harder, longer.

And there was another problem.

Professor Garner's book would show readers what his project had unearthed and explain the import of these discoveries. The most interesting to a broad readership would of course be the mummified Roman soldier. As had Rosalie, readers would want to know about Horatio, about his life and especially about his death. Regarding his life, Professor Garner could tell a tale based on the knowledge that archeology had collected about activities of those legionnaires posted to frontier forts, but he depended on Tad to gather evidence from which he might construct a story, speculative to be sure but supported by archeological data, about the death of the Last Centurion.

Tad had no such evidence. The dates were such that it seemed clear that the fort was being abandoned and that Horatio was part of some rear guard. But why was he so far from the protection of the walls? Why was he alone, if he was? How had he been ambushed, if he had? Or had he sprung the surprise attack? Had he chosen to make a stand? He was at the far end of the bridge, where he could block an advance of numbers. As had the Horatio of Livy, he could confront the enemy two or three at a time and use their bodies to hamper the movement of the others—Tad the soldier had seen that at once. But unlike the legendary hero, this Horatio had no river by which to escape.

Had he yearned to return home, or had he no real home to return to? Had he known he was going to die? Would that awareness have consoled him?

Would he have known that he'd have no funeral, no transforming flames?

Tad had no data to apply to any of these questions. He had no suggestions for Professor Garner. He had neither the inclination nor the time for conjecture.

Horatio had died a soldier doing his duty. To Tad Fellows, who recognized a comrade in arms even two thousand years past, nothing more need be said.

That afternoon, on his way, late, to tea and a tart and Rosalie, Tad stepped for a moment into Horatio's room. The dark form behind the glass appeared not only a human body but also an abstract shape, a primitive representation that gestured toward the ancient and elemental. The mummified head seemed bone and flesh gathered around the arrow jutting from an eye socket. Tad recognized the configuration of his headaches.

You too, he thought.

"It's all right to talk to him." Gray Miss Eversly stood in the doorway. Her smile was small, gentle. "Lots of people do. But if he answers, that might be rather a problem."

Tad had spoken aloud, it seemed.

"We wondered, when you didn't come in yesterday—the director feared you might be ill."

He saw then that Miss Eversly, with her small, bent frame and thick spectacles, was a kindly woman. He had not been aware of that. He had not been aware of so much about people. Because people were difficult, could be burdensome, injurious, wearying.

"I've been sent to fetch you," she said.

Tad followed her gray shape across the foyer and up the stairs. Shown into Professor Stuckey's office, he discovered that the director was not alone.

"Ah, Fellows." Rupert Quarles sprawled in a wingback chair, his corduroy-covered legs jutting over the carpet. His bony pate shone as brightly as his boots. "Queer speech the other night. Ginny found it amusing. Daft, I had it."

Tad said nothing.

Quarles grinned. "Daft as biking to Waterby in the middle of the night. Lucky a car didn't bang you into a slough."

Tad felt, under the weight of the pouch in his pocket, the lingering soreness in his thighs—bicycling.

Professor Stuckey fit her fingers together, laying her clenched hands on her empty desktop as if they made a weapon. "You appear to be finished cataloging the recent dig materials, Mr. Fellows."

She could know that only by going into his files. So nothing was secure. Tad sensed himself surrounded. He felt the beginning of a headache.

Professor Stuckey took a deep breath. "Perhaps you could explain why I haven't received a copy of the entries for this year's activity."

He had not thought to send her the information. "I forgot."

"Forgot, Mr. Fellows?" She leaned forward aggressively in her chair. "You consider the interests of the English people of so little conse-quence that you can't be troubled to account to anyone for your activ-ities? Or is it that you don't wish to document your theft?"

Pain, faint, seemed to float in Tad's head, not an attack so much as a reminder, a warning.

"I'd like to find the catalog attached to an email in my in-box by the end of the workday. Can you manage that, Mr. Fellows?"

"Yes," he said.

She sat back, glancing at Quarles. The baronet seemed bored. Then she said, "How long before you've finished your work with the site records?"

"A month," he said. "Maybe less."

"And when does Bob Garner plan to begin shipping material to America? I assume that he will want to spirit it, and Horatio, out of the country as soon as he can, before the government comes to its senses."

"I don't know," Tad said.

"Don't know or won't say, Mr. Fellows?"

"Don't know."

"I find that hard to believe, especially since—"

"Let it be, Sylvia," Quarles interrupted. "Twit's not going to tell us anything."

"He'd better. He's using my—our facilities, working with English artifacts, we have every right—"

"He's nothing," Quarles said, crossing his legs languidly. "Hasn't a clue."

Professor Stuckey squared her shoulders. Under her fawn sweater, the action forced her breasts up and out, as if in challenge. Her jaw set.

"Mr. Fellows, I want the completed catalog. Will you see to it?"

"Yes," Tad said. He noticed then that the papers on the table behind her were fewer, and neatly organized and laid out. She seemed in control of herself as well.

"And you maintain that you have no idea what Professor Garner's specific plans are for the artifacts?"

"Ha!" Quarles laughed sharply. "Wouldn't tell us if he had."

"Is that correct, Mr. Fellows?" Professor Stuckey looked at him, strangely satisfied.

"Yes," Tad said.

"There's loyalty, Fellows," Rupert Quarles snorted. "And there's stupidity."

Professor Stuckey's satisfaction swelled. "You're not concerned that I'll be writing a letter for your dossier, that your professional prospects will be nil—"

"Let it go, Sylvia. We don't need him," Quarles said brusquely. He offered Tad a grin that slowly sagged into a sneer. "Soldier on, you dumb bastard."

"We're finished here, Mr. Fellows," Professor Stuckey said, echoing Quarles's tone. "Please go away."

After leaving the office, for a moment Tad stood outside the director's door, under the quiet gaze of Miss Eversly. He didn't know what had just happened.

"She works too hard," the small gray woman said quietly. When Tad did not respond, she added, "She doesn't mean . . ."

Tad waited, but Miss Eversly could not quite finish the thought.

He went back to the basement, pulled up the catalog on the computer, and sent it to Professor Stuckey. As he worked he thought that he ought to talk to Robert Garner. He wondered then why the professor had not yet spoken to him about his schedule, the state of their project, the plans for the future.

Bicycling to Waterby in darkness—why had he done that? And Waterby the estate or Waterby the village? He could almost remember: black land, yellow headlights, shadows, breaking glass, the small, clean, empty room.

He decided not to go to the teashop. He would see Rosalie after the Panto rehearsal. He wanted now only solitude and work.

His headache came and went like puffs of hot gritty breeze before a storm.

ON HIS WAY to the theater that evening, Tad for the first time took real notice of Christmas decorations—strings of lights sagging from eaves, wreathes hanging on doors, cutout figures of Santa or Bethlehem crèches leaning on lawns. The holiday had never meant much to him. He remembered the winking lights his father had hung in the market window. He remembered their Christmas tree, tiny, plastic, set on a coffee table. He did not remember giving or receiving.

He hadn't thought about this Christmas. He didn't need Rosalie to tell him that he should buy her a gift. He had no idea what might please her.

Tad, approaching, saw her standing alone before the entrance to the theater. She seemed, from a distance, slumped, dejected. He was nearly upon her before, as if rising out of reverie, she lifted her head and turned and saw him.

"Oh, you're here. I was beginning to think—did I misunderstand? You weren't here last night."

"I had a bad headache," he said. "I'm sorry."

"No, no, you never really said you'd be here every night, did you? You have work to do, and you have other ... friends. I have no claim on you. Do I?"

Her last two words hung between them, burdened with a world.

He touched her cheek, warm under his cold fingertips.

"I'll be going back to America in a month or so," he said slowly. "Will you come with me, or do you want me to go ahead and set up a place for us?"

She frowned, as if faintly pained. "Tad ..."

"You'll need a passport."

"I have a passport," she said, "I—are you sure? I mean, it's just seemed like a ... game, a fantasy. America."

"What would you like me to give you for Christmas?"

She looked at him. Then she took his arm, leaning into him as if for support. "Something small, Tad. Something small that I can hold in my hand and look at and think of you."

He felt the weight of the pouch in his pocket. He thought—but no, he had to return it. The coin. He hadn't thought to do so that day.

They started down the street. Rosalie quickly became her chatty self, talking about the Panto, the dress rehearsal the next evening and then the opening, and about the difficulties she'd had with a costume—the story was set in King Arthur's Camelot, the characters were outfitted in medieval gowns and tunics, which had been a task to create, given the puny budget. The actors were good and the show was funny, lots of topical humor, some bawdy but obscure, so that little children wouldn't understand. Tad would like it. He'd especially like one skit, she said, tugging at his arm, but she wouldn't spoil his fun by telling him about it. As for Christmas, she usually went with her parents to dinner with her aunt and cousin in Peterborough, she was sure they would be happy to have him join them, although frankly it would be really dull, and maybe, well, she was a grown woman, wasn't she, and her parents needed to get used to her being on her own, so maybe they, the two of them, could go to one of the restaurants that would be serving dinner, lots of them did these days—they could talk about it, work something out, but not now, now she didn't feel like talking anymore, she didn't feel like going home, maybe they could go to his room for a while, she just wanted to be with him, alone.

At Mrs. Ball's, the television cast a flickering lavender light into the shadows in the parlor. Two heads seemed perched on the back of the sofa like shooting-gallery targets: one shapely, dark and nappy, the other freshly shaved but for the strip of stiff hair down its center. Neither head turned as Tad guided Rosalie across the foyer to the stairs.

He had hardly shut the door to his room when, before he could switch on a light, she turned to him, mouth and tongue, hurried hands. In the lambent illumination from the street, they came together. Quickly naked, she seemed in the dimness a dream creature in the desert night, pale and shadowed, attacking. Her lovemaking was at once wanton and desperate, as if her body moved under some dark compulsion. She thrashed below, heaved above him, grasped and stroked and clung, labored over him, forced his servitude. She grunted, whined softly, once nearly growled. She seemed not there, Rosalie. She seemed someone, something else.

When she was finally quiet, he dozed, awakening to find her risen and, when he switched on the bedside lamp, dressed in bra and panties. She slipped into her blouse, but not quickly enough to keep him from seeing the graying blotches on her upper arms.

He got up and dressed and, neither having spoken, they stepped into the dim hallway and down the stairs, past the dark parlor, out into the cold December night.

Halfway down the block, she stopped. "I wish you'd say something."

"I have nothing to say, Rosalie."

"I just wanted you to . . . I've been with blokes. You know you're not the first. I just wanted to do all of it with you. To make it all right."

"It *is* all right," he said.

"I just want to be free."

"Yes," he said.

"I— Do you feel anything for me, Tad? Do you care, at all?"

In the cold, in the empty street, in the night, they stood silently.

Then he said, "You're my only chance, Rosalie."

He didn't know quite what he meant. He only knew it was true.

She seemed to know as well. She took his arm. "In America, in California where we'll be, it never snows, does it? I don't think I'll miss it."

Tad walked her home. At her door he said, "I have a lot of work to do. I may not see you for a couple of days."

"But we're going to the opening of the Panto, right? The evening after next?"

"Right," he said. "To see that skit you won't tell me about."

He walked back. Once, at the far end of a street, tires screeched as a vehicle, a smudge of white, spun its tires on the pavement and streaked off. Before the B&B, a silver BMW idled. As Tad came near, one of the doors opened. Robert Garner climbed out into the street, went around to the sidewalk, and opened the door for Mrs. Ball. Both stood smiling.

"Out late," Garner said. "Probably you haven't been working."

"No."

"She's a nice girl, Rosalie," Mrs. Ball said. "Is it serious?"

"Yes."

"Good for you. And good night to you both." She lifted a finger and pressed its tip against Garner's chin. Then she turned and stepped up to the door. The Americans watched silently until she was inside.

"We need to chat, Tad," the professor said. "I'm jammed up, trekking down to London tomorrow, I've got meetings here, and then there are my . . ." He grinned. ". . . social obligations. And I'll be flying out on

Boxing Day. I was hoping, if you haven't made plans, that you and your young lady— Rupert and Rowena Quarles are hosting a Christmas dinner at the pub in the village. Waterby needs a lot of work before the new baronet can entertain there, but he owns a piece of the pub, so he— You'll be receiving an invitation. We might meet there early. We can take care of business and then enjoy an English Christmas."

Tad nodded. Soldier on, you dumb bastard.

"I—pardon me?"

"Nothing, nothing," Tad said.

The professor smiled, patted Tad's good shoulder. "Good. And I'm glad you and Rosalie have hit it off. Have you figured out how you're going to conduct an international romance?"

"She's coming to America," Tad said.

"It's that serious, is it? And she doesn't want you to stay here?"

"No."

For a moment Garner was silent. Then he said, "So I'll see you on Christmas, noonish." He climbed in the BMW and revved the powerful engine, only to ease the car carefully away from the curb and down the street.

Inside, Mrs. Ball waited for Tad in the parlor. "You should know, Mr. Fellows, that I'll be gone over Christmas. I'm off to Jamaica the day after tomorrow, and I'll return on New Year's Day."

She seemed especially pleased.

"Mr. Mobuku will keep the house open on the holiday," she said. "We have a couple from the States come to visit their daughter for Christmas. Once they leave, Mr. Mobuku is flying to Nigeria for a visit. He'll shut the place up. You and Mick can get your own breakfasts. You don't mind?

"No," Tad said.

"Chan will look in from time to time."

Tad said nothing.

As Tad turned toward the stairs, she stepped closer. He could smell her scent, something floral mixed with a faint aroma of gin and tobacco smoke and sex. He could feel the heat of her. Her mouth was freshly red, loose.

"Thank you again for getting Rob—Professor Garner to come here, Mr. Fellows. He's promised to call the university housing office and speak on my behalf. I'll be back on their approved list." She smiled. "Next semester's lodgers will pay for my trip. My Christmas gift to myself, but from you two as well."

She gripped, nearly stroked his arm. She was, he saw, tipsy.

"I'm beginning to think more highly of Americans." She squeezed his arm, tugging so that pain scraped across his shoulder. "While the house is shut up, you and Rosalie—well, I don't encourage overnight visitors, but in this case, as there's only you and Mick . . ."

"There's Chan," he said.

She mistook his meaning. "Our Chan. No, he's not for Rosalie, is he? He can't take her to America. And he'll always be just a lad."

A lad with a key to the house and the rooms in it, Tad thought. But he wished Mrs. Ball a good night and stepped up the stairs.


"SOMETHING'S GOING ON."

Mick Curtain sipped his coffee, watching Tad.

In the army Tad had learned that something is always going on.

Mick's sources told him that Rupert Quarles and Sylvia Stuckey were meeting often, that Sir Rupert had also met with the English Heritage Board and the board of directors of the museum. Professor Robert Garner had met with the boards as well, and of course he and his daughter were staying at Waterby.

"Looks like our new baronet is trying to dismantle the Horatio deal, while his guest is working hard to prevent him from succeeding." He paused, giving Tad a long look. "He could do it, an MP. He could make promises, cut deals."

Tad rose. "I have to go to work."

He was at the museum until well past midnight. Fighting off a headache, he walked back to Mrs. Ball's through the frosty, star-strewn night, slept a few hours, breakfasted on a slice of toast he ate going out the door, and hastened back to his task. By five o'clock he had gotten enough done to encourage him that he might finish in time. He felt the kind of confidence that had raised his spirits when with his fire team he set off on patrol—he knew what had to be done and how to do it. Only fate could have him fail.

At Mrs. Ball's, Mr. Mobuku offered a large smile as he handed Tad a small envelope embossed with a flowing W. The note inside, written and signed by the fluid hand of Rowena Quarles, invited him and a companion to Christmas dinner at the Lion and Lamb in Waterby. A postscript informed him that Sir Rupert would send a car to the B&B at eleven that morning.

Mr. Mobuku smiled again, happily. Mrs. Ball was winging her way to Jamaica, and the couple from Alabama had decided to take their daughter to London for the holiday, so Mr. Mobuku had been able to move his flight to Nigeria up to the next morning. He would see that all was secure this evening. His voice sounded even more musical as he said, "Happy Christmas, Mr. Fellows."

Rosalie, when he picked her up, also was in high spirits. The dress rehearsal the day before had gone well—exceptionally well from her perspective. The costumes were beautiful, fit perfectly, and functioned properly. She wouldn't be worrying during the performance and would be able to enjoy the show. When without her instruction Tad admired her dress, she laughed out loud.

Busing to the theater, she told him of the row she'd had with her mother about Christmas dinner. "But it's not dinner, really. She knows I want to leave. She thinks she can't run the tearoom without me, but plenty of girls can wait tables. She'll have to pay them more. I mean she takes out for my room and board, I'm like a slave—but she can't expect me to spend my life there, can she?"

As Mrs. Ball had two nights before, she squeezed Tad's arm. "I'm so glad to have that settled. Finally."

He thought to tell her of the invitation to Christmas dinner at Waterby, but just then the bus hissed to a stop. With two other couples, they got off and moved to join those clustered before the theater doors. Soon they were seated in the center of the hall.

"They hate to give away expensive seats," Rosalie told him. "But I insisted. It's the only payment I get for my work. Well, there are the photos for my portfolio, but nothing other than that."

Tad had seen the portfolio—glossy images of costumes, some worn by actors, others adorning dummies or spread over pillows. The photographs would get her a job in America, she'd said.

The theater filled with old folks and children and couples and students. "I love Panto," Rosalie smiled. "Everyone's always so happy."

The room warmed. Voices swelled. Then the lights flickered and dimmed, and the curtain rose.

Tad had not understood, despite Rosalie's explanations, that Panto was pure silliness. The story mixed into farcical confusion the adultery of Lancelot and Guinevere, Percival's quest for the Holy Grail, and Gawain's adventure with the Green Knight, as well as figures like Saint George and Boudica, all interrupted by songs and skits featuring deaf dons, gay Nazis, clumsy Chinese acrobats who were actually computer hackers, a bear, assorted dancing girls, and a pair of wandering minstrels who sang risqué versions of old pop songs or the tunes of the Beatles and the Stones and Elton John. The actors were young and talented and charming. Much of the humor was homosexual, some topical, and all of it well received. Those in the audience shrieked, yelled advice and warnings, applauded pratfalls, and expended nearly as much energy as those on the stage.

Beside him, Rosalie squirmed in her seat, her face flushed, damp. At one point she took his arm in both her hands and said over the uproar, "Why aren't you laughing?"

He smiled at her. "I am."

After the intermission, the nonsense continued. Then, as Sir Gawain went out to meet the Green Knight, the promised stroke of a blade on his neck, and, surely, death, Rosalie leaned into his ear. "Here it is."

To this point, Gawain had been foppishly attired in spangled tights over a crotch grossly stuffed with something other than genitals, as well as an embroidered tunic to which were attached anachronistic epaulets. Now, entering what a cardboard silhouette of a tree told all was a forest, he wore American army camouflage—pants, blouse, and boonie hat.

Tad tensed. His boonie hat—was it? But it couldn't be. His hat was at the bottom of the River Cam, or riding the currents of the North Sea. It couldn't be.

Gawain burst into song, lewd lyrics sung to the tune of "It Had to Be You," describing how the United States had "incessantly abused / screwed, blued, and tattooed" the United Kingdom, for which its citizens should be profoundly grateful.

Beside him Rosalie whimpered with glee.

The uniform the actor wore had the stiff, glossy look of the new. But the hat? Was it somewhat softer, crumpled, long used?

Stepping onto a small wooden arch over a shine of blue wrapping paper, Gawain announced that he was come to the River Cam prepared to give his all, to have his head lopped off for honor of Arthur and Camelot, for George Washington and Barack Obama, for Donald Trump and Bill Gates, for Wall Street capitalists and Hollywood personalities, including Lindsey Lohan and all the Kardashians, and for Ebay, Amazon, and Starbucks. The audience loved it.

Tad understood. That was his boonie hat.

"What?" Rosalie leaned back to look at him.

He shook his head.

From the other side of the stage then appeared the Green Knight, green legs partly covered by a kilt of green plaid, bare chest bearing a green tattooed map of the United Kingdom, hair gelled into green spikes, carrying a Roman short sword. With an accent so thick Tad couldn't understand a word, the green man confronted the American soldier. Then he sang, to the tune of "Yesterday," a lament for the destruction of the old ways and values, the traditional forms obliterated in the relentless advance of American material and popular culture.

At the song's end, the orchestra built a dramatic flourish, then fell silent—time for the stroke of the blade.

The audience had earlier watched Gawain whack off the head of the Green Knight during a Christmas party at Arthur's court. The Green Knight, who had simply picked up his head and walked out, now would deliver a reciprocating blow. But Gawain, dressed as an American soldier, began to plead cravenly for the audience's help, whimpering that the contract was the work of shysters, begging for a pardon, promising foreign aid and fast-food franchises and rap lessons from Eminem. The audience hissed, booed, cried for his blood.

Tad could not take his eyes off the boonie hat. The hat was his, it was real in a way that all else was not.

Finally the soldier—Gawain—laid his head, reluctantly and after several feints and hesitations, on the rail of the bridge. The Green Man raised his short sword to deliver the contracted blow. Kettledrums and then an oboe swelled out of softness. The audience fell into suspenseful silence.

The Green Man turned to the audience and winked.

Grabbing the boonie hat, he hurled it out into the hall. As if in the same motion, he dropped his sword, grabbed the soldier by the chest and thigh, and upended him, so that he somersaulted onto the blue paper.

After a moment, Gawain leaped up, the Green Man leaped down, and the two bowed, linked arms, and skipped off into the wings.

Once the laughter and applause began to subside, the stage became a swirl of activity as the scene was changed.

Tad had followed the flight of the hat. Three rows in front of him, a young man had stood and caught it. Tad fixed the student's face, his shape, in his memory.

"Tad?" Rosalie was looking at him, her uncertainty edging toward alarm. "Tad, it was all in fun."

"My hat," he said.

"Tad . . ." She took his hand in both of hers. Her voice was thick, beseeching.

He had nothing to say.

The show went on. Then it was over and the hall began to empty. Tad ushered Rosalie out. He waited for the young man who now wore the boonie hat. He looked at it.

No CIB pin. It wasn't his hat.

His hat was gone.

Rosalie explained. They bought the hats, one for each scheduled performance, from the local army surplus store. She thought he'd be amused. Turning the incident at the bridge into comedy showed their, well, not affection exactly, but maybe a kind of sympathy. Panto only mocked what the audience cared for—that's why all the jokes about the royals, for example. And they weren't making fun of him, not him personally. They were joshing British and American relations, so complicated, ironic—colonies and wars and submarine bases and nuclear missiles and movies and money. He shouldn't be angry. Not with her, anyway.

"I'm not angry," he said. "Where did they get the sword?"

"On line," she said. "Three or four companies sell them. They're reproductions, but they're supposed to be exact copies."

"Seemed like it," he said.

"It wasn't sharpened. Even so, the actors were cautioned." She paused. "I— Cast and crew are meeting at the pub for a drink. We don't have to go, though."

"It's all right," he said, "if you want."

"No, no." She took his arm. "Let's just . . . be together."

He told her then what Mrs. Ball had said about staying the night.

"Yes," she said, clearly relieved. They had moved out of uncertainty. She now knew what to do. "I'd like that, to actually sleep together."

At the B&B, a faint light shone behind the front door. Otherwise the house was dark. They made their way to Tad's room. Rosalie watched as Tad removed his amulets from his pouch and arranged them in a row on the desk. She watched quietly as he removed his clothes and slid into bed. Tonight she didn't try to conceal the bruises on her shoulders as she undressed for him.

"Billy Knox," he said.

"When he comes around, I have to— Chan I can put off, he's simple, you know, but I can't stop Billy. I— Do you understand?"

"Yes," he said. "Does he hurt you?"

"Hurt me? No," she said, slipping into bed beside him. "He isn't cruel. I just— You know how easily I bruise. It isn't about pain. It's about . . . he does what he wants because he can. These—" She shrugged, as if to shed the contusions. "He's tried to make me get a tattoo, but I won't. So he does this. He's just leaving his mark."

Like a dog, Tad thought.

"I suppose," Rosalie said. She nestled into the curve of his arm. "I feel that way, with him. Soiled."

Once again Tad realized that he had spoken aloud.

"But we're all marked, one way or another, aren't we." She drew a fingertip gently across the scars along his side. "Not like you, but . . . I have scars, too. They just don't show."

She snuggled deeper into his arm. The top of her blonde head brushed against his chin. She seemed to speak to his wounds.

"Did it . . . was there much pain? I— You never talk about it, the war,

★    170    ★

or getting blown up. You don't have to, it's fine if you're uncomfortable . . ."

He saw the black burqa, the black eyes, the sudden inevitable grasping for the instrument of death.

"I didn't feel the bomb. When I came to, I was full of morphine, so even though I hurt, it was like it was someone else's pain. I actually felt—"

He remembered struggling against the light, seeking to return to the shadows. In a hospital bed in Germany. In Jesus Green, as snow fell.

"I didn't want to come back."

"You mean from being unconscious? Or drugged."

"Not . . . that. I just felt that I'd been away, in a different world. I've been there since, a few times."

"I don't understand," Rosalie said.

"When my headaches are really bad," Tad said, "I slip off, into myself. I don't know where I go or what I do. When I'm back, I have the sense that for a while I was my real self, who I really am."

Rosalie traced with her fingertip the stiff tissue, as if to account for him by the shapes of his scars. "You've been this way—the way you are—since you were blown up?"

"Yes," he said, "but sometimes I feel like I've always been this way, deep down."

Her breathing changed. "Have you never ever . . . cared about anyone?"

"Not the way other people do," he said. "Or say they do. I've never really had anyone to care *about*. Even my parents—they were like ghosts."

"What do you feel for me, Tad?"

After a long silence, he said, "I'd die for you."

"Die? I don't want you to die. I'm not talking about dying. I'm talking about loving."

"Then serve. I would protect and defend and serve you. I'd do the same for my country. Even if I knew I was going to die doing it. Even though I know that America and you and I don't matter, not really."

He had spoken with an unusual urgency that silenced them both.

Finally she said, her breath warm on his chest, "Would you do all that for her, too? For Ginny Garner."

He had given the American girl little thought recently. He wasn't sure why.

"Maybe. I don't know."

"So she doesn't matter either? You're not . . . in love with her, in your own way?"

"No," he said.

She rose up onto his chest to look at him. "But if nothing matters, how can you go on? Living, I mean? What's the point?"

"I don't know what the point is. I don't know if there is a point." Tad picked up the worn paperback from the bedside table. "Marcus says that everything is all for the good, even if what happens to us individually isn't. We should embrace the lives and duties that Fate has assigned us. I was a soldier and now I'm a graduate student. I was alone and now I'm with you. What happened doesn't matter because we can't change it, and what will happen doesn't matter because we can't know it. Nothing matters except . . . Marcus did his duty. He calls that virtue."

"But . . . what about love, Tad?"

"I don't know. The Romans talk about love only in the abstract," he said. "For them—for the men, anyway, the fighters—what was important was not what one felt but what one did. Not love but loyalty."

After a pause, he said, "I tried to explain to the VA doctors about duty, loyalty, after my headaches started. They thought— I never was able to make them see."

"What did they say?"

"They said the mind does complex things in order to protect itself, builds walls and fortresses. One said I had too few memories of growing up, like I only let myself remember what gave me some kind of comfort."

"Is that true?"

After a moment, he said, "How could I tell, Rosalie?"

"Yes, well," she said, "what did they say you should do about it?"

"The usual," Tad said. "Drugs. Counseling."

"But you aren't being treated, are you? Why not?"

"I am what I am." Popeye.

"Popeye? Is that a person?"

"A cartoon character," Tad said. "Never mind."

"But . . ." He could sense her struggling for language. "Don't you want to be . . . like other people."

"I want to be completely, wholly what I am, Rosalie."

This was the longest, most intimate conversation Tad had ever taken part in. As he lay in the darkness, he sensed the presence, distant, fleeting, of another self, the Tad Fellows he might have been.

After another long silence Rosalie said, "So you'll never tell me you love me."

"I don't know what love is," he said. "But I'll always be here for you."

After a while, she moved her hand. "That might be better."

A BUILDING HEADACHE awoke him in the middle of the night. He took aspirin. Waiting for it to work, he sat at his desk and looked at the peach pit and clothespin and lipstick cap, the piece of shrapnel, the shilling, the stone, and, at the end of the line, the Marcus Aurelius 194. The denarius seemed to him to complete a pattern, to make a whole.

Rosalie stirred in the bed. After a moment she padded softly to where he sat. With one hand she held together the counterpane she'd wrapped herself in. The other hand she placed on his bad shoulder, not noticing his wince.

"When I was small, I had those. Private things. I kept them in a little box made of balsa wood. I didn't carry them around, the way you do yours, though."

He nudged the peach pit with his fingertip. It didn't move.

"They're keepsakes, are they? Reminders of things that happened? Of people?"

"Reminders?" he said. "No."

"Charms, then? What do they call them—talismans?"

"These don't work magic, Rosalie," he said. But as soon as he'd spoken, he knew that was wrong. "Not in the normal sense. They just connect me."

"Connect you to what?"

He shrugged, wincing again. "They're artifacts."

He didn't know why he'd said that. He only knew it was true. "I— it's . . . hard to explain."

"I'm sorry," she said. "I didn't mean to pry." She bent and kissed his ear. "Come back to bed."

"Yes, in a minute."

He looked at the row of objects on the table. Then he stood at the window, waiting for the pain in his head to withdraw. He saw something move, a human shape in the shadows. Or perhaps it was a wind-bent bush. He felt a sudden powerful urge to be out in the shadows himself.

Rosalie, in bed, sighed deeply.

He returned to her.

CHRISTMAS MORNING came gray and cold. Smooth-bottomed clouds lay low over the city. During the night, snow had fallen lightly, and now the wind swept the dry flakes into brief feathery plumes on the street. Tad watched from his window as gusts shaped and reshaped the snow.

He was alone in the house. He hadn't got to bed until long after midnight, and he had awakened with a headache, which the aspirin he'd swallowed was holding off. He was thinking of the work he had yet to do. He felt as he had sometimes when waiting to set off on a mission, focused so intently on obligations that he was disoriented, adrift in the larger, the alien world. He rubbed his fingers over the pouch in his pants pocket.

He hadn't seen Rosalie for two days, instead spending long hours at the museum. He would finish on schedule, he was persuaded, so long as he could work uninterrupted. She understood. She planned to spend their time apart encouraging her mother to accept the inevitable—things change.

When he'd told her about the Quarleses' invitation to Christmas dinner, her eyes had widened. "Dinner with a baronet? Not likely!"

"I'm sure—"

"I shouldn't be able to move, or open my mouth, for fear of making a fool of myself." Her head swiveled like a mechanical doll's. "No. No. I wouldn't really be wanted."

He showed her the invitation. She took it between her thumb and forefinger, as if fearing she might mar the heavy, expensive paper. "This isn't my world."

"I have to go," he said. "I'd like you to be with me."

Rosalie frowned, shaking her head.

Tad took her hand. "The old ways don't mean anything, Rosalie, unless you want them to. Think American."

She looked at him. Finally she said, "All right, Tad. I'll go. For you. Even though . . ." Anxiety twisted her small smile.

Now the wind shifted the snow as Tad waited for the car Quarles was sending. He again wore clothes he'd bought with Rosalie. He carried in his coat pocket a small, neatly wrapped box containing a cameo broach, one of those she had admired in the antique store weeks before. His headache retreated, became a faint reverberating call across an abyss.

A dirty red Land Rover pulled up across the street. The driver got out, turned, and rested his bare tattooed forearms on the hood. He looked up at Tad as if he knew exactly where to find him, and he grinned.

Billy Knox. Sir Rupert Quarles was sending Tad a message. Happy Christmas.

Tad locked the door to his room, then the door to the empty house. When he started across the street, Knox came around the Land Rover. The tattoos on his arms and neck and face seemed more vivid, as if refreshed by the bright white teeshirt he again wore beneath his tattered vest.

Tad almost remembered—shadows narrowing to nothing, a white shield.

Knox made a show of opening the passenger seat door. "Happy Christmas, Squire."

When Tad stepped silently past him and got in, Knox laughed.

The Land Rover was old, its seats cracked and littered with papers, and its floors scattered with tools and food wrappers, stained with grease and mud. The heater fan, on high, groaned.

Knox drove carelessly, as if he owned the road and all it passed through. Other drivers, at intersections, deferred to him. When he turned the steering wheel, the muscles in his tattooed forearm quivered and bunched.

They were nearly to the tearoom before Knox spoke again. "You don't remember, then?"

"Was it in an alley?"

"Sodding drunk, laid out a wreck you were. Disappointing, really. I thought you were better than that."

Tad ran his fingers over the pouch in his pocket.

"It would have been easy. I was tempted," Knox said, sneering. "But only for a moment. No fun that way. I want you wide-eyed and shitless.

I haven't actually killed anybody yet. You'll be the first. A fucking American—how great is that!"

Tad offered no comment.

"I heard you talk about Fate, destiny, that shit. A wonder how it works out, ain't it—Fate sending you to me, me being your destiny? Your doom. Never been anybody's destiny before. I want to do it up right, Yank."

Tad looked at him. "Maybe I'm *your* destiny."

Knox laughed, deep in his throat. "There you go. That's better." Then he said, "So are you enjoying our fat Rosie, now she's all broken in for you? Sweet, her cherry was."

Tad reached forward and switched off the heater's fan. In the sudden quiet he said, "Leave her out of this."

Knox laughed again. The ink on his face shifted like night shadows. "Can't. Consorting with the enemy? She knows what comes for that. But she'll give you up, mate. In the end, you'll see."

He pulled up before the tearoom.

Tad sat for a moment. Then he said, "In the alley. I wasn't drunk."

Knox's grin faded. "You get . . . what? Attacks? Epilepsy, like that?"

"Headaches." It must have been pain that reduced him to a heap.

"Not only a gimp but ill too. You think that makes a difference?"

"No."

Tad got out and climbed the stairs to the Cushes' apartment.

Rosalie's dress was green with thin vermilion stripes, a simple sheath that slimmed her hips, lay white and bare the round tops of her breasts, and deepened the color in her throat and cheeks.

"Admire me, Tad," she said.

"You look like a Christmas present."

"I just hope I don't humiliate you." Her smile was at once apprehensive and eager, her voice fluty.

"Not much chance of that," he said. Then he took out the small wrapped package. "Speaking of presents."

With almost childish eagerness, she opened the box. The cameo had a noble-looking female profile set against an onyx background, all bordered by obsidian edged with gold.

"Venus, the shop girl said."

"Tad, it's lovely, isn't it?" She smiled, kissed his cheek, and pinned the broach to her dress.

"I've a gift for you," she said, "but you won't be wanting to carry it around during dinner. I'll give it to you later."

He helped her into her coat. Her scent was heavy, musky, exotic. Then, before they stepped out the door, he said, "The car Quarles sent—it's a little dirty, an estate vehicle. I can call a taxi."

Her frown dug deep lines into her forehead. "Taxi? Good lord, the expense!"

"The driver is Billy Knox."

Her face emptied, as if the young woman she was had gone into hiding.

"It has nothing to do with you," he said. "Quarles is sending me a message."

"A message?"

"I can call a taxi," he said again.

"No, no, that would just make it . . ." Color seeped back into her cheeks. "It's too late. He'd know."

Tad wasn't certain that he understood. "It's up to you, Rosalie."

"If it were up to me, we'd be on our way to Peterborough with my parents, wouldn't we?" Her voice thickened with something like despair.

"Rosalie—"

"No. Let's go," she said, forcing a smile as she opened the door. "Christmas with the swells."

On the street she stopped, looked at the red Land Rover, at the blue-haired and tattooed driver leaning against the fender, at the gray snow stirring on the pavement, at the gray, smooth clouds.

"Billy," she said with straining brightness, "Happy Christmas."

He stood, affected a bow. "And to you, Miss." He grinned and opened the rear door. "I cleaned it out a bit. Don't want to dirty your pretty Christmas clothes."

As Rosalie bent to slip through the door, he put a hand on her arm. "Allow me."

Tad, standing behind them, thought he heard Rosalie say something, but the sound whipped away on the wind. He got in beside her.

They drove to Waterby in silence. Passing through the flat fields, the boxy Land Rover swayed and stuttered in the wind. From time to time, Knox met Tad's gaze in the rearview mirror and smiled. At one point, Rosalie took Tad's hand. He felt her relax, slowly. When the Waterby estate came in sight, she looked at him and smiled. Then they were passing the cottage in which Billy Knox had grown up.

"Ah, there it is, the old place." Knox, finally speaking, turned his head, allowing his gaze to linger on the small, sagging building. "You remember it, Rosie. Where you and me used to have all that fun." He grinned into the rearview mirror. "Playfellows, we was, Yank. Remember our games, love?"

Rosalie's hand stiffened in Tad's. "I remember your mother being kind to me."

"A sweetheart, Mum. Everybody loved her. Day or night. A pound coin on the dresser."

"You have to smear everything with filth, don't you?" Rosalie spoke with spirit. "Even your mum."

"Put a turnstile on the door, the way the johnnies came and went." He laughed again. "Speaking of doors—somebody broke in the place the other night. Don't know why. Nothing but rubbish and dust. Now why'd somebody do that, Yank?"

Tad remembered a clean, empty room.

"Ginny Garner's apartment got broken into as well, I hear. Not at your post behind that tree, were you, mate? Some guard you are."

That's how Ginny had known Tad was standing watch. Billy Knox had told Rupert Quarles. They—the baronet and the Pict—knew everything about him. He had been careless.

Knox pulled up before the main entrance to the inn. Again he made a show of attending the door. "Accepting no gratuities, Squire. Not from guests of His Worship."

Knox took Rosalie's elbow, as if to help her out of the vehicle.

"Take your hand off her," Tad said quietly.

Knox ceremoniously removed his hand. Then he grinned.

Just inside the inn, Rosalie stopped as if she'd been struck. "I shouldn't be here."

Strings softly played Christmas music on the sound system. From the dining room came the clink and clatter of midday feasters and the rich aroma of roasted meat and baked goods. The hallway they stood in was warm, wainscoted, hung with old paintings of pastoral scenes, and now festooned with holly and tiny winking lights.

"Please, Tad, take me home," Rosalie said.

"All right," he said, "We can go to—"

"There you are." Ginny Garner stepped from the bar, smiling. She laid a hand on Rosalie's arm. "Merry Christmas."

"I—yes," Rosalie managed. "Happy Christmas."

"Dad's waiting for you in the bar, Tad," Ginny said. Then she addressed the English girl, "Let's get rid of your coat and get you a cup of cheer."

Smiling wanly, Rosalie allowed herself to be led away.

The professor sat by himself at a table in the corner. Tad joined him, accepting the cup of coffee he poured and offered. Robert Garner smiled his innocent, engaging American smile as he lifted his own cup. "Merry Christmas, Tad."

Tad returned the gesture and salutation.

The professor's expression took on the contours of concern. "You look tired. I understand you're working early and late."

"I'll finish in time."

"I know you will," Garner said. "Or, to be exact, I know you would have, had it been necessary. But it isn't, not anymore."

The professor encircled his coffee cup with his large, strong, farm-boy hands. Like those of Rupert Quarles, they were fit for holding tools or weapons—spades, trowels, knives, swords.

"It's not official yet, but there's been a slight change in plans."

Tad stilled, waited.

Garner smiled again. "No need to be alarmed. Your prospects haven't changed, not significantly at any rate. The work you've done—well, even Sylvia Stuckey admits its professional competence. But . . ."

Garner spoke with his usual assured charm, language issuing from him as easily as it had when he'd talked of murder and copulation. Much of what he said now was background, or explanation, or evidence, all part of a presentation, Tad realized, that the professor had made to various audiences. As if selecting primary targets in a narrow street crowded with advancing enemy, Tad picked out the new, dangerous information.

Horatio would not be moved to America.

There would be no museum or wing in California.

There would, however, be a wing on the museum in Cambridge, an Anglo-American undertaking. The university would construct the addition on the now-empty lot stretching to the river. American philanthropists and foundations, led by the Schumacher family, would pay for it.

The Roman artifacts, including the Last Centurion, would remain in England, under English control.

Professor Garner would write his book about Horatio and the dig, publication coinciding with the opening of the new wing, a couple of years off at least. He might also host a television special about Horatio. Then, his renown firmly fixed, he would retire to write his memoirs.

Professor Stuckey would provide an introduction to the Horatio book, extolling the virtues of international cooperation and celebrating the British wealth of ancient Iron Age and Roman sites. She would supervise the expansion of the museum facilities. She would receive credit for the accolades the museum would no doubt receive.

Sir Rupert Quarles would score political points for putting aside his antipathy toward all things American and brokering the compromise, for getting the deal done.

And Tad would earn his PhD and take an assistant curator job in Cambridge, working for Sylvia Stuckey, helping to plan the layout and displays in the new wing, setting up future Anglo-American digs at various British sites, and spending summers easing artifacts from the earth.

"So you see," Garner smiled, "everybody wins."

Everybody but Rosalie.

"Rosalie?" Garner paused. "I don't understand."

After a startled moment, Tad said, "She wants to go to America."

"Well, you'll be there for a few months, as soon as you finish up here."

"She wants to move there permanently."

"Ah . . ." The professor leaned back. "I'm sorry, Tad, if this causes difficulties in your personal life. But you can see how, professionally, it removes all objections. It's such an obvious solution—at least it was obvious once Rowena Quarles proposed it."

"This isn't official yet?"

"Nearly. A few small bribes have yet to be actually accepted."

Corruption, Tad was to understand, was the way of the world. He did in fact understand. Rot.

"And papers require signatures. Papers always require signatures, don't they? But Sir Rupert assures us that there will be a public announcement by New Year's or shortly thereafter."

Tad had a week, then, to prepare Rosalie for the news.

Professor Garner reassumed his concerned expression. "I know you've been under a strain, Tad. In fact, you look worn down. Are you having headaches again?"

Tad's headache was gathering strength even then. "Only one bad one."

"And you ... went off, the way you did before?"

"I lost a day. Rupert Quarles says I went for a bike ride. And I sat in the snow."

Tad fell silent. He knew that Robert Garner was studying him.

Finally the professor, brushing a hand at his silver hair, said, "And your meds. Do you need a new prescription? Do you need to see someone, or can it wait till you get back to America?"

"I have everything I need," Tad said.

"At any rate, now you can relax, the pressure's off. No more stress." Garner drained his coffee. "Finish the work at your leisure. I'll talk to Mrs. Ball, you can stay with her through the spring semester. I'll move some grant money around to pay for it, and to cover a little travel, if you and, uh, Rosalie are inclined."

Tad suddenly, for a moment, did not know where he was. He did not know who he was. Where was his squad, his fire team? How had he come to be alone?

"You've been at it, unremittingly, since you got out of the army. Take a break, Tad. England is lovely when things start to green. Even though you've been here several times, you haven't seen much of it. You might start to get a sense of what it would be like when you settled here for good."

England. England.

"Yes." Garner again brushed at his hair. "I know that you and Professor Stuckey have had . . . differences. Is there any reason why you couldn't work for her?"

"No," he said.

"Whatever else she is, she's a fair woman. Professional and fair." His smile quivered. "At least she tries."

"Yes," Tad said.

"It was a misunderstanding, with the two of us at that conference. The stuff of bedroom farce. I said one thing and she heard another. Who knew she'd respond so fiercely. I mean, visiting lecturers and winsome young assistant professors, well, that goes on all the time, doesn't it?"

Professor Garner seemed to expect Tad to agree. Tad said nothing.

"At any rate, you don't need to be here forever. You might be able to use a Cambridge job to step up into something in the States. Eventually."

"Eventually," Tad said.

"Yes, well . . ." The professor rose. "If anything changes—I don't expect it to, mind you. Sir Rupert has control of almost everything at this point, and he's a man who gets what he wants. But should anything change, I'll let you know."

Tad slipped from his chair.

Robert Garner placed his hand carefully on Tad's bad shoulder. "I'm wondering what your girlfriend is going to say to the news. If you're going to stay in England, will that . . . well, it's none of my business, is it?"

"No."

The professor grinned. "Nothing but plain speaking from you, is there, Tad? Your friend Marcus would be proud of you. I've often admired the way you've been able to structure your life on his principles. Duty. Loyalty. Honesty. All that."

He paused, his hand still on Tad's shoulder. He seemed to be waiting. He seemed to want something.

Tad said nothing.

The professor removed his hand, his grin fading. "All the same, if

Rosalie won't have you unless you take her to America, that doesn't augur well for the relationship in either case."

Garner thought that Tad, for Rosalie, was merely a ticket to America—why else would she attach herself to one such as he?

"You've been talking to Mrs. Ball," Tad said.

Robert Garner grinned again, broadly. "Indeed I have. At my age, give me a woman of experience every time."

THE QUARLES PARTY was in a private dining room at the far end of the hallway. This space too was wainscoted and decorated with holiday tinsel and winking lights. On the walls were large old oil paintings of hunting scenes—men and dogs, wild creatures, gore.

The new baronet stood before a small crackling fire. On the wall above the hearth, a smoke-stained canvas had a magnificently antlered stag, arrows jutting from his side and chest, at bay before a pair of dogs; a lackey was about to fire another arrow as a gentleman on a horse looked on imperiously. Around Sir Rupert congregated three men who looked remarkably alike, thin-haired, red-faced, overfed, in their fifties, and a blonde woman twenty years younger whose bare shoulders Quarles obviously admired. Near the table two middle-aged women in more modest attire stood with Ginny Garner beside a seated, black-clad, elderly lady, white-haired and thin, the bones of whose face preserved the structure of a former beauty. In a corner Rowena Quarles huddled with Rosalie.

"Ah, Garner. Fellows." Rupert Quarles offered perfunctory introductions. The three men were a German hydrological engineer with whom Quarles was planning a new series of diversion ditches, an ex-Oxford lecturer and member of the English Heritage Board, and an MP from Yorkshire who served with Quarles on a committee inquiring into English agricultural practices. The women were their wives.

The elderly woman was Lady Millicent, widow and apparently sole mourner of the late baronet.

"My sister's consoling your friend, Miss . . ." He trailed off, as if Rosalie's name could not be of consequence.

"Cush," Tad said. Now, looking across the room, he saw that Rosalie was distressed, her eyes bright with tears.

"Little incident." Quarles might have laughed. "My mother."

Tad made his way to the two young women. Rowena Quarles held Rosalie's hand in both of hers. She withdrew one, patting Rosalie on the shoulder before extending it in greeting to Tad.

"She's a little upset," she said as they shook hands. "My mother, she—well, she's not completely round the bend, but she gets confused. She took Rosalie for a servant of some kind. We couldn't get her to understand."

"It wasn't her fault," Rosalie said. Her eyes were still wet and bright. Her makeup was damaged.

"Of course it was." Rowena patted Rosalie's hand as she spoke to Tad. "She kept calling her 'girl.' Kept asking me what was wrong with 'that girl'?"

"No, it was me," Rosalie said. "I didn't react properly. I mean, I knew, I could see she was, as you say, confused. But I got confused too. I thought . . ."

"Never mind," Rowena said. "Let's go fix your face before they start to serve."

Ginny Garner came up. "How anyone could take you for a waitress is beyond me. Not in that dress. It's beautiful."

Ginny's own dress, pale fruit colors, apricot, lime, was cut of cloth that hung beautifully from her shoulders and breasts and hips. Rowena wore taffeta and silk, simple, elegant. Rosalie turned to Tad and smiled, her first real smile of the day, and when she moved he saw the new bruise on the inside of her arm, just above the elbow.

Tad and Ginny watched the two young women leave the room.

"It was embarrassing for her," Ginny said. "But kind of funny too. The English take their place and class stuff far too seriously, those at the top and bottom both. What they all need is a good dose of American who-gives-a-shit."

She looked at her father, who was listening intently to the German hydrologist. "Did Dad tell you about the changes? Horatio? The new wing here?"

"Yes," Tad said.

"You don't mind?" When he didn't speak, she went on. "You know what it's really all about, don't you? It's all about that stupid chair he didn't get."

"Ah," Tad said.

"Officially, the wing will be named after my mother, Tiffany Schumacher Garner, but of course everyone will call it the Garner Wing. And in academia, a wing trumps a chair every time."

Tad knew that Ginny was right. Professor Garner had admitted that he wanted to be recognized and remembered.

Petty. Vain.

"I believe that's the first time I've ever heard you say anything negative about him, Tad." She smiled.

Tad was looking at a painting. A bloodied boar fought a pack of dogs, several of which already lay ripped and dying, while another, trailing viscera, flew through the air. A man in the dress of an eighteenth-century squire advanced on the animals with an ax.

"Only the English would think that staring at dog guts would add to the pleasure of one's meal." Ginny grinned. "They're bizarre, these people. Maybe that's why I feel so comfortable with them."

Rosalie and Rowena came back into the room. Ginny patted Tad's arm. "We're seated together. We can talk. We need to."

The room warmed. Voices thrummed. Then after a nod from the maitre d', Rupert Quarles announced that the first course was ready to be served, and all sat, in the process Rowena Quarles switching place cards so that she and not the brassy German woman sat between Rosalie and Lady Millicent. As Tad took his seat, the waiter served a steaming soup.

Ginny raised her spoon. "That's a lovely cameo Rosalie is wearing. Victorian, isn't it? Your Christmas gift?"

"Yes," Tad said.

She smiled. "Are you going to give me a gift, Tad? I can tell you what I want. Although it was already given to me once, so it wouldn't really be a gift from you, would it?"

Her eyes were bright, her complexion high. She looked as she had the day he saved her from sexual assault and had felt the working of fate.

"When I discovered it was missing," Ginny said, "Rupert had a man check the CCTV. You need to go back to burglary school, Tad. It's hard to see how you could have missed the cameras."

On the walls, creatures fought and bled and died. A log shifted in the fire. Waiters hovered. The diners spooned soup and exchanged remarks.

"Oh, don't worry, the tape is so grainy that positive identification isn't possible." She cocked an eyebrow, amused at his expression. "At least it wouldn't stand up in court, Rupert says. But the way you move, the way your arm hangs from your shoulder, it's distinctive. To me, at least."

On her other side, the Yorkshire man spoke into Ginny's profile. The American girl ignored him. Instead, after a spoonful of soup, she said, as if sharing an especially delicious secret, "Rupert was pissed about you being in my apartment. I mean enraged. I didn't care. In fact, I thought it was kind of sexy, in a creepy sort of way, you in my bedroom, rummaging through my things, even though you're, you know, the way you are. But he doesn't understand about you, about us. I've told him that all your efforts are protective."

She smiled. "Is that why you took it? So I wouldn't be caught with it?"

"I don't know," Tad said. The boar in the painting was doomed, he saw, yet the beast fought on in a pure and perfect rage, doing what a boar must do.

"Do you still have it?"

He resisted the impulse to touch the pouch in his pocket. "Yes."

"I'd like you to give it back to me, please."

For a long moment Tad said nothing. The ache rose in his head like the sun from the sea. Then he said, "I'll return it to the collection."

She folded her hands. A waiter quietly removed her soup dish and, without asking, Tad's as well. When Ginny spoke again, it was with the same smile, the same confidential tone.

"It belongs to me. I want it back."

Tad felt as Rosalie had. He ought not to be here.

"I'll buy you another," he said. "There's one in the coin shop on—"

"I don't want another," she said, easily. She might have been asking the waiter for more soup. "Just give me back my coin, Tad."

He had always known that her sense of right and wrong was utterly subjective, centered on her self and her own well-being, but because he was virtuous, her amorality hadn't mattered. He had never refused her.

"No," he said.

The waiters served salad. The diners chatted. Rosalie smiled at Rowena Quarles. The German engineer tried to distract Rupert Quarles from his wife's shoulders. Lady Millicent muttered into her dish. The disemboweled dog flew through the air.

"I'll return it to the collection," he repeated.

For a moment he thought she wouldn't reply. When she finally spoke, she did so in a different voice, not so much cool as empty. Things would never again be the same between them. "But you haven't returned it yet? You've had it for days. Why not?"

"I don't know," he said.

"Rupert thinks you intend mischief, some sort of extortion. If you told people where you got it, reputations would be jeopardized. Mine—well, you can't hurt me, Tad. But my father's is different."

"I don't intend mischief," he said. "I don't intend anything."

"But you won't give it to me?"

Tad looked at her. He would die for her. He would kill for her. But he wouldn't, he couldn't give her the coin that belonged with the coins that had been buried where once had stood a small shrine to a local Celtic god.

She took up a fork. "If there's another coin, why don't you buy it for yourself and give me back mine."

"If I did, how would you know which was which?"

"You'd tell me."

Tad had no response to that.

She smiled an empty smile. "You're bringing it on yourself, Tad."

He didn't ask her what she meant. Instead he said, "He sent Billy Knox to drive us out here."

"The blue-haired creature?"

"He wants to kill me."

The American girl brightened. "Really? Knox, you mean?"

Tad nodded.

"Rupert might, too. He's a killer at heart." She smiled the same empty smile. "He wouldn't do it himself, though. He'd want to, but finally he'd just have it done."

The waiter poured wine. She took a sip. "The rumor is he's old Sir Quarles's son, Billy Knox. Positively Victorian, isn't it? Be a shame if it wasn't true."

She took another sip of wine. "And now you're going to be stuck here with these people. England may be your destiny, Tad. Mine too."

But she was not suggesting that they would share a future. They would never share anything again.

THE MEAL PROCEEDED, traditional English fare. When it was done, the men milled and drank coffee or brandy. The women, two by two, left and returned. The Yorkshire couple excused themselves, having another engagement. At that point, Rosalie caught Tad's eye, pleading silently.

Tad went to her. She stood awkwardly, bare arms folded, hiding from him the fresh bruise. He took her hand. "I have a headache."

"He gets these," Rosalie told Rowena Quarles. "They're fierce. Nothing helps, really, but a lie-down. I'll need to get him home."

Miss Quarles offered standard condolences. Tad thought she actually meant them.

They moved to the hearth, where Rupert Quarles again stood. The baronet sent for the maitre d' to order a taxi, as the car was unavailable —the driver, he said, was sharing a Christmas pudding with family.

"Friend of yours, Billy?" He looked at Rosalie, at her round face, her round shoulders, her round breasts.

She flushed under his stare. "From when I was a child," she said.

"A man with the ladies, I hear."

Her flush deepened. "I . . . I hear that as well."

Quarles grinned. "Rumor is, he's the old baronet's bastard. Comes by his wenching honestly, if so." Then his face changed, as if Rosalie no longer existed, and he turned to Tad.

"Doesn't care for you, Yank. Thinks you're a thief. Haul off our old stuff. Our women. Culture. National honor." He smiled. "Men are killed for less."

Tad said nothing.

Quarles laughed. "Think it over, Yank. A couple of days."

Professor Garner had joined them. Learning of the situation, he insisted on driving Tad and Rosalie back to the city. Unsmiling, he seemed distracted, troubled.

As they waited in the hallway for their coats, Rowena Quarles came up, again offering conventional sentiments, which again seemed to Tad to be sincere.

Once out in the cold, Rosalie shivered into her coat. "She's the only human being in the bunch."

"She's kind and generous. Her mother of course is not responsible." Professor Garner gave Tad a grim look. "And Rupert—what does Marcus say about aristocrats? They're cold?"

"'Somehow lacking in affection.'"

"That's Rupert. Not perhaps the best influence on rich, spoiled American girls? But Rowena balances it out."

At the BMW, Rosalie, before she got in, said, "He's a liar, too. Billy Knox doesn't have any family."

They drove into town. Overhead, the smooth bank of cloud had roughened. The wind had picked up, the air warmed. Rain soon would fall.

Rosalie talked quietly, envy scuffing her voice, about the dresses the women at the dinner had worn. What must it be like to work with that kind of fabric? When they reached the ring road, she asked to be taken home. She wanted to give Tad his Christmas present. And she should be there when her parents returned from Peterborough. It was Christmas, after all. And she might like a bit of time alone before they arrived. It had been a day, hadn't it?

At the tearoom, Professor Garner waited while Tad escorted Rosalie up to the flat. Once inside, she threw off her coat and hurried into her bedroom, returning with a carefully wrapped and ribboned package, long, narrow, and, in his hands, comfortably weighted.

"Happy Christmas, Tad."

She smiled. Then, as he watched her, the smile faded. She was near tears.

He nodded at her arm, at the bruise he couldn't actually see. "Is it Knox? Is that why you're upset?"

Instinctively she clamped her elbow to her side. "No. If it was only him . . . I mean, these fade away, don't they?"

"What then?"

"I'm sorry, Tad," she said. "I just—I know I let you down. But you don't understand how it is here, not really. Lady Millicent, she thought I was a waitress. Well, she was right, wasn't she? That's what I am, and she saw it right away. And the baronet, ogling me, using Billy to put me in my place. If it hadn't been for Miss Quarles, I don't know what . . ."

She stopped, flushed. "Tad. Your present. I'm sorry. I'll shut up. Open it."

He untied the ribbon, peeled back the wrapping, opened the end of the box, and tilted it. The gladius slid out into the light. Removing the leather scabbard and attached baldric, he held up the sword—steel blade, hardwood pommel and grip and guard. Simple. Lethal.

The gladius fit familiarly into his hand. Its form and heft moved muscles and tendons in his arm and shoulder and torso into inevitable arrangements. This was his sword, and always had been.

"I know it's an odd gift for a girl to give a bloke. Some people might think so, anyhow. But you're— Well, I thought you could mount it on your wall or something."

With his thumb he tested the dull blade. The carbon steel would take a keen edge. He extended his arm, twisting his wrist, and watched the light play on the tooled metal.

When Tad did not speak, Rosalie began, nervously, to explain. She'd heard him admire these swords, and when she saw the one the prop people ordered for the Panto she'd felt, well, inspired. She'd found websites, there were several, and several kinds of swords, she didn't know which one he'd like, but this one seemed right.

"It's perfect," he said. He touched her cheek. "Thank you, Rosalie."

She seemed to be waiting for him to say something more. He didn't know what else to say. He said again, "Thank you."

Her eyes filled, sparkled. "You'd better go. The professor is waiting."

He put the gladius back in its box.

"Yes, stick it away," Rosalie said, now oddly agitated. "You don't want to come charging into the street with that in your hand."

He opened the door and stepped into the hall. Rosalie placed a hand on his arm, exerting pressure.

"I wasn't going to ask you, Tad, but I have to. Is it true? You'll be working here, in Cambridge, not in America." Her eyes turned the question into an assertion. "Ginny told me," she said. "It's true, isn't it?"

After a moment he said, "If you want to live in America, Rosalie, we'll live in America."

"But your job, the one you want, it's going to be here in England?" Before he could respond, she added, bitterly, her round mouth twisted, "They don't care, do they, your Professor Garner and his precious daughter? Everything's for them, no matter what it costs the likes of us."

"Rosalie . . ."

Now her words came in a violent eructation. "You're just like me, Tad. We don't count. Except you Americans don't know it. You think you're equal, but all you are, to them at the top, is nothing. We serve their tea and fight their wars and take what they give us. Don't we? Don't you?"

Her face flushed, her round eyes brimmed. He had never seen her like this—angry, despairing. "They can't be trusted. Promises mean nothing to them. They do what it's to their advantage to do."

"Rosalie," Tad began, "I'll do—"

"Your duty," she interrupted. "What you always do. What you have to do."

He did not deny it. He did not disagree with anything she'd said. When had it ever been other?

She spoke again, now quietly, even as she moved so the door

became a shield, "I'm sorry, Tad. I just have this feeling like every-thing's crumbling. Like there's no America for my sort. *They* won't allow it."

Tad felt the weight of the gladius in his hand. He had a weapon, but what was there to defend against?

"What can I do?"

"I need to . . . adjust. Things are going so fast, I need— Give me a few days."

Alone.

"Yes. I need a little space right now, time," she said, unable, quite, to look at him.

"Nothing's changed, Rosalie. Not really."

"No," she said. "Everything has changed.

PROFESSOR GARNER didn't ask Tad about the gift. He drove back to Mrs. Ball's, not speaking until he pulled the BMW to the curb. "The young Pict, Knox? Do I understand that he bears you ill will?"

"He wants to kill me."

"Kill— My god, Tad!" Garner was genuinely shocked. "What makes you think that?"

"He told me."

"But—" The older man struggled to comprehend. "Why?"

"Murder and copulation," Tad said.

"No, no. That was just . . ." The professor sat, stunned. At last he said, "I've been coming to England for forty years, but I still feel, now and then, a stranger in a strange land."

Tad sat silently.

Robert Garner roused himself. "Look, Tad. This all has to do with Rupert, I know. I heard him threaten you, and that Pict is—well, some say his illegitimate brother. I don't know about that, but he does odd jobs for him, seems to have free use of one of the estate vans. But there's nothing important enough in this matter that anybody should get hurt, let alone . . ."

He flushed with feeling. "For god's sakes! All we're talking about is an old Roman coin!"

Tiny drops of rain began to dampen the windshield. Garner gathered himself, sighed. "It isn't rare. It isn't especially valuable. It's just . . ."

He glanced at Tad. Tad watched the rain.

"Ginny took a fancy to the coin, so I gave it to her," he said stiffly. "In so doing I violated a basic rule of our profession, one everybody is especially touchy about these days. In the real world, of course, no one cares. There are denarii aplenty out there. But among archeologists, well, you know what someone like Sylvia Stuckey would do with that information. A stupid coin, a spontaneous gesture, and a ruined reputation. There goes my ability to get fat cats to open their wallets. There goes the museum wing."

A wing trumps a chair.

After a moment, Garner said, "Ginny pleased herself with that formulation. Perhaps it is all an exercise in vanity, and revenge. At least it began that way. But . . ."

Rain smeared the windshield, distorting the world.

"Rupert's got political capital invested in Horatio, Tad. I want that wing, yes, but he needs it built, here, where his constituents can see it. His career hangs on it at this point, and he won't allow anything or anyone to place the project at risk. I've assured him that you would never do anything to injure me, but he isn't persuaded. He thinks you have mercenary motives."

"I'm going to put the coin back with the others," Tad said.

Raindrops grew finer, became a faint drizzle, hardly more than mist.

"I know what your word means to you, Tad," Garner said at last. Everything.

"Yes, everything." The professor extended his hand.

Tad took it.

"I've done the best for you that I could, under the circumstances," Garner said, brushing absently at his hair. "I'm sorry about Rosalie. But choices had to be made."

"Yes," Tad said.

Robert Garner managed to smile. "I'm flying out tomorrow. After a brief stop—I suppose I can tell you I'll be in Jamaica for a couple of days—I'll be back in the US settling matters with some of the groups providing funds for the wing. So let me wish you a Happy New Year."

"Yes," Tad said, "you too."

STEPPING INSIDE THE FRONT DOOR, Tad stopped, suddenly alert. The air in the foyer held a hint of foulness—anxiety, sweat, and something else. A small clump of mud clung to the carpet on the stairs. Tad listened intently but heard only the house complaining of age and weariness.

He climbed to his room and, opening the door, stepped into a shambles. All his belongings—papers, books, computer, clothes—had been flung about in a hasty, angry search. His copy of *Meditations* had been destroyed, the pages torn from the binding and ripped into small pieces that were strewn over the mess. In the center of the room, his blue blazer lay crumpled on the floor. On it was a pile of human excrement.

For a while Tad sat on the bed. Then he took out the sword. Hanging the baldric over his bad shoulder, he stood, extended his left foot, braced himself with his right, and he drove the blade out and up.

He had no shield, no protection, no balancing weight, but he wouldn't have been able to hold one up anyway. He would need to angle his attack, find stable positions from which he could fight aggressively. He would have to hack and slash as well as thrust. He would be alone, not a function of a complex unit but isolate, pure intent. Against a force of any size, he would not last long. Like Horatio.

The sword felt right in his hand. The coin felt right in the pouch in his pocket.

He shifted his shoulders, settled into a comfortable crouch. He moved his feet, felt his equilibrium imperiled, leaned, moved his feet back. He tested, tried his body. He dipped, pivoted, bent, twisted, slid, attacking. As if teaching himself to dance to the rhythms of the pain in his head, he moved carefully around the filth in the middle of the room. He moved slowly. He had plenty of time.

T HE NEXT WEEK Tad worked and he walked through the cold fog that had settled on the city and he watched.

The work went well. Hours vanished, days plummeted into the past, the future remained an absence on a far horizon, and he thought of nothing but what he was doing.

Once Professor Stuckey came down to his room. She watched him sort through photos of an excavation of what had been the stables, the earth removed so as to create tiers, like a small stairway into antiquity. Tad thought she had come to gloat, but instead she seemed, watching him, befuddled. At one point she started to speak, then didn't. Instead she turned and stepped through the door and disappeared down the hall.

Each day, leaving, Tad visited Horatio. Sometimes the dark and beheaded mummy seemed impossibly alive, other than Tad the only real thing in the world.

They had been soldiers, the two of them. They had served, fought, functioned. Now neither had a unit into which he might integrate. Each had only the other. Horatio had died, as would Tad, doing his duty.

One day, as he gazed at the bog man, he thought of Boudica, the redoubtable foe of Rome. Inspiring Professor Sylvia Stuckey, she remained a presence in the world, nearly alive. Like Horatio, she had had an honorable death. To a soldier, what else mattered?

At night he walked down streets and alleys become his own. The cold fog seemed to seep into his skull, numbing his now-perpetual headache. He made his rounds. Sometimes forgetting his promise, he stood behind the tree across from Ginny Garner's apartment, even though the windows were always dark, even though she was out at Waterby relaxing after riding horses with Rowena Quarles or dining, Mick Curtain told him, with Sir Rupert and whomever the baronet happened to be bending to his will at the moment. Other times he stood where he could see the bakery and tearoom and upstairs flat, and one night as he watched a white van pulled up and Rosalie got out and hurried into the alcove and up the stairs and the van swung suddenly around so that Tad was caught in the lights and the van gave a little toot of its horn and sped away down the street. He stood outside the museum, or he walked around it, sometimes catching a flicker of light from Johnson's flash, sometimes stopping to listen until what might have been the sound of something not right became just another groan or squeak of the old city. And he stood in the doorway of the pharmacy and watched the Blue Boar, he watched the enemy enter and leave the pub, and he estimated their numbers, and, recalling the layout of the booths and tables and bar, he calculated where they might be standing and sitting, resentful old men, angry young Picts.

He slept two or three hours a night. When he couldn't sleep, he arranged his fetishes in a line on the desk. The Marcus Aurelius 194, which felt in his pouch in his pocket so inevitable that he forgot he was going to return it, made all whole. Or he took out the sword and he danced.

One morning he found himself sitting on the museum steps, as he had his first morning in Cambridge. He didn't know how he had come to be there.

One afternoon he walked past the tearoom. It was more crowded than usual. Rosalie, he saw through the window, was busy with customers at the cash register. She gave no indication of seeing him as he passed.

The next afternoon he went to a bookstore and bought a copy of *Meditations*. That night he read: "Be like a rock against which the waves of the sea break unceasingly. It stands unmoved, and the feverish waters around it are stilled."

It was difficult to be a rock, to stand unmoved in the wave-tossed water.

"Why the book?" Mick Curtain had asked. "The excrement I understand, but why the book?"

Mick had returned at dawn on Boxing Day, just as Tad was sitting down to a meal of cereal and diced fruit. As he ate, he listened to Mick's account of his drive down from Hull through the fog. He'd had a good Christmas with his parents, Mick said, then asked about Tad's holiday.

Tad told him tersely of the dinner hosted by Sir Rupert Quarles. He told him of the change in plans for Horatio. He told him what he had found when he returned from the Christmas dinner.

Mick sipped his coffee thoughtfully. "Well, now we know what all the meetings were about, don't we? But the vandalism—you sound like you know who did it."

"Billy Knox, for Quarles," Tad said. "The filth was probably Chan."

"Did you report it?"

"Chan has a key, so it wasn't breaking and entering. He could say it was a joke. He wouldn't implicate Knox."

Mick nodded. "Do you know why?"

Tad felt the pouch in his pocket. With the weight of the Marcus Aurelius 194, it was real and whole.

"Yes," he said.

When Mick perceived that Tad would say no more, he asked about the book.

"It wasn't with the others on the desk. It was on my night table. That made it special to me."

Mick nodded. "So is it Rosalie? Is she what the fuss is about?"

"Not really, except as spoil," Tad said.

"Spoil?"

"I'm the American enemy, the invader, the occupier."

Mick shook his head. "There's a lot of anti-American sentiment around these days, yes. Some of it, from the left, is ideological. Some is just because it's so easy to blame the US for everything. But it isn't universal. We're ten years beyond 9/11, most of the good will generated then your government has squandered, but a lot of people still support America—especially those in the technological, entrepreneurial communities. We aren't all *Guardian* readers."

"No," Tad said. "I don't mean that. It's . . . personal."

Mick seemed uncertain. "England is full of Americans like you, Tad, students and military personnel and businessmen, and all of them chasing English lasses. It's been going on for decades. Centuries."

"That isn't what I mean," Tad said. "And they aren't like me. I can't put it into words. It's just . . . "

"Fate?" Mick smiled. "Destiny?

Tad nodded, unsmiling. "Yes."

Mick shifted the subject. "The compromise over Horatio. It seems reasonable."

"Yes."

When nothing more was forthcoming, Mick said, "So, at the Christmas nosh Sir Rupert didn't happen to mention where he's getting a sudden infusion of cash? I hear he's asking for bids on a major refurbishment of Waterby Manor."

"I don't know anything about that," Tad said, rising. "I have to go to work."

"Why today, at this time of morning? I thought there wasn't any hurry anymore."

"I said I'd finish by mid-January. It doesn't matter to anyone else now, but . . ."

He attended to his dishes. He knew Mick was watching him, puzzled. He went out into the fog.

THE DAY BEFORE New Year's Eve he went to the tearoom. He sat in his usual spot and watched Rosalie serve a young couple. Her movements were abrupt, jerky, as if she were in constraints. Her smile, when she came to his table, was tense. "This isn't a good time, Tad."

"For tea and a cherry tart?"

"No. I mean, yes, that's okay. But we can't really talk here. Now."

"All right," he said.

"Yes," she said. "Tea and tart."

She prepared and served his tea. As he ate the pastry, he watched her busy herself about the shop, avoiding him. He saw then what he hadn't before. Her round face was thinner, round bones more prominent. Her eyes were deeper, darker in their sockets. It occurred to him that Rosalie's involvement with him was somehow doing her injury.

When he paid for his meal, he said, "If you don't want me to come around anymore, I won't."

"It's better, for a while," she said. "I just need— I'm feeling a lot of different things, Tad. I need to sort them out. I need time."

Her smile was small, round, hopeless.

He knew he should say something more. "You can depend on me, Rosalie."

"I know, Tad," she said. "It's not you I'm worried about."

A pain as if from a blade stabbed into his bowels, rose into his chest.

"Happy New Year's, then," she said.

"Happy New Year's."

He didn't return to work. Instead he walked along the River Cam, where trees were shadows in the fog, where pedestrians and bicyclists emerged from the gray like dream figures. Darkness fell. In the glow of street lamps, the fog floated, particulate. He walked.

Finally Tad went back to Mrs. Ball's. Chan Hackett was watching television in the parlor. Beside him sat Mick Curtain. On the screen a pretty young man mugged for the camera as an even younger couple screamed at one other.

Mick shook his head. "Why would people expose themselves to ridicule like that?"

"Hey, they're on the telly, ain't they?" Chan looked around, as if in the empty room he might find someone who would confirm his proposition. "They're famous, like."

"They're cretins," Mick said. He offered the young hooligan a small smile. "They're the type who would defecate in a bedroom in his aunt's bed and breakfast."

Chan smirked. "Hey, you can't prove it was me done it."

"As soon as she hears what happened," Mick said, "she'll know, won't she?"

The smirk stiffened with anxiety. "So who'll tell her?"

Mick let his glance deliberately drift from Chan to Tad, who said nothing.

"Hey, it was just for fun," Chan protested. "Nobody got hurt."

Tad looked at him. Then he said to Mick, "Time for a pint at the Blue Boar?"

On the screen, the couple had come to violence, the young woman clawing at him, the young man slapping at her hands. Men in muscle-strained teeshirts watched carefully, as if making sure that nothing interrupted the mayhem.

"Mr. and Mrs. John Bull," Mick said, rising. "This from the people who gave the world *Macbeth*."

On the walk to the pub, Mick asked if Tad was going to speak to Mrs. Ball. Tad shrugged, painfully. He'd straightened up the room fairly quickly. He'd gathered the torn pages of Marcus Aurelius. The blazer and its foul load he'd taken out and dropped in a trash bin. He'd sprayed the room with disinfectant air-freshener.

"Chan isn't the problem," Tad said finally.

The pub wasn't crowded. Vacant spaces seemed to deepen the bar smell of funk—stale beer and ancient tobacco smoke and unwashed bodies and anomie. As Mick bought pints, Tad settled into a booth and reconnoitered.

A pair of Picts threw darts at the board just off the entry. Men occupied a booth and a couple of tables. Three men and a solitary woman sat at the bar. All seemed in transit, as if they had been trapped here on their way somewhere else, somewhere better.

Tad considered the corner formed by the bar and the wall. Billy Knox from that position would command a view of the entire room. Protected, he could attack suddenly; he could also escape, if necessary, down a narrow hall that led to the loo and, Tad surmised, a rear entrance. If Knox were in the pub, that is where he would wait.

Mick returned. They sipped beer. Then Tad asked, "Is there anything special I need to know about Billy Knox?"

Mick immediately understood. "That's why you mentioned the Blue Boar in front of Chan. He'll tell Billy. You expect Knox to show."

"That's the plan," Tad said. "Might not work."

Mick looked around the pub. "He'll be merciless."

"Eventually," Tad said. "He'll be alone?"

"Hard to say. He's a leader, isn't he? But he's also a loner." Mick rubbed his knuckle thoughtfully across his chin. "He's not stupid, Tad, not like Chan. He just doesn't want to think. He lives in his body and he knows he's going to die and he doesn't care. He doesn't analyze what he feels. He acts."

Tad nodded. "In the army, there were men like that. They were great in the field. Not so great in camp, in town."

"It's too bad he couldn't join Prince Harry over in Afghanistan. He'd get his fill of fighting." Mick looked into his glass for a moment. Then he looked up at Tad. "If he gets you down, you'll be finished."

"I'm finished anyway."

"Has something happened?" Mick asked.

"Rosalie thinks Professor Garner has betrayed me."

"Has he?"

Tad's answer was slow in coming. At last he said, "The only promises that matter are mine."

Around them, voices ground at the silence. With a soft thump a metal dart stuck into the board. Then the door opened, and three more tattooed young men came in. One of them was Chan Hackett, who approached, swaggering, aware that all in the pub were watching him. "Billy's outside. He'd have a word."

"A word, yes," Tad said. "But inside. Tell him."

Chan looked at Tad.

"I'm not going to say anything to Mrs. Ball, Chan."

The young man frowned, as if sorting through conflicting orders. He looked around the pub for assistance, meeting only stares. He rubbed his hand violently back and forth over his Mohawk. "Okay," he said. "Okay. Right."

Tad and Mick watched Chan out the door. Mick finished his beer, but he made no move to get another. "Are you sure you want to fight him, Tad?"

"Fight him? I don't want to fight him," Tad said. "I just want to give him a message."

Chan Hackett stepped back inside, followed soon by Billy Knox, who, much as Tad had, scanned the room for potential threat. Then he went to the bar, waited as the bartender pulled three pints, and carried them to the booth where Tad and Mick sat, watching.

"My treat, gents." He set the beer on the table, pulled up a chair, sat, and took up a glass. "England for the English."

Tad raised a glass. Mick smiled. "God save the Queen."

Knox laughed, drank, and wiped foam from his lip. "You have some-thing I want, Yank. Wasn't in your room. I didn't know then that you carried it around with you, in a little sack of junk. You give it to me, I may let you walk out of here."

Rosalie.

"Right." Knox smiled. "So give."

"Tell Quarles I'm going to put it back tomorrow," Tad said quietly.

"Sir Rupert, as he is now, won't have me tell him anything." The fanged creature on his face, Tad noticed for the first time, was a dragon. "I don't bring him what he wants, he'll be unhappy. We don't want a unhappy baronet, now do we?"

"It belongs with the others. I'll return it. You have my word."

Knox grinned. "Your word. What's your word to me?"

"What matters is what it is to me."

Knox set his glass on the table, clenching and relaxing and clench-ing again his fist. "Look around, Yank. Counting the geezers who'd like a bit of fun, it's about a dozen to one. We won't include your friend here. He does nothing—only writes about those that do."

"The only important one is you," Tad said.

"Problem is," Knox said, "I've got this job to do."

"Quarles, or his sister, or Miss Garner can come to the museum in the morning and watch me put it in with the others and indicate such in the records."

"You've got it in your pocket," Knox said. "Why don't you save your-self some pain and hand it over."

"No."

Beside him Mick Curtain stirred. "Tad, I don't know what you've got, but how important can it be? What can be worth all this fuss?"

Billy Knox smiled again, took up his glass, and drained it. "Look at him, scribbler. Such a sweet, innocent face—shame I have to ugly it up. Our poor fat Rosie will be— Oh!" He feigned recollection. "That's right. She's dumped him. Revealed all his secrets. Can't deal with crazy gimp Americans."

He rose, grinning. "Told you, didn't I, Yank? That she'd turn on you."

"You can come too, to watch me put it back."

Knox turned to Mick Curtain. "He's crazy. You see that, don't you? One crazy American!"

"He's . . . different," Mick said. "He's . . ."

"Yeah, even the word man can't find the right word for him." Knox finished his beer. "No reasoning with a crazy man. But we aren't after abusing the *non compos mentis,* are we? War done him in, Rosie says. Gave him headaches and odd habits. In the service of his fucking country what thinks it rules the fucking world."

"Billy," Mick Curtain said, "let him be. He said he'd make it right in the morning. You know he will."

"Yeah, I know," Knox said. "I'll be there, at the museum. Making sure. Saying hello to my old pal Horatio, while I'm at it."

He turned, took a step, turned back. "Horatio. You got it figured, Yank?"

"White van," Tad said. "Work on the house in Waterby, the repaired window, the new power line—to keep him in good condition." The clean, empty room.

Billy Knox laughed.

Tad nodded. "You bribed Johnson to fix the alarm system, then clubbed him. He couldn't tell them who did it without implicating himself."

Knox grinned at Mick Curtain. "He's crazy, maybe, but he ain't stupid."

Everyone in the pub watched the blue-haired Pict walk out. Three tattooed young men followed him. Two others, one of them Chan Hackett, took up darts. The patrons of the pub turned to each other, as if to consider what they had just witnessed.

"Are you going to tell me what that was all about?" Mick's sense of story had been stoked.

"No," Tad said.

"Rosalie?"

After a moment, Tad said, "It's not her fault."

Mick nodded. "And that about Horatio? It was Billy who tried to steal him?"

"With Chan and one other. For Quarles. Maybe Professor Stuckey was in on it, too."

"If only we had real evidence of that. The best stories are always the ones I can't tell." Mick smiled over his spectacles. "Well, at least you saved yourself a thumping."

Tad hadn't thought the large man was quite so naïve. "Excuse me," he said.

He made his way to the hallway, which did in fact end in an unlocked outside door. In the loo he removed the pouch from his pocket and tucked it in his underwear, behind his genitals. Then he washed his hands. Looking in the small dirty mirror above the sink, he recognized an old friend.

If he could strike first, he could do some damage. Then he'd take a beating, but Knox wouldn't find the coin and so couldn't kill him. Not yet.

He went back to the booth. "It's time."

He and Mick, making their way through the pub, again stirred up silence. Chan Hackett stopped the dart game, watching warily while Tad stepped past him.

As Tad pushed open the door, behind him Mick grunted in pain even as a hand shoved Tad, hard, out onto the sidewalk and into Billy Knox's fist.

He was stunned, shocked.

Hands grasped him as harsh voices shrieked. Measured blows fell on his face, torso.

He heard the crack of bone, tasted blood. He was down.

He began to slip away, into brown fog and pale yellow light and black shadows.

From far above came voices like animal cries. He descended into a deepening darkness, a gathering silence, out of which then, slowly, a shadow took shape, became burqa-clad, fixed him with bright hard eyes and reached within herself and as before brought into the world blinding white light and then nothing.

NIGHT. FEN SHADOWS. Shush of wind, stir of reeds, rush of water. A narrow twist of dirt through sump and mire, quicksand and current, and ahead, in the darkness, the darker shape, the bridge, the end.

He awoke in pain. He went back into the shadows and slogged on toward the bridge.

He awoke in pain—head, ear, nose, shoulder, ribs, groin. Shadows paled. Dark went gray. The bridge dissolved into a thick, soothing haze.

He awoke in pain, drug-dulled, familiar. A nurse was talking to him. Now a doctor. He went back into darkness but couldn't locate the bridge, the fen, couldn't hear the wind or the water.

Finally he awoke. He heard the sibilance of a steam radiator and the groans of restrained voices. The air felt heavy with heat. He hurt, it seemed, everywhere.

He was in a narrow bed enclosed by a white curtain on a ward in a hospital. He was pinned to a drip system. He was alone.

He was alive and alone. But he was not back, not quite, not all the way.

Eventually they came, nurse and doctors, eventually they explained. He had been out for nearly a week, two days in a coma, then several more days simply, deeply asleep. A retreat, a doctor told him, his psyche adjusting to the physical and psychological trauma.

He had been brought in with a dislocated jaw, a badly broken nose, and an ear nearly torn off. Doctors had put the jaw back in place, set the nose, and sewn the ear back together. His bad shoulder had been severely wrenched and would hurt him until he had another operation. His two cracked ribs and torn cartilage had been taped up but would continue to hurt until they healed. His bruised kidney would for a while have him passing a little blood and give him pain. His testicles might have been crushed but for the small pouch of curious objects stuffed in his drawers.

He had been battered by fists and brutalized by boots, kicked in the ribs and groin and especially hard in the head. He had been badly beaten. He would mend, but it would be some time before he would again be as he was. If ever.

One of the doctors, who had been in Afghanistan, recognized Tad's scars. He nodded as Tad told him, haltingly, carefully working his realigned jaw, about the bomb, about PTSD. The doctor seemed to understand why Tad didn't take his medications. He understood about the headaches. He asked about other concussions, and Tad told him of the blow he'd taken from Billy Knox on the bridge. He asked how long Tad had been talking to himself. When Tad told him that nothing seemed quite real, the doctor nodded again. Painkillers, he said, opiates. But also, he thought, Tad suffered from Second Impact Syndrome, the effects of a serious head injury following an earlier trauma—memory lapses, OCD, headaches, confusion, and loss of identity. Drugs helped, but not a lot. Medicine had much yet to learn about concussions.

A nurse unhooked him from the drip system. She slid away the curtain. He was in a long room lined with beds filled with men who looked about to die.

She helped him out of bed. It took some time. Standing hurt him, and walking, and breathing. In the bathroom, the discolored, misshapen, patched and bandaged face in the mirror seemed that of another, an ancient, newly human species. He peed pink.

He asked after his belongings. His clothes had been laundered and were in a drawer beneath the bed. His wallet and little chamois pouch were in a drawer in the bedside table. That night, before he slept, he removed the items from the pouch and laid them out in a neat row ending with the Marcus Aurelius 194.

The next day a detective constable came to sit beside his bed and ask questions and write in a notebook. Tad identified his attacker as Billy Knox. He said that their dispute was over a woman. He gave the DC Rosalie's name and address. He hadn't really seen any of the others clearly enough to describe them.

The officer told him that Mick Curtain had also fingered Billy Knox. However, Mr. Curtain hadn't actually witnessed the attack, having been involved in a scuffle in the bar with two young men whom he was unable to identify. And the seven bar patrons insisted that Billy Knox, after sharing a beer and a word with Mick and Tad, had remained in the pub while the attack was occurring. Mick had said there were more than seven in the bar—could Tad confirm that? Yes. Could he identify them? No. Neither could Mick. Could Tad identify the two that set upon Mr. Curtain? Tad said that he hadn't seen the encounter.

The policeman asked Tad why he had a small pouch filled with coins and other objects hidden in his underwear. Tad told him they were primitive charms. The DC asked if they had to do with sex and Tad said they had to do with everything.

Tad asked why he wasn't dead.

Luck, the DC said. Patrolling officers had happened onto the scene. The sight of their car caused the assailants to scatter. Pure dumb luck.

Fate.

The DC said that Tad could call it that, yes. He said that the authorities would be in touch if they discovered any way to break Billy Knox's alibi or the witnesses' story, but he wasn't optimistic.

A nurse brought him a tray of food. He looked at it. She told him to eat or she would feed him herself. He struggled to keep down a spoonful of mashed potato. A little later he ate a bit of pureed vegetables. Taking up the tray, the nurse told him that a Mr. Curtain had several times enquired about his condition.

Three days later, as she passed, the same nurse told him that he had a visitor.

Rowena Quarles came down the ward, to each of the men she passed offering a soft smile, which each man seemed to think a gift. When she saw Tad, she slowed to a halt. Her expression changed. She seemed not so much sympathetic as deeply saddened.

She moved to stand by his bed. "I'm sorry, Mr. Fellows. Tad. I'm so sorry."

Her long woolen coat was open against the heat of the room, revealing a silk scarf at her throat above a gold and teal sweater. Her head was bare, her hair up, her face only lightly touched with cosmetics. The softness around her mouth, the glimmer in her eyes made Tad think of children's stories about the fairy princess.

"Will you be all right? Is there anything you need? Anything I can do for you?"

Tad discovered that her mere presence was a comfort. The air around her seemed softer. "I'll be all right. I'll be leaving tomorrow."

She scanned his face, frowning, as if his condition argued the impossibility of his intent. "My brother is responsible for this, isn't he?"

"Yes," Tad said.

"We didn't know, you see," she said. "There was nothing about the attack on the news or in the paper. Ginny only learned yesterday, when her father phoned. He seems to have heard of it from Professor Stuckey. But it turned out Rupert already knew. He said it was a fight over a girl—Rosalie, I assumed. But that isn't true, is it? Rupert set that blue-haired monster on you."

"Yes," Tad said.

"Yes," she repeated. Her voice shifted into a mode of intimacy. "I— Ginny told me what happened to you in the war, your wounding, your psychological . . . state. And now this—it's hardly fair, is it?"

Fair?

"I know," she said. She reached out, placed her hand on his arm. "It's just that, well, one wants to think that everything ultimately balances. Guilt, I suppose."

"Everything that happens is for the good of the whole, Marcus says." Tad paused. "Even if it's not always good for the individual."

She smiled ruefully. "Rather easy for him to say. He was the emperor of Rome, the most powerful man in the world. Do you think he was right?"

"Sometimes," he said. "Sometimes I'm not sure."

She smiled again. "Ginny told me that you believe that you have a special fate in store. A destiny."

"Yes," he said.

"She's in London with Rupert. Tomorrow they announce their engagement."

Tad was not especially surprised.

"She joked about it. Her destiny is to be a character out of Henry James."

He had never read Henry James, but he thought he understood what she meant—"She needs a big world."

"Believing you are destined—that's a kind of destiny in itself, isn't it? Or maybe it's just mindless confidence. Profound selfishness. My brother has an abundance of both. Ginny, too. One can't really reach her. She's protected by the shell of herself. "

"Yes," he said. As for most of his life he had been.

"One can only love her."

Tad knew that Rowena Quarles had said what she had come to him to say.

"My brother is a brute, of course. But she'll give him as good as she gets, won't she? And then, I'll be there to see that she comes to no real harm."

They were silent for a moment. Then she smiled again. "You do look quite frightening, you know. What must Rosalie have said?"

Tad didn't answer.

"Oh, I—I'm sorry," Rowena said, seeing. "I should mind my own business, shouldn't I?

"It's all right," Tad said.

As he spoke, he detected movement at the wardroom door. Mick Curtain, in his customary tieless three-piece suit, came in, saw Rowena Quarles, hesitated, and then advanced. "You look a mess."

Tad nodded. "You, too."

A bruise yellowed on Mick's cheekbone beneath his wire-rimmed glasses. He smiled broadly. "Slipped and banged the corner of a table."

Tad introduced him to Rowena. Mick confessed his occupation, mentioned all the rumors swirling around Waterby—of refurbishing the manor, of improving drainages, as well as suggestions of intimate relationships and political intrigues—was any of it accurate? Rowena declined to speak about her brother's business. Quickly she said her goodbyes. The two men watched her move down the aisle and out the door.

Mick smiled. "I don't suppose you know about any of that?"

"An announcement tomorrow, she said. An engagement."

Mick nearly smirked. "The American heiress. That's where the baronet gets the cash to restore the manor. The professor sells his daughter to get his museum built, and the daughter becomes an irreverent

Lady and, just maybe, down the line, mistress of 10 Downing Street. A perfect match—a raging arsehole and a spoiled brat."

Everything fit, finally.

"So," Mick said then, "you survived."

Mick enquired after Tad's injuries, and, as Rowena Quarles had, seemed to doubt his assertion that he would be discharged the following day. Mick could tell Tad little about the incident at the pub, having been waylaid by Chan Hackett and his tattooed pal, who had shoved Tad through the door.

"I'd like to say that I got my licks in, but it wouldn't be true. On the other hand, once I slipped and was on the floor, neither of them seemed to know what to do. They just stood over me, hollering obscenities."

"You didn't identify Chan to the police."

"I thought I'd let Mrs. Ball take care of things, which she has. Young Mr. Hackett is even now out on the North Sea on a fishing boat."

Mick talked about the police investigation and the alibi provided for Billy Knox. He wanted to know if Knox had gotten what he was after. He wanted to know if Tad would ever tell him what was going on. He wanted to know if anyone other than Rowena Quarles had been to see him. Each "no" Tad uttered seemed to hang in the warm air like a visible emptiness.

When Mick made to leave, Tad got out of bed. He did it more rapidly, with less pain. Mick helped him into a hospital robe, and Tad walked with him, slowly, to the ward door.

"One more question," Mick said. "You knew Knox was waiting for you outside. Why the hell did you go out there?"

"It was time," Tad said. He saw that Mick didn't understand. "I wanted to get it over with. He was just better than I was."

"I should hope so. You're one-armed. He might have killed you."

Yesterday sperm, tomorrow a mummy or ashes.

"Yes, yes, I know," Mick said. "Marcus. Life is short. Then you die."

"Yes."

Mick hesitated. Then, quietly, he said, "You need to talk to somebody, Tad, somebody professional, about the war. Or there are support groups, veterans like yourself . . ."

"I am the way I am," Tad said. "I keep telling everyone. But nobody listens."

THE NEXT MORNING, after an hour with forms and administrators, Tad filled at the hospital pharmacy a prescription for pain pills before allowing himself to be rolled in a chair to the main entrance. He had thought to walk back to Mrs. Ball's, slowly to be sure, but while he was in shadowland a heavy snow had fallen, melted, and frozen before all was whitened again by another storm. The day was bright, the sky blue, the air cold, the snow on the sidewalks hard-packed and treacherous. Heeding advice, he took a cab.

On the Cambridge streets, vehicles crushed and scattered frozen slush. In the city center, walkways were crowded, students eager for the new term to start. Tad too was ready to get to work; he would need one more good push, but he could still finish his tasks in time.

At Mrs. Ball's, a tune with a Caribbean lilt drifted through the partly open door of the landlady's apartment. She reclined on the parlor couch, head back, eyes closed. Tad thought she might be asleep, but as he quietly shut the door, she rose up and turned to look at him. Her mouth shaped into a silent O.

"Yes, then. Do you feel as bad as you look?" She got to her feet. She was, for the first time in his presence, wearing no makeup, which made her look somehow younger. "You'll be long convalescing. I'll try to help. It's the least I can do."

The B&B had been reinstated, she said, placed back on the list of university-approved accommodations. She'd already had inquiries and taken applications, and she would soon let long-empty rooms.

Robert Garner had done as he promised, and she was grateful to him. To Tad as well.

"And thank you for keeping our Chan out of the nick. I enticed a fishing boat captain of my acquaintance to take him on. It's time the lad grew up. He won't be bothering you anymore."

Bob Marley sang a jaunty, happy song.

"Yes, then. I am indeed changing my mind about Americans. But your telly don's really a man of the world, isn't he? He understands give-and-take. You're lucky to have him looking after your career."

"Yes," Tad said.

Her smile grew confidential, nearly conspiratorial. "And you, I don't really think of you as an American, especially now that you don't have that army hat. I—well, you know what I mean. The way you are."

"You'll have my room, too," Tad said. "I'll be leaving in a week to ten days."

"Leaving? But ..."

"I'll finish my job. Then I'll go."

Understanding seeped into her gaze. "And Rosalie?"

"I don't know," he said.

After a moment, she said, "Yes, then. Thank you for the notice. I'll— You'll tell me when your plans are finalized, the date of your flight, all that?"

The music ended. The silence wanted breaking.

"About Rosalie," Mrs. Ball said quietly. "If you don't know, you know."

Tad climbed slowly to his room. All was as it had been. He took a pain pill. Then he picked up the gladius, unsheathed it, felt its familiar weight. He put it back in the scabbard and lay down on the bed, thinking to rest briefly before he went to the museum and began work.

He awoke to darkness. For a moment he thought that he had returned to the land of shadows. Then, feeling the bed shift beneath him, he realized that he had slept. He felt, rising, refreshed, as if this was the first real sleep he'd had since the assault. He needed another pill, but he recognized that the pain he felt was less, more distant than it had been. He stood at the window and looked out at the night and knew he needed to be out, at least briefly, in it.

He had to move carefully on the icy snow. Even so, small slips and jerks after balance sent pain stabbing into his ribs. His testicles and his kidney ached. His shoulder scraped, his ear burned, his jaw was sore and his nose clogged and painful. Picking his way down cold, shadowy streets, he began to comprehend how badly he was hurt. He had no business being out in the cold this night. Yet out in the cold he was.

He walked to the tearoom. He stood in the cold for a long while. Then he walked back to Mrs. Ball's, his boots squeaking on the packed snow, his breath coming in gasps.

In his room he laid his treasures out in a line. Then he undressed and got into bed and took up his new copy of *Meditations*. He opened it and read: "You will soon forget everything. Everything will soon forget you."


HE FELT, THE NEXT MORNING, reinvigorated. Shaving, carefully, he saw a different face, still bruised a mottled black and purple and yellow, still taped and bandaged, but clear-eyed now, sentient. At breakfast, Mick remarked on the improvement. "You look almost human."

Tad attended to his meal. He chewed slowly, carefully, but he ate heartily. Mick drank coffee and consumed a muffin and talked, rehashing the situation with Horatio and the museum wing, going over the goings-on at Waterby. He might have been pitching a story to an editor. Then he eased into another consideration. He had an idea, he said, that knowing what he knew and suspecting what he suspected, he might be of service to the baronet. He could make certain that all he was privy to was placed before the public in a positive form, making certain as well that all he suspected was left uninvestigated, obscured, or secreted away. He could write stories celebrating the aristocrat who got things done, the man of principles who would bend in beneficial compromise, the Englishman who despised all things American but not all Americans. He could step away from smut-gathering and muckraking, put on a tie, and become a public-relations man. "Hardly more respectable, a flack," he said, grinning, "but better paid."

Tad finished his coffee.

"What I need, of course, is an entrée," Mick said. "You saw how enthusiastically Miss Quarles accepted my questions the other day. And I couldn't get within ten offices of Sir Rupert's lair in London—unless, of course, someone was to lobby him on my behalf, someone close, even intimate. Let's see now—do we know anyone on intimate terms with the baronet?"

"If I see Ginny, I'll ask," Tad said.

"You can assure her that their story will delight all with its fairy-tale wholesomeness, and that certain darker aspects of it will never be pursued—venality among bureaucrats, sexual shenanigans in the crumbling old manor house, that sort of thing."

Blackmail.

"Not precisely, no," Mick said, rather shamefaced. "A mere listing of pros and cons."

"Billy Knox will be waiting for *you* outside the door next time," Tad said quietly.

"Yes, well—I'll take my chances," Mick said, but Tad was on his way out.

He walked, slowly, carefully, to the museum. The day was again bright and clear and cold. Snow again squeaked under his boots. His pain now was a dull soreness, which even tentative movements stretched and thinned. He was improving, he knew. He was, as he shuffled along, feeling better in body and spirit. He was going back to work, to a job done well and now nearly finished.

He arrived at the museum a bit later than usual. He met no one on his way to his basement room. At his desk, he took out his chamois pouch and emptied its contents. He placed the objects in a straight line. Then he gathered from the lab a saucer of distilled water, a small vial of cleansing solution, a set of fine brushes, and a soft rag. With these he slowly, lovingly worked on the Marcus Aurelius 194.

Soon the coin was as clean as the others they'd found in the cache, with which it now rested, bagged and boxed. The records duly noted that the missing coin had been found that day.

Tad sat at his desk, looking at his other things. As he had when he lost his boonie hat, he felt powerfully incomplete. His throat ached. His eyes filled with tears. He suppressed a sob. He hadn't understood that he could feel such loss, he who so deliberately felt so little. But now it was all he could do to remain seated, not to rise and retrieve the coin and place it at the end of the row.

He was still sitting at his desk when Miss Eversly appeared. She was, despite herself, obviously shocked by his appearance. Finally she said, "Should you be here, Mr. Fellows? Are you . . . able?"

He discovered that he was too weary to answer.

She stared at him. Then, blushing, she turned her gaze from his face. She looked about the room. "You're very tidy."

When he didn't respond, she said, "The director wishes to speak with you."

As they made their way up to the director's office, Miss Eversly, as if unable to bear the silence, offered a series of freestyle observations— the heating system was acting up, the director was in much better spirits these days, the number of visitors was higher this quarter, Horatio continued to be a significant draw, they were so fortunate that Tad had foiled the attempted theft.

For a moment, at the director's door, she stopped. She smiled a small soft smile. Then, with a sigh, she showed him into the director's office.

Professor Stuckey was at the window. In the bright sunlight, her gray pantsuit shimmered silver, like armor. She turned, hesitated at the sight of Tad, and then moved to sit behind the dark empty expanse of her desk. The long table behind her was also empty.

Tad could see what had drawn Miss Eversly's comments. Sylvia Stuckey looked younger, fresher, healthier, eyes and complexion clear, posture upright, movements at once energetic and controlled. Her expression, as she gazed at him, mixed resolution with something like triumph. She did not invite him to sit.

"You've been badly beaten," she said. "I'm sorry. America isn't the only country to breed thugs."

Tad said nothing.

With some ceremony, she removed from a drawer a sheet of paper. "This was sent to me anonymously. I've had it verified. It's a police report about the incident outside the pub, the assault on you. It records the items on your person when you were brought to the hospital. One of these items is a Roman coin, a Marcus Aurelius 194—the same coin that was listed as missing from those found at the Horatio site."

Tad said nothing.

"Do you deny that the coin you had was in fact the one missing?"

Tad looked into himself.

At last he said, "No."

Professor Stuckey smiled. Her smile was quietly, calmly victorious.

"The coin is now with the others," Tad said.

"But it wasn't then, was it? According to the police, the coin was in a small pouch hidden in your, uhm, groin." Her gaze darkened. "We won't concern ourselves with what sort of perversion you may have been indulging with such an arrangement."

When Tad remained silent, the director flushed, as if she were the one caught out in an act of obscene pleasure.

"Personal appropriation of archeological materials violates a basic principal of our profession, to say nothing of the law."

Tad remained silent. He could only have told the truth, which would have been to betray those to whom he had pledged loyalty. Not that it would have made any difference for his professional prospects. He was finished.

The director continued officiously. So as to prevent scandal from attaching to the museum, she would not involve local law enforcement. She had informed both his PhD committee, from whom he would soon receive notice of his expulsion from the graduate program, as well as Professor Garner, whose irresponsible mentoring contributed to the situation. As of that moment, Tad's connection with the museum was severed. He could leave his keys with Miss Eversly on his way out.

Once in Afghanistan, as he was returning from chow, a bomb had exploded a hundred meters across the compound. The shock assailed him in waves as sound retreated into the distance and dust obscured the world. For a long time he had stood outside his tent, feeling the tremors wash over his body, deafened, blind, helpless.

Now, eventually, he said, "I'm almost done. A few more days."

"You're done now," she said.

He stood there. Then he said, "Please."

"This is your own fault, Mr. Fellows." For a moment, a small sympathy settled in her gaze. "I'm sorry. But you knew better."

He thought of something. "The artifacts from the dig belong to England, to English Heritage. But the records, the timelines and narratives, do not. That's what I've been working with. I'm nearly finished."

"I can't allow you to continue working here," she said, slowly shaking her head. "It would require that I also post security personnel down there, to make sure that you didn't try to steal something else."

Tad looked around the room. He was alone.

"Your coat has been brought upstairs," Professor Stuckey said. "Please give your keys to Miss Eversly."

Tad said nothing. He didn't move.

After a moment, she said, "Do I need to call security, Mr. Fellows?"

"No," he said then.

"It's really all for the good. For England. For our profession."

For good of the whole.

"Yes. Social action and all that."

Tad stood very still.

Professor Stuckey went on. "You know about the decision to keep Horatio in England, I believe. The plan was that you would come here, as an assistant curator under my supervision. But it would never have worked, surely you see that."

He didn't see. But it didn't matter.

It was finished, all of it.

HIS HEAD HURT.

Tad sat again on the bench on Jesus Green. The slant of the winter sunlight told him that he had lost several hours. He remembered leaving Sylvia Stuckey's office and allowing Miss Eversly to help him on with his coat. But that was at midmorning. He didn't know where he'd been or what he'd done since then.

His head hurt. He reached into his pocket for his pills, chewed one, and, returning the plastic tube to a different pocket, discovered that he still had his keys to the museum. He forced himself to relax his neck and shoulder and abdominal muscles as he waited for the pain to be pushed back.

Narrowboats rested unmoving in the quiet dark water. Pedestrians and bikers made their way along the path. The day dwindled.

Like the bog man, Horatio, he was in a far country. He was following orders he did not understand, defending a land not his own.

It came to him then, again—he was finished.

Professor Stuckey was right. It was his own fault.

Why he had not returned the coin immediately he would never be able to explain. Had it felt right in his pouch in his pocket? Had it completed, made whole the straight line he was wont to construct of his charms? Who would understand? He himself did not understand.

He had thought that he was protecting, guarding, making things right. But now both his project and his purpose were obscure. Protecting what and whom? From what and whom? His head hurt and he couldn't think.

He was finished. Yet better he than Robert Garner, the man who had given meaning to his life after war.

So many men and women he served with had returned home to find that they had no home. So had he. So many of these men and women had survived Afghanistan but could not survive America. Robert Garner had given him the means, and the will, to go on. He had given Robert Garner loyalty.

He did not blame Robert Garner, who was but human.

He did not blame Ginny Garner. How could she have done other than she did, being what she was? Fated. Destined.

He did not blame Professor Stuckey either. He had broken the rules, and her response may have been particularly harsh, but it was not unwarranted. He had no cause to appeal.

He did not blame anyone for anything, not for what he had done, not for what he was going to do.

He did not blame Rosalie. He remembered sensing that his presence in Rosalie's life gave her injury. He would make up for that.

His head hurt. The pill seemed to be having little effect. He rose and began to walk into the dying light.

He didn't know that he was going to the tearoom. The windows were empty of cakes and pastries. The room was dimming to darkness, but a light that made the kitchen entryway a frame suggested that someone might be there. Tad rapped softly on the door, and rapped again, and Rosalie, a dark shadow against the yellow light, came to look out. For some time she didn't move. Then she stepped back into the kitchen. The light went off, and she quickly reappeared, moving through the darkness to open the door and step out.

She wore a soft blue cardigan, but she nevertheless hugged herself against the cold. "I'm so sorry, Tad. You look . . . you're hurt bad, aren't you?" She raised her hand, as if she would touch his face. Then she let the hand fall. "I know it's my fault. But at least he didn't kill you."

His mistake.

"I can't talk," she said. "My mother's waiting for me upstairs."

"I came to say goodbye."

"Already?" She was surprised. "You finished your work?"

"No," he said. "But I'll be gone in a couple of days."

She didn't say anything for a moment. Then, as he watched her face, he saw her accept her fate.

"I'm sorry, Tad."

He did not respond. She hugged herself more tightly. "I'll never get to America, I know that. You were right. Things don't change. At least not for girls like me, they don't."

He didn't say anything.

"You deserve better than me."

"No," he said.

"Yes," she said. "I—I had to tell Billy that you kept the coin in a pouch in your pocket."

"I know," he said.

She stepped back, pinched the lapel of her sweater between two fingers, and pulled it back and down, exposing the pink of her sleeveless blouse and, on the white flesh beneath it, a tattoo. In the waning light Tad strained to make out the small image. Was it a head with a tangle of vines and leaves for hair, and dark blue outlining patches of red and green?

"Like in the story. He gets his head cut off and they kick it around like a football."

He wanted to touch her cheek. He didn't.

"I'm sorry, Tad," Rosalie said again.

He moaned, faintly.

He turned and walked off down the street.

His head hurt. He walked.

AT ONE POINT, finding himself on a residential street lined with semidetached houses and tiny lawns, Tad realized how in England everything fit. Everywhere he looked he saw layers of history. The society was layered as well, everyone neatly in his place, houses all in a row. America, America was a chaos of change, of destruction and development. What, in America, was there to defend? Where in America could a last defender make a stand?

What had he to return to?

Later he stood in the shadows and watched the door of the Blue Boar.

HE AWOKE in his room, in his bed. He rose and dressed and took a pill and went down to breakfast. His headache robbed him of any appetite, but he knew that he needed to eat, to keep up his strength.

Mick Curtain had heard of his dismissal. "The word is that it involves stolen artifacts. But if that's the case, then you're taking the rap for someone else. You wouldn't steal a pin."

Tad said nothing.

"You'll be leaving soon, then."

"Yes."

"I'll miss these spirited conversations," Mick joked. When Tad said nothing, Mick went on. "I'm sorry."

Tad finished his coffee and left.

The day was gray, the city befogged. Tad walked in it. At a hardware store, he bought a whetstone. The blue-gray stone pleased his eye, the weighty round shape fit his hand.

He returned to his room and took out the gladius and slowly, methodically began to rub the stone against the steel edge. The stone felt right in his hand. Its faint gritty oiliness made it seem somehow alive. The sword responded.

THAT EVENING he received an email from Robert Garner. He had done the best he could for Tad. His room at Mrs. Ball's was paid for through the end of the spring term. His voucher for a plane ticket was still good. And the professor would see to it that, in his book on Horatio, Tad's contribution to the effort would be publicly acknowledged. He said too that his immediate impulse, upon hearing from Sylvia Stuckey, was simply to tell the truth. He had been dissuaded by Rupert Quarles. Sir Rupert had been especially insistent that a confession would do Tad no good, given that official records had the coin in his possession, but would destroy Garner's reputation and the prospects of a Garner wing. Rupert, Professor Garner suspected, had had the police report sent to Professor Stuckey. Rupert, he was beginning to understand, was a man not to be crossed.

Nevertheless, Robert Garner said, if Tad wished him to tell everyone exactly what happened, he would.

Tad replied to the email: "Don't."

HIS HEAD HURT CONSTANTLY NOW. Pills removed the immediacy, the urgency of the pain, at least for a while, like a defender holding off the probing of patrols before a major assault. More and more, however, respite was brief. That night he walked, and for some time he stood in pain that was a kind of despair watching the enemy camp, the Blue Boar, and he walked on again.

The next day he went to a bank, where he spoke to an assistant manager. The woman was clearly disturbed by his appearance and behavior—pain bunched up his muscles, contorted his expression, turned him jittery. About his identity and inclination she was dubious.

However, she agreed to try to authenticate the first and, having done that, to satisfy the second.

He was no longer able to escape the pain.

The pain was changing him, reducing him to brute.

That afternoon he went to an Army-Navy surplus store on Regent Street. He had passed it before, on occasion stopping to look at the gear and weapons and uniforms, both actual surplus and used. Now he went in. They had a shelf of boonie hats. He found one that fit, but finally he put it back. It was stiff, new, didn't feel right, wasn't his.

On the counter sat an old cigar box that held a number of pins and ribbons from military units of different countries. Tad's twitching fingers found the CIB almost immediately.

Who, having earned one of these badges, would allow it out of his possession?

The salesman frowned, uncertain whether he had been addressed. He knew what the CIB meant. He wouldn't let Tad pay for it.

Tad took the badge back to his room and attached it carefully to the scabbard of the Roman sword.

Then he took out the whetstone and slid it over the steel blade, watching the edge grow keen. He applied the stone in slow small circles. The action seemed to connect him.

The pain seemed to connect him.

After it had been dark for some hours, Tad went out. Under his coat he wore the gladius, the strap of the baldric pulling down his shoulder, the scabbard stiff against his side. They felt right.

He walked to the museum. The fog was thick and cold. He might have been in the underworld of the ancients, all gray and dim and shadowed. The museum loomed. He walked around behind the building and tried his key, which turned smoothly in the lock.

Either the director did not know he still had his keys or she had forgotten to order the locks changed or bureaucratic inertia had delayed the work. But he could not depend on that continuing to be the case. He would have to act soon.

It was time.

He walked to the Blue Boar. He watched the enemy pass in and out the front door. At one point he slipped out of his shadowed alcove in the entry to the Boots pharmacy and moved across the street and down a dim alley to the rear of the pub, where a half dozen vehicles were parked. The back door to the pub was again unlocked. He returned to his lookout position, from which he commanded a view of the mouth of the alley. No vehicles entering or leaving could escape his notice.

He watched until the pub went dark.

He walked.

In his room, he took out his pouch and removed his charms but he could not align them in a straight row.

He opened *Meditations* but found no words, only ink in obscure patterns, gestures of a culture long passed into oblivion.

"JESUS, MATE," Mick said. "You look terrible. You—we need to get you to the hospital."

"Headache," Tad said through clenched teeth.

He didn't know how he had come to be in the breakfast room. Had he slept? He noticed then two young women, Indian or Pakistani, who from a table across the room were watching him with concern, perhaps even fear.

"I'll call a cab," Mick said. "You're . . ."

"No," Tad said, rising. "It's too late."

Mick looked at him. "You're in bad shape, Tad."

Tad, struggling, at last understood that Mick was his friend. He had never had a friend. He didn't know what to say to him.

He turned and walked out.

He walked. The fog thinned, lightened, and then resettled, grew grayer.

THE NEXT DAY—was it?—the assistant bank manager had papers for him to sign. The transaction would be complete by the following day. His account in the American bank would be closed, its contents electronically shifted to a new account in Cambridge, in the name of Rosalie Cush. The assistant bank manager would send Ms. Cush a registered letter informing her of the account balance and asking her to fill out various forms.

Something hard pressed against his ribs.

Oh, the sword.

The assistant bank manager begged his pardon.

"Nothing," he said, rising. "Nothing."

At the hardware store, he bought a liter petrol can. At a Shell station he filled the can. In the fog, he carried the can to the museum loading dock and slid it beneath a sorting table.

HE WALKED. The fog felt coarse against his skin, tasted of the distant sea. Sounds blurred, as if from a great battle raging far away. Once he heard an eerie peal of laughter, triumphant or mad. Once he heard moans, whether of pleasure or pain he didn't know.

The fog thickened and the day darkened and all became shadows and he was in a doorway, crumpled, beaten down by pain that was pure pain as the sun was pure light and life and he could do nothing but accept the pain, give himself to it, become pain himself, until there was only pain and no pain and shadows.

He rose and stepped into the shadows for good. For the good of the whole.

THE PETROL CAN was where he had placed it. The key turned again in the lock.

In his basement room he got a flashlight and a screwdriver.

Horatio greeted him.

With the screwdriver, he removed a glass panel. That was enough. The wooden frame would burn well. Johnson, the security man, once alerted by the smoke alarm, would arrive in time to prevent serious damage to the room. But Horatio would be ashes.

He poured the petrol carefully over the mummy. He lit a match and tossed it and Horatio burst into flame.

THE WHITE VAN sped down the street, turned sharply, and roared in the alley.

THE LAST CENTURION removed his coat. He crossed the street, turned into the alley, and entered the back door of the pub, drawing his sword.

# ACKNOWLEDGMENTS

★ ★ ★

I WISH TO THANK Christine Kelly and her editorial staff—Wes Reid, Curtis Vickers, and Molly Albert—for the careful, thoughtful work they did on the manuscript that I submitted to Baobab Press. Their efforts produced significant improvements. And I especially want to acknowledge the contribution of Margaret Dalrymple, whose instincts for what the text needed and didn't need proved unerring.

I also want to thank those kind souls who read and commented on various drafts of the novel. My gratitude goes to Bill Baines, Michael Binard, Kathy Boardman, Danny Goeschl, Robert Merrill, Gaye Nichols, and John Pettey.

I owe particular thanks to Myles McCallum, who saved me from several serious errors in the treatment of some of the "bones and stones" material. His comments and advice proved invaluable. He and others familiar with the sort of dig with which the story is concerned will recognize that I have taken a few small liberties with archeological procedures and protocols. I've made these modifications for thematic and narrative reasons, and I am wholly responsible for them.

# ABOUT THE AUTHOR

★ ★ ★

Born and raised in Deadwood, South Dakota, BERNARD SCHOPEN attended the University of Washington, and the University of Nevada, Reno, where upon receiving his Ph.D. in English, he taught for many years. He is the author of three Jack Ross novels, as well as a study of the novels of Ross McDonald. His latest novel, *Calamity Jane*, was released in 2013,